Little Toy Car

A Novel

Gabe Oliver

Disclaimer

ONE

Fall 1997

Knock! Knock!

I heard the sound echoing from the front of the house to the back of my bedroom as my ears perked and an electrifying chill delivered itself to the extremities of my limbs. I looked down at the little toy car I had acquired from the neighbor's house only hours before. The open blue cardboard packaging with a clear plastic casing that the car used to sit so comfortably in, was laid out on the floor like a wet newspaper on a busy metropolitan street curb. I tightly squeezed the little car in my hand, lifting it from its previous joy ride through the streets of my dusty bedroom floor. I brought it up close to my chest with a single string of misplaced hair caught between its wheels, listening tentatively to comprehend the sounds that would follow the *knock*.

I was five years old at the time and lived in an old faded blue house in the outskirts of downtown Denver. The house was covered with leaves from the trees that coddled its sides and shaded its rooftop with their towering embrace. There was a five foot splintered wooden fence that surrounded the backyard and pinched the sides of the house, dividing the back yard from the front yard. The grass, yellow and dry like strips of hay, poked up skyward from the ground to support the leaves resting gently on its tips. The windows were lined with dirty white frames struggling to keep their white flakes of paint from succumbing to the ground below.

The streets in front of the house were worn and cracked like a piece of paper forced out flat after being previously crumpled in the tight grip of a vengeful hand. Rows of houses in similar conditions to mine stretched out as far as you could see, only divided by a cross street every twelve houses or so. Trees grew in every yard shedding leaves that blew through the cracked streets like children chasing after each other in a crowded schoolyard. There were cars parked along the curbs that would exchange places as the people came and went in their daily routines. It was a place where dreams stood above you slightly out of reach, but always close enough to continue reaching.

Inside, the house was divided by dirty white walls and a faded wooden floor sanded from years of dusty shoes trampling its fragile plane. As you entered the front door, you were greeted with an open living space -

small but spacious. Beyond the living room was a small kitchen area with a window overlooking the backyard. After entering the house, to the left was a tiny hallway that led to the only two bedrooms. It was a nice economic accommodation aged to an elegant feel like an old bottle of whiskey.

I lived with my mother Anita. She was a short delicate woman with dirty blonde wavy hair that flowed with the length of her spine. Her eyes matched her hair with a brownish tone. She had a stiffened walk as if she had to prove her legs were worthy of each step they took. Her stance was upright without slouch like that of a valiant warrior goddess but lacking the height and physical strength to be accepted for this position of honor. It was just the two of us and I couldn't quite remember how it ended up that way, but sometimes I would have these dreams, like déjà vu, and I would spend days analyzing them for validity.

I heard subtle creaks from footsteps moving towards the front of the house and with each step they took I felt the subtle vibration tickle my buttock as I sat criss-crossed on my bedroom floor. The un-oiled hinges on the front door made their presence known in a loud confident threat, giving me certainty that the door had opened. I heard distant conversation but could not make out the words. It was a harsh male voice followed by a raspy female voice I wasn't familiar with.

The conversation dragged on in the background with a lack of clarity until I heard a sudden shout "Gene!"

The voice of my mother, clear and concise, made my heart start pounding the inner wall of my chest like a rabid animal in a tiny cage desperate for freedom. I knew that a response wasn't necessary because she wanted me there quickly and a response would only reveal that I was not moving fast enough.

***

Carlos was a neighborhood kid that lived a few houses down from mine on the corner of a cross street. He was tall for his age with almost black hair. He had told me his parents were from Mexico but that he was born here in the United States, which he said automatically made him an American. He always wore an extra large basketball jersey that swallowed his skinny frame with shorts that sagged to his shins. He was fourteen, much older than myself, but would request my company every so often for various reasons.

Only hours before the *knock* he had come to my house looking for me to help him with something and giving me a promise of a reward. I always liked to spend time with him as it made me feel like I had exclusive access to an otherwise restricted club for my age.

Carlos walked with the confidence of someone that knows exactly what they want and how to get it. I followed him attentively as we paced down the streets of the neighborhood.

"Here," Carlos spoke with certainty in his words.

Carlos pointed to a splintered wooden gate entryway piercing the side of a faded yellow house surrounded by towering bushes naked without leaves. We proceeded towards the entryway through leaves spread across the ground making a loud crunching sound with each step we took. He looked at me and signaled for me to open the gate with his eyes and a slight tip of his head upward. I pushed on the gate lightly at first, with caution, peering through the crack that became more exposed the further I pushed. The gate was open and Carlos galloped forward ahead looking back at me waving his hand with a repeated sweeping motion as a signal for me to close it. I closed the gate and ran towards him anxiously.

Carlos bent over and picked up a cigarette butt he found from within the mess of the leaves on the ground. He then reached into his back pocket pulling out a lighter and holding it up to the sky as if it was a diamond that he had just dug up. Placing the cigarette butt in between his lips and arching his hand over it like an umbrella, he brought the lighter to the tip of the butt and aggressively thumbed the lighter shooting off sparks till the butt had a neon orange glow to its tip. He lowered his head and locked his eyes to mine while pulling the cigarette butt from his mouth and exhaling a cloud of smoke into the open air.

"Here, try it," Carlos spoke generously, holding the cigarette butt out as a gift. "It's good for the nerves."

I gripped the cigarette butt between my thumb and pointer finger bringing it hesitantly towards my lips as my eyes followed it till they were cross-eyed.

"Now take a deep breath," Carlos calmly told me like a father teaching his son to swim.

A drought filled my mouth as a fire dove down my throat swimming purposefully into my lungs leaving a charred trail scorching everything in its path. My eyes widened and I let out a harsh expulsion of coughs while begging with my shaking hand for Carlos to take back the cigarette butt.

"Was that it? Was that the reward?" I said in a disappointedly raspy tone.

Carlos looked at me, smiled and then laughed.

"Of course not!" he said as his laugh trailed off.

Carlos tilted his head to the left signaling me to follow him. He led us to a sliding glass door on the back of the faded yellow house. He peered into the house through the glass door, forehead pressed to the glass and both hands covering the sides of his face in order to shield the light from interrupting his view. He grabbed the handle of the sliding glass door and swung it to the side.

Carlos turned and looked me in the eyes with one hand on my shoulder and the other outstretched and pointed to a specific location in the house. I followed the length of his arm with my eyes revealing the location his pointer finger was locked on. I saw a wooden staircase that led to a basement and at the end of the stairs was a transparent plastic box with a thick white plastic lid covering its contents. The house smelt of fresh pine wood as if the owners had just installed that staircase this morning.

“That’s the reward,” Carlos said confidently and with dramatic emphasis. “Go get it and bring it up to me.”

That is when the thought crossed my mind that maybe we weren’t supposed to be here. Chills filled my body as my nerves woke up from their slumber. Curiosity overtook and replaced that feeling that had awakened before sending it gradually back to sleep. I felt the blood in my body start to move like the starting of a large assembly line. I tip-toed quietly into the house making my way towards the wooden staircase. As I got closer, the scent of fresh pinewood grew stronger. Once my feet touched the pine wood stairs, I scrambled my way down the staircase ignoring my previous intentions of keeping quiet. I tightly gripped the sides of the transparent plastic box, lifting it quickly as I raced up the stairs to the sliding glass door.

Carlos had closed the door! I tried to rip it open with one arm while holding the box in the other but it wouldn’t move. I couldn’t get out! I was frightened instantly and the once sleeping chills in my nerves woke quickly with the violent pounding of my heart against the insides of my chest. I tried the door again but this time set the box on the floor and ripped open the door with all my might. This time the door slid open as fast as if a tightened rubber band had snapped in two.

Carlos was laughing hysterically. He had been holding the door as a prank.

"You should have seen yourself!" Carlos bursted out barely breathing from laughter.

I turned red in the face and started laughing along with him, reluctantly trying to hide my face by turning around and grabbing the box I had left on the floor. He swiftly took it from me, holding it in one hand and opening the white lid with his other. I surveyed the contents that were fitted perfectly with clean symmetrical rows as if that transparent plastic box had been made specifically to hold what it contained. The rows were made up of individual blue uniformed cardboard packages with clear plastic casings that held various models of toy cars comfortably fitted inside.

"Pick one," Carlos insisted.

I reached inside, scanning the different car models with my finger tips examining them carefully in my mind with hopes of choosing the perfect one. There were pickup trucks, vans, Mustang convertibles and a variety of other models inside. I chose a candy red Porsche but when I had finally made my selection Carlos took it from my hand and traded it for another one.

"That's your reward. Now let's get out of here," Carlos demanded while making his way to the gate we had entered before.

We exited promptly and Carlos ran off without me tightly holding the box of cars under his arm against his side. I didn't feel a rush now that I had the car in my hand so I made my way casually back to my house studying the new car I had just acquired. This car wasn't as cool as the Porsche but it was still a toy car and with that I was content.

***

I jumped to my feet releasing the toy car from its tight squeeze and allowing it to hit the ground harshly, stumbled to my bedroom door and squeezed the door handle swinging it open quickly and carelessly as I ran across the living room to the front door where my mother had called me. A police officer stood steadfastly hands on his hips slightly tilting his head to look at me as I approached my mother and started tightly hugging the trunk of her right leg. Behind him was a blonde lady with pale white skin and blotchy red blemishes staring with contempt directly at me hunched over slightly with her fists punching the sides of her hips. Her eyes burned with fury searching deep into the depths of my mind through my pupils, holding tightly to her unspoken accusations like an up-stretched hand waving violently in the air.

"Is this your son?" The policeman asked my mother assertively.

She nodded her head slightly acknowledging the officer's question with a hint of undeserving guilt and disappointment. I couldn't tell if she was disappointed in me or in herself because she hadn't been able to keep me from doing what I had done.

The police officer squatted and looked me directly in the eyes, "Can you bring me the little toy car that you took from this lady's house?" he asked firmly but in a childish tone.

I knew exactly what he was talking about; of course. I walked shamefully back to my room where I had left the toy car and snatched it swiftly from the dusty floor and gripped it with a tight squeeze in the palm of my hand. My face tensed up making my temples fill with painful pressure. I tried to swallow the huge lump of air lodged in my throat keeping me from taking a much needed breath. A tear dripped from my eye like a struggling drop of juice squeezed out of a used dry lemon. Even though I had let out some tears, I kept trying to hold them back.

It was just a stupid little car. It was just a stupid little toy car but it represented so much more than that. Every single toy that I owned my mother had received from donations; a ripped one-eyed teddy bear with dirty white stuffing that fell out of its face after every squeeze and an action figure missing a leg. They were toys that the other kids didn't want, and with good reason. Old broken toys that I still played with, but nothing like this new packaged model toy car, nothing like the feeling of ripping apart that fresh cardboard box and holding my very own toy that no one else had previously tainted with their hands.

I stood in front of the officer holding the little toy car in outstretched hands like a peace offering of my complete surrender as he stood towered above me. The woman stepped towards me, her eyes staring at the car with disgusted disbelief.

"He opened it!" she shouted angrily. "That was a goddamn collectors item worth big money. Do you know how much these are worth? Your son is a thief! A thief! This is going down on his record for the rest of his miserable life. The police will make sure of that."

"Please ma'am, I know you're upset," my mother pleaded desperately. "It was wrong for him to have stolen this car from you but please, he is just a five year old boy. Is there a way I could pay for the car in exchange for you not pressing charges? I truly apologize."

The lady was so furious that her otherwise pale face turned bright red. She crossed her arms tightly slowly turning her eyes to the police officer then glaring back at my mother with growing disgust.

"One hundred dollars," the woman stated firmly.

"Please ma'am, the car can't be worth more than twenty dollars," my mother sounded even more desperate with this second plea. She looked at the police officer to search for some validation that the woman's demand was, in fact, ridiculous.

"One-hundred dollars," the lady restated while nudging her head in the direction of the police officer. "Or he puts your son down as a thief on his permanent record."

I watched as my mother's head dropped, nodding to submission. Her hands were shaking violently as she turned around and walked to the kitchen where there was a small portable metal table that her purse sat on top of. She rummaged through the little plain gray purse searching desperately for some cash. I watched as she pulled out some bills; a couple twenties, a crumbled up ten, eight fives, six ones and a handful of change. She counted them slowly and painfully.

I couldn't bear to see her like that, and all because of me. Why did I have to do things like that? Why did we have to be so poor? Why did Carlos ask me to help him? Why did I go? Why? There was a twisting in my stomach like the wringing out of a drenched rag that made me feel nauseous. I felt an open misty air passing from my stomach to my mouth like a foggy humid morning before a coastal California sunrise. I wished I had never done that.

My mother placed the cash in a little plastic sandwich bag and brought it to the woman, handing it to her carefully, hoping not to disrupt the woman's mood. The lady snatched the cash from my mother's hand and walked off. The police officer scribbled something in his notebook and spoke on the radio using code which I didn't understand. He then tipped his head towards my mother and then to me signaling that his work here was finished. The door creaked shut and an uncomfortable silence filled the room that made the air heavy and hard to breathe in.

My mother didn't say a word-she didn't have to. I could hear her disappointment speaking loudly enough through the deafening silence. She sat on one of the metal folding chairs at the kitchen table studying a piece of paper which she held carefully in one hand. She was still shaking and that's when I realized it wasn't just disappointment that she was feeling, but worry. The paper was a rent statement and I didn't even need to see the amount, whatever it was, her eyes clearly stated that any and all hope of making that payment was gone. It had been carried away in a little plastic bag abruptly and mercilessly, leaving us drowning from the outcome of my blunder.

Ashamed, I opened my hand slowly revealing the little toy car. It no longer felt like the new toy that nobody had played with before, that I had only hours before seen it to be; no. Now it was a symbol of regret, a harsh lesson and the first piece of rubble from my self-inflicted wounds and bad life decisions.

TWO

Spring 1998

I sat with my hands perched on the inside ledge of the front passenger side window of a 1990 Volvo station wagon staring out the window as the sun started to glide over the peaks of the Rocky Mountains shooting rays of blinding light in every direction. The sky was blue with a few stringy clouds stretched out like trails of cotton candy being pulled from their sugary hive. Once the sun had risen, I sunk back deep into the front seat of the car with my head resting on the door beside me, alone with my thoughts.

It was nothing like the brand new model toy car I had held in my hands months before but it carried the same feeling of regret. It shared the same harsh lesson as the little toy car did, only it was larger and more real than the toy car could ever be. The paint on the exterior of the car was peeling off like the dead skin of a severe sunburn. The seats in the back were pushed forward at a forty-five degree angle spearing out to the front windshield. The front seats had a dirty beige worn out rag wrapped around the yellow sponge looking foam, shedding pieces all over the interior of the car. A pile of old wool blankets with black, green and white triangular patterns lay bunched up and unorganized in the back of the station wagon. Two little plain brown pillows were mixed up in the pile as well. It was a drastic change to the last home we had once occupied. It was as if I had traded our old house, our old life, for that little toy car.

I still thought about it every day, about how it was my fault that we hadn't been able to make the last payment and, therefore, had lost the house. All for a stupid little car that I no longer even had. My mother had tried to maintain a positive demeanor, though I could tell she was sinking on the inside, tired as if she was constantly trying to stay afloat.

My mother and I had developed a fairly steady routine, at least as steady as it could be living in the back of the station wagon. We would wake up at sunrise and crawl our way up to the front seats of the car. My mother would take the driver's seat and I, the passenger's seat. Then we would stretch our arms out backward with a back bend curve in our spines. My mother would yawn, grabbing the car key from the middle cup holder, sliding it into the ignition and turning it while the car engine cranked a few times. She would wait a few minutes for the windows to defog and then start the drive to the elementary school where she would then leave me for the day while she went off to work. Later, she would pick me up from the elementary school sidewalk curb and drive us to the fitness gym parking lot where we would go to take showers but never to work out. She bought a membership there for the sole purpose of using the showers and bathrooms as it was actually affordable compared to the rent prices that were impossible for us to afford with her current salary. After our showers, we would eat from the weekly rations we received of free expired food from the grocery store up the street. The sun would set behind the mountains and we would cuddle up in the back of the station wagon until we drifted to sleep, awaiting the new day to repeat this all over again.

I hated the elementary school. It was a tall brick building alternating between brown and red bricks in rows that wrapped around its towering walls like that of a prison gated off around the perimeter. School buses would arrive lined up in the front parking lot each morning, disrupting my peaceful solitary wait on the school side curb, with a flood of children screaming, laughing and talking about who liked whom in such-and-such class and who had the coolest backpack. There was a large grass area where everyone played soccer or gossiped during recess.

Inside, it had a large hallway lined with lockers and doors that led to various classrooms connected at either end in the shape of a giant square. Teachers would stand outside their doorways waiting for the children to fill their classrooms before shutting the doors, leaving the hallways empty and quiet. The bell would *ring* each hour signaling the changing of classes and a fifth bell rang that would signal the start of lunch time. The same boring routine each and everyday for the whole school year.

Making friends was the difficult part of school as everyone shared so many things in common such as the neighborhoods where they lived in or the sports clubs that they went to. I shared none of these things, as sports clubs were too expensive and none of them lived in the parking lot of the fitness center.

I lifted my head from the window ledge turning it to the back of the car where my mother was starting to wake up from a deep sleep. I watched as she rubbed her eyes and threw back her hair. She then proceeded to crawl into the driver's seat. She woke up a little later than usual, disrupting our daily routine, which is why I was already in the front waiting for her. As usual, she grabbed the key from the middle cup holder, slid it into the ignition and turned the key as it cranked a few times to start. The windows had already defogged from the sun as it had had more time in the sky to do so. She took a deep breath and set her hand on the steering wheel but then paused for a second to think.

"Why don't we take a day off today? No school, no work, just Anita and Gene," she said abruptly as if releasing a breath she had been holding for too long.

I turned my head to face her and saw that she had a slight grin from the idea as she turned to me as well. I could see she had already made up her mind as she hadn't really phrased the statement as a question but more as an introduction to a quest.

"Okay," I nodded and showed approval with a slight grin.

We drove down a long interstate highway that consisted of a couple lanes going in our direction and a couple going opposite to us. The highway led us to a long winding road that ascended up a tall mountain as I rested my chin on the inside window ledge watching as everything below seemed to become smaller. The smell was like a forest of Ponderosa pine trees and a tiny hint of vanilla emitting from their bark. Large rock boulders and pine trees blurred as we drove past. We only passed a couple of cars going the opposite direction. I assumed most people were at work or school during this time; in fact, that was where we should have been as well, though I found this was much better.

My mother started to slow down and pull off to the side of the road. We were really high up now and everything below looked like a miniature model of what it really was, like you could reach out and pick up the little houses, cars, people and trees and place them wherever you wanted. The car came to a complete stop facing the edge of the mountain and my mother turned off the key and pulled the hand brake. We both flung open the car doors and stepped out onto the gravel road beneath us. The view was magnificent! I felt as if we were floating with the clouds as the wind gently blew refilling the air with a new fresh scent of pines. I watched as my mom hopped up onto the front hood of the car landing on her buttocks and swinging her legs off the edge. I imitated her and sat next to her. We sat there in silence staring at the world below us and contemplating its beauty and complexity.

It was nice for a change to break the routine and explore a place that didn't constantly remind me of my mistake, but instead allowed my mind to wander and drift to a world that I could arrange however I dreamed. I thought about all the lives we were gazing down upon, how much detail each and every one had and I contemplated how, if in some way, they were all connected. Sitting there on that mountain made it feel like it wasn't so bad living in the back of the car. Maybe it wasn't a punishment but a reward, like Carlos had told me in the backyard of that faded yellow house. I guess I would never really know; the other life, the one that we had left in that little plastic bag, had been traded for this one.

"Gene," my mother said as if she hadn't completely finished her thought.

"Yes?" I replied with curiosity waiting to hear what she had to say.

"Know this, Gene. Know that I will always love you and will always want the best for you. No matter what happens," she told me, letting her emotions show.

"I know," I replied and nodded softly.

"Life can be tricky and complicated sometimes. . ." she continued, "hard to understand fully, but it's important for you to know that I'm always thinking of what's best for you."

She finished briefly, I nodded with acknowledgement and we both sat silently for a while, still gazing down at the little world below.

***

I was seated upright in one of two hard wooden chairs and both were facing a large desk. On the desk was a clutter of papers, folders, pens and pencils and a golden plated name tag that stared directly at me with the words PRINCIPAL chiseled into it in all capital letters. Behind the desk was an older man with short wavy gray hair, square framed glasses and a rough face with a maze of thickened lines that had developed from his old age. He was staring at me sternly.

As I sat there quietly waiting my mind flashed back to the freedom I had felt only a couple weeks prior when I was gazing off the mountain with my mother. I remembered our conversation and how she told me she loved me and was always thinking about what was best for me. I thought about how maybe the outcome of my mistake was actually better than how it would have been if I hadn't taken my reward for helping Carlos, but that I would never really know. I thought about how my mother had told me that life could be complicated and whether I really even understood what she meant by that. I pondered these thoughts while waiting for the man to speak.

"What on earth were you thinking?" the man questioned in disbelief.

Only moments prior to me entering the principal's office, my first grade teacher was briefing the principal on what had happened in her classroom. She was a tall pudgy middle aged woman with brown curly hair that cut off at the end of her neck just before touching her back. Her body was covered in brown speckles of various sizes and blue trails of veins were just barely visible throughout the rest of her skin. She wore a loose red dress covered in blue and black thin lines like a bunch of thread strands scattered throughout the dress. I hated her class and the way she taught it. She would single out students in the classroom and crown them as favorites, always giving them preferential treatment.

The principal was irritated and impatient with my absent response to his questioning.

“This is not good, Gene, not good at all,” he said firmly, shaking his head left to right as he spoke, “We’re going to have to call your mother to take you home. I can’t let you continue the school day like this.”

The day had started out routine like every other day before it. My mother dropped me off on the curb outside the school, I waited for the school buses to arrive and then we would all scramble our way into the first classes. All the kids in the class would stand for The Pledge of Allegiance of the United States with their right hand over their heart and in unison recite it mindlessly fumbling through the words. We would all simultaneously sit back down in our seats and begin to listen to the lecture the teacher had for the day.

“Today we are going to start with twenty minutes of silent reading,” my first grade teacher stated in a sleepy monotone voice.

The classroom was a small square room with four by five rows of beige desks each accompanied with a little brown chair. There was a giant black chalkboard which covered most of the wall. There was a larger wooden desk for the teacher situated to the far front left corner of the classroom and the door to the classroom at the back. On the right side of the classroom was a large bookshelf full of an assortment of books.

I stood up slowly from my desk and made my way to the bookshelf to pick out a book. I started scanning them with my fingertips and studying the pictures to choose the perfect one. Another boy was also looking at the books with me. He was a little taller than I was with short messy brown hair and light brown eyes. I ignored his presence and kept looking until my finger landed on the perfect one. It was a bright blue book with a colorfully drawn out picture of a racing motorcycle. As I was gripping the book and pulling it closer to me, the little boy reached out and snatched it quickly from my hands while trying to offer me a different one in exchange.

My mind flashed to the backyard of the faded yellow house where I had selected the Porsche and Carlos had taken it from my hands and gave me another. Back then, I had just accepted the trade happily, but it felt different now; I wasn't just going to accept that this time.

"Here take this one," the boy offered optimistically.

"No! Give it back!" I shouted not realizing how loud I actually was.

He shook his head left to right to show his decline of my demands, turning around quickly and sprinting back to his desk.

Right then. I remembered how harsh the punishment had been for stealing something that wasn't mine. How taking that car had changed everything; forcing us to live in the back of that Volvo station wagon. I remembered the lady's reaction and how she showed no mercy as my mother pleaded for forgiveness. I thought about how maybe the world didn't really care about what happened to criminals as long as they were punished. How my mother's plea for forgiveness went unheard to deaf ears. I thought maybe I should punish this kid for stealing from me too.

I sprinted to the desk the brown haired boy had retreated to, cocking back my arm like a medieval catapult. I clenched my fist tightly and then forced it forward to the boy's face with all my might. My fist struck him right on the nose making him lose his balance. He dropped to the floor. He let out a high pitched scream and tears started to fill his eyes. His nose started leaking with little drops of bright red blood like the tips of icicles in a blistering sun towards the end of a long cold winter. I bent over and reached down to the ground picking up the book he had dropped. I started walking back towards my desk non-regretfully until I was stopped by my first grade teacher, who had rushed to the scene. She reached out her hand attempting to take the book from me. I stretched my arms back over and behind my head and then kicked her in the shin. She let out a subtly muted scream and her face turned bright red with fury, the same type of face I had seen on the blonde haired lady I had stolen the car from. The rest of the class stood staring at what was going on in disbelief with jaws dropped and mouths wide open, some even had both hands cupped over their mouths shielding their reactions.

"Principal's office NOW!" my teacher shouted in aggravation.

That was how I ended up here, silently waiting, seated in the wooden chair facing that old gray hair man.

***

The ride back was silent, just like the faded blue house the day I stole that stupid little car. It was almost time for bed. The street lights burned bright. The stars in the deep black sky battled with the haze of light covering the parking lot. My mother and I laid staring up out of the side windows with our feet stretched out to the back. It had been a long day and I felt bad that she had to come home early from work to pick me up from school. I felt like what I had done wasn't completely wrong but the feeling I felt from my mother's disappointment confirmed that it was, indeed, wrong.

I continued staring out the window reflecting on the day that had passed and thinking of what I could have done differently or if I was justified in my actions. I thought about the future, wondering if my mother and I would live in this station wagon forever and if my actions would always keep us here. I wondered what my dad would have said to me. I wondered why I couldn't remember what he looked like or what he sounded like. What made him leave if he ever was once together with my mother and I. As I began to ponder these thoughts, my eyes became heavy as more weight was added to them from the sleepiness that was overtaking me. My body was completely relaxed and it felt weightless underneath the wool blankets. I tried to keep my eyes open to see if my mother had shut hers already but, as hard as I tried, I couldn't. I had surrendered to the night.

I was sitting on a cold hard wooden floor wearing a bulky white diaper. I held onto a baby bottle in my tiny left hand. My short stubby little bare feet rested in front of me. There were tall dirty white walls towering over me. To my left was an entryway to what looked like a kitchen area and, to the right, an old wooden door that led outside. I could see outside through a little window beside the door. The air in the room was cold and dry and I saw a woman walking from the room where I was into the kitchen. I brought the bottle to my lips, cocked my head back and started sucking milk out of the little rubber tip.

Whoosh! Slam!

I jolted abruptly like I had just been shocked by electricity. I released the suction of my lips from the rubber tip of the bottle and dropped it out of my hands down to the floor. I stared wide eyed at the front door. A man stepped into the house and started walking eagerly towards the kitchen. He wore a dark gray sweatshirt with a hood that covered his head, a pair of white tennis shoes and dark black jeans that were frayed at the ends. He shouted something I couldn't understand and the woman yelled back. They were both in the kitchen so I couldn't see what was happening until the man took a retreating step backwards into the room, followed by a frying pan swinging viciously in his direction.

Ding!

The frying pan struck his right temple. His body stiffened and collapsed just like Goliath in the Bible after David had struck him with the stone. The woman stood over the motionless corpse victorious but shaking violently from the shock of the conflict. I watched as she walked to the kitchen and returned back to the room where the man lay motionless. She had a light blue telephone in her hand.

Not too long after this, I turned my head to the window and saw the reflection of blue and red flashing lights on the glass. A group of uniformed men stormed into the house through the open front door with a rolling white bed supported by an adjustable yellow and black frame. The men heaved the motionless man onto the white bed. They tightened three black straps together to secure him to the bed and then rolled him out the door rapidly. The woman talked expressively to a uniformed police officer while he wrote in a little black palm sized notebook. I continued to watch while concentrating on the scene but the police officer and the woman started to fill with a dark fog and blur from my vision. The dark fog slowly covered everything like a dark storm cloud moving in to consume a clear blue sky.

I woke up in the back of the station wagon and slightly pushed my shoulders and elbows back, resting my upper body weight comfortably on my forearms. I turned slightly to look out the back door window, the sun hadn’t come out yet but I had awakened early to attempt to analyze the dream I just woke from. Who was that man? The woman? The house seemed so familiar as if it had been the faded blue house we used to live in. I mean, I guess a lot of houses had wooden floors and technically were all very similar but it felt like I had been in that one specifically, like that dream was real. Could this dream have been a déjà vu? It was always so hard to determine which dreams were based on reality and which were completely fabricated in my head.

***

“Ahhhh,” a man blurted out softly, motioning for me to imitate him with his mouth open. He held a wooden popsicle stick and a little black light pointed into the back of my throat.

He was a doctor and he wore a classic white lab coat with a checkered red tie and a light blue collared shirt visible from underneath the coat. He had a long face and slick black hair combed back with gel and his jaw was defined with a five-o’clock shadow. He spoke with a deep roaring voice but was kind and gentle with his words. He had a bright blue stethoscope dangling from his neck that matched the color of his eyes.

After examining the inside of my mouth, he asked me to hop up on a hospital table cushioned with a leather blue covering in which he proceeded to tap my knee with a tiny triangular hammer, making sure my leg swung out towards him. He continued checking various functions throughout my body asking me to move my arm this way or that and do the same with my legs. When he was finished, he asked me to wait and stepped outside of the room.

The doctor re-entered the room and signaled my mother to sit down on the black chair near the door. He was examining a small stack of papers that I assumed were his notes.

"After reviewing my observations with other specialists, we have concluded that your son suffers from a hyperactive form of Attention Deficit Disorder, also known as ADHD," the doctor said gently and continued with some reassurance, "It is nothing to worry about really, as he will function normal in life. We have prescribed him some medication called Amphetamine Aspartate Monohydrate commonly known as Adderall, that will help him focus and assist with normal cognitive function in his day to day life."

"Okay," my mother responded cautiously.

The doctor then guided us out of the room back to the front reception area where we had originally registered and bid his farewells. My mother stood in the lobby area, examining the papers the doctor had given to her with deep concentration. She then walked to a long row of chairs and we sat together. I peered over her shoulder and looked at the papers that she was holding. Among them was the prescription. She folded it in halves until it was the size of a business card. She grabbed my hand and tugged me out towards the automatic sliding glass door. Outside the building, there was one of those circular trash bins that had an ashtray on the top. As we walked passed, I saw my mother toss the folded up prescription into the mouth of the lid on the trash bin discreetly and smoothly. She didn't even stop. We made our way through a large parking lot back to where the station wagon was parked.

***

I find it interesting how when people reached an all time low in their lives they would almost always, without fail, turn to God or a higher power. They seek a power that is beyond them simply because they feel too weak or powerless to overcome the struggles by themselves. It is almost always a desperate reach for God and never a voluntary one. This, at least, was what I had learned from eavesdropping on the stories that people shared with my mother on Sunday mornings at church. From my observation, I believed my mother wasn't much different than the stories I had heard. She sought out refuge in the church from her troubles and worries of our situation as well.

It was a large church. This made it easy to mix into the crowd without attracting too much attention, though attention was almost unavoidable because everyone was in search of an open ear to share their testimonies of salvation with. There was a large parking lot where my mother would park the station wagon while we attended the service. She always parked as far away from the church building as possible, away from the multitude of newer nicer looking cars. We would enter the church through a long narrow hallway that branched off into various meeting spaces and even a basketball court towards the far end of the hallway. Halfway down the hallway was a large open space with five propped open double doors. They led to a massive stage with neat rows of pews. The pews were stacked three stories high. There must have been thousands of people flooding in to attend that church every Sunday morning, like ants to an ant hill.

Personally, I thought the church service was rather boring, but I would still pay attention a little because there was really nothing else to do anyways; playing with the little clear plastic communion cups and red hard covered hymnals got old pretty quickly. The pastor would walk causally to the large podium in the center of the stage. He always dressed in a clean cut suit and carried a large black Bible in one of his hands. He would start by reading some passage of Scripture with an emotional passion and then a large choir would sing some hymns. Soon afterwards, they would stop singing and pay attention to the pastor as he began his sermon. I distinctly remembered one Bible verse that the pastor would recite every Sunday morning. He recited it as he called on the people in the congregation to come forward to what he referred to as "the altar". There, they would kneel, heads bent facing the ground and hands held together in prayer. The Bible verse read,

"For God so loved the world, that he gave his only begotten Son, that whosoever believeth in him shall not perish, but have everlasting life."

With this verse he would announce passionately that anyone that wanted to could say a prayer and ask God for forgiveness of their sins. This, he said, would guarantee a place in Heaven after death. I guess somehow this spoke to my mother as I remember she accepted his offer and walked up to the front of the pastors podium and did just that. I wasn't convinced that it was that easy to get to Heaven but I saw that it made my mother feel good so

I decided to go up to "the altar" to show her that I was still there with her. I remembered what she had said that day up on the mountain top,

"Know that I will always love you and will always want the best for you, no matter what happens."

I guess her prayer had worked as I noticed it somehow made her smile more often than before. Even through the cold nights sleeping in the back of that old station wagon and the times the grocery store didn't have enough food to spare. Through all of our struggles from then on out she always kept a smile.

It wasn't more than a couple weeks after that prayer that my mother started inviting a man to come sit beside us in church each Sunday. He was a skinny pale man with black curly hair and thick glasses exposing the lack in his vision. He always dressed in a clean long sleeve button down collared shirt with a tie of various colors tucked into a pair of brown dress slacks. He spoke in an awkward giggly tone, always forcing a smile into each one of his words, though he didn't speak often. His name was Jacob Nelson.

I was cautious towards Jacob at first because I wasn't used to having a man with us, but he slowly chipped away at my cautious attitude each Sunday when he would take us out to eat food at a fancy restaurant. I always looked forward to this. The food in those restaurants was incredible; like nothing I had ever tasted. Everything was fresh and the food was served hot with visible steam rising from the top. I would eat until my stomach could hold no more food and still tried to eat a little more as if to save it for the week that followed. I hoped that I wouldn't have to eat as much free grocery store food. I didn't mind Jacob. I was pretty sure at this point that he was my mother's boyfriend.

***

The sun was glowing bright in the middle of a pure blue sky and there was a slight breeze that tickled my hair and gave me a soothing cool brush through my skin every couple of minutes. I was standing next to my mother and Jacob in the middle of the church parking lot next to where the nicer cars parked. Beside us was Jacob's car which was a cranberry red, almost brand new, four door sedan. I had overheard my mother and Jacob talking about us driving into the mountains to have a picnic for lunch. He told her that he wanted to take us to Trail Ridge Road; a beautiful long winding road, which happened to be the highest paved road in the United States.

"What do you say Gene, do you like the mountains?" Jacob asked me in an excited rhetorical way followed by a little awkward giggle. He already knew my answer.

I nodded and gave him a little smile. I really did love the mountains, especially the day my mother had taken me to gaze down on the world after I had skipped school; and eating up there sounded even more exciting as the food with Jacob was always so delicious.

Jacob wasn't wrong, the road was beautiful. We had driven so high and deep into the mountains that the little houses and cars were long past and all that remained was herds of wild elk and deer prancing through the rugged terrain. There were wild flowers blanketing the mountainsides blooming vibrantly with yellow, red and light blue petals. The breeze would blow them slightly making it seem as if the blanket of wild flowers was actually a flowing sea. The air was thin, crisp and slightly frigid due to the twelve thousand foot elevation.

I sat in the back seat of his cranberry red four door sedan on the drive up. It had clean black leather seats and a little arm rest that pulled out of the middle seat that held two cup holders at the end. The entire car was spotless. It smelled fresh, as if the car had only been bought the day before.

Jacob pulled the car off to the side of the road into a small parking area that held about seven cars. We all got out of the car and started walking on a little trail that was marked by a sign and a little dirt pathway. The path led to an open view of the mountain range and just below was a crater still full of white snow with a light brown tint of dirt as if someone had gotten some overspray of paint on it from a spray brush. On another one of the many mountain ranges was a family of elk munching on the grass. While I was fixated on the view of the mountain range, Jacob and my mother approached with the large bag of food from the trunk of his car. I was sitting on the stone wall ledge that had been built around the viewing location.

I watched as Jacob pulled out large sandwiches made with fresh French bread loaves from the bag and big juicy dark purple grapes and three cans of soda. He then pulled out a dark green blanket and laid it out for us to sit and enjoy the meal. I grabbed the sandwich in both my hands with eager excitement but right as I was about to take a bite Jacob blurted out. . .

"Wait! We have to pray before we eat."

I tilted my head with a bit of confusion but lowered the sandwich acknowledging that I had heard what he said. He started to pray,

"Dear God, We gather here today grateful for the gorgeous day you have provided to us. I am grateful to have the company of Gene and Anita. We ask that you bless this food and drink and bless our bodies. In Jesus' name, amen."

An uncomfortable feeling came over me sending static through my veins after the prayer was finished. It felt really strange to me to say a prayer before eating food when we were not at church with the grape juice and crackers, but I ignored the feeling and started chomping down on my French bread sandwich.

I liked Jacob but he was an awkward guy and not just because of the prayer; though that did spark my mind to start thinking about all the strange behavior he had. Some of the things he did seemed a little OCD and I noticed his teeth would start grinding a bit if he noticed something was not the way he wanted it to be. He wouldn't start the car until he personally turned around and checked that everyone inside was wearing their seatbelt properly. One time, I whispered to my mother during one of the church services and he hushed me with his pointer finger over the center of his mouth telling me not to talk during the church service. While we were eating at one of the restaurants, I had my elbows on the table and he told me in a firm tone to remove them because he said it was a very rude thing to do. It wasn't like these things were really that big of a deal, but they felt strange when they happened.

"Yes!" my mother shouted loudly, shaking me from my thoughts.

I turned to see what was happening as it seemed I had zoned out while deep in my thoughts and didn't realize what was going on in front of me. Jacob was knelt down on one knee. My mother was standing with her hands cupped over her mouth and dripping a few tears from her eyes. She reached out her left hand towards Jacob. He took it gently and pushed a sparkling silver single diamond ring onto her finger. She brought it closer to her face in admiration. They both stood up holding hands, smiling as they gazed into each other's eyes. I sat staring at them not really knowing how to feel or what to say. I wasn't sure if I should smile, stand or clap so instead I just sat there quietly observing with both of my hands cupped around my face supporting my chin and elbows resting on my crossed legs.

THREE

Fall 1999

The leaves were dropping from the trees again like brown, yellow and orange stars falling from the sky. The air was starting to become drier and colder but the sun still warms the air making it just the right temperature. I sat outside on a wooden bench dangling my legs back and forth as I scanned the landscape around me. Behind me was an old white steeple and church with a large golden bell hanging from the top. There were people gathered inside chatting with occasional bursts of laughter.

I was dressed in black slacks, a white collared shirt and a black bolo tie fastened around my neck. It was the type of uniformed attire selected for the men of the wedding.

As I sat on the bench, I thought about all that had happened so quickly and how life was constantly moving in different directions. I pondered the idea of whether or not we really had any control over the direction of our lives or if we just blew in the direction life took us like the leaves submitting to the winds. It hadn't crossed my mind before today but I started to think about love and what it really was from watching my mother and Jacob as they prepared for their wedding. I thought about all the Sundays that had passed since Jacob's awkward proposal on the mountain top. I remembered all the times I had noticed the worry on my mother's face from the ways Jacob had treated me when I failed to appease his demands. Her reaction would disappear promptly with a forced smile whenever he turned in her direction. She always made sure to impress him and keep him content with her behavior, never questioning his authoritative manner. Observing these things made me question if love was an undesired submission to the demands of its first contender or if it was something you could actually desire.

I hopped off the bench and started walking towards the church where the ceremony was about to start. My mother had given me a role in the wedding. I was to carry the wedding ring on a little white fluffy pillow down an aisle lined on both sides with wooden church pews to the podium where the preacher stood. My mother and Jacob stood facing each other slightly in front of the podium on a little platform. Standing beside me was a little girl about my age with black curly hair that flowed down her back. A little white headband kept the hair off her face. She wore a white dress and held a colorful bouquet closely to her chest. Her face was pale white with powdered red circles on both cheeks.

The music started and both of us slowly walked to the beat of the music together down the church aisle. As we arrived at the front we separated to opposite sides of my mother and Jacob and waited while the preacher gave the traditional wedding speech. My mother and Jacob recited their vows followed by the unveiling of my mother's veil, the exchanging of rings and a kiss that ended the long, traditional, drawn out ceremony.

That was the day when everything changed. Drastically. Once again just like it had when we left the faded blue house for the back of that old Volvo station wagon. This time, we were moving back into a house. We were leaving those days of cuddling up in the back of the car behind.

***

Jacob's house was way bigger than the little faded blue house and not even comparable to the back of the old station wagon. When you stepped inside the house, there was a fuzzy light beige carpet lining the whole living room area. It spread until it abruptly got separated by a skinny metal strip in which the floor changed to hard wood. This wood floor was nothing like the one in the old faded blue house; it was shiny and clean with no scratches or dust. It stretched throughout the whole kitchen area, which was very spacious. To the left of the front door was a staircase that led up to two medium sized bedrooms and an ensuite room.

The neighborhood was quiet for the most part until around four in the afternoon when all the kids came home from school. It was surrounded by a seven foot brick wall with a white strip painted horizontally down the center. All the houses were uniformly white and had green window shades. Each one of them had a little yard and a five foot light post that lit up once the sunlight was gone. A gray cement path led you to the front door.

Life, living with Jacob, was a lot different than it had been when it was just my mother and I. I slept in my own room and I had a little dresser and so much space to move around. There was even a closet that was big enough for me to step inside. Jacob had bought me some new toys. They were new, like the little toy car. He didn't really talk much, but when he did it was usually to reprimand me, or a one-word response to questions my mother asked him. He had a lot of strict rules; no talking at the dinner table because "children were to be seen and not heard", needing to be home by five for dinner and in bed by eight. The neighborhood kids always played a game of football after school at four thirty so I never got to finish a game. I always had to leave before the game finished. The awkward prayer had become a routine before every meal and he would make me say it most of the time. If I didn't refer to him as "dad" he would get very angry and punish me by not letting me go out and play with the neighborhood kids. Living with Jacob had its perks but there were definitely a lot of downsides as well.

My mother, on the other hand, had adjusted quite well to living with Jacob and seemed to be enjoying the new life of basic luxuries like having a kitchen to cook in and a bathroom that you didn't have to share with a bunch of sweaty people like the one at the fitness gym. She always came home with new clothes that Jacob would buy for her and some things for me as well. She would use the kitchen to cook meals for all of us and would dance and sing to herself as she tended to whatever was cooking on the stovetop. She smiled a lot more often than before and moved around as if she was one hundred pounds lighter, when in reality she had actually gained a bit of weight. She even started attending college to pursue a degree for herself. I guess that all of the things the pastor had said proved to be true for her. God had apparently provided for all of her needs and desires shortly after we started attending that church every Sunday. She seemed to be content.

FOUR

Fall 2001

Ruth lay there screaming and crying while her little arms and legs shook back and forth frantically. Her eyes were sealed shut and her face crumpled up from the never-ending screaming that was coming from her little teeth-less mouth. She wiped away the streams of tears with her little hands like windshield wipers on a car. She wore a tiny green hat that covered her head and a matching onesie. Ruth was the newly born daughter of my mother and Jacob.

I was starting to get used to the routines and how to deal with Jacobs' intricate expectations. I figured out ways to get around some of his strict rules to start playing with the neighborhood kids more. I simply told him they were strict Bible believing Christians and that they wanted me to join them for their religious meetings; which never existed unless you considered a rough game of American football a religious meeting. I never worried about him finding out or asking to come with me because his antisocial ways were embedded deep within his core. I was certain that any type of social gathering instantly made him uncomfortable. He would try and force me to be interested in things that I really didn't care about. He would even get angry and tell me I was disrespectful if I expressed to him that I found his hobbies boring, like building little models or watching him fly remote control airplanes. I eventually realized that if I just agreed with everything he said with my words, regardless of how I truly felt, then everything would go more smoothly and I could return to my "religious meetings" with the neighborhood kids faster.

School was a lot better than it had been when we lived in the back of the station wagon because I was actually able to relate to the kids at school and talk with them about after school football. We didn't live too far away so I walked to and from school by myself everyday. There was a street that I would follow to the right as I exited the neighborhood that would lead to a little park with a playground. Then, I would turn onto the street to the left and follow it until I reached the school building; about a ten minute walk. The school was surrounded by a gray chain link fence that wrapped around the entire property including a large football field that was marked with white spray paint like the professional football fields, but not as clean and well maintained. The building itself was a light grayish blue color with cranberry red doors. I was in fourth grade now, only another grade away from becoming a middle-schooler.

It felt strange having a half sister in the house as almost everything revolved around her now. We would delay our mealtimes if she was hungry or wake up if she started crying in the middle of the night. I was always expected to help take care of her and try to calm her down if she started to cry. I think Jacob felt proud to have a child that was actually his, versus myself who just happened to be left over baggage that my mother was carrying around with her from whatever life she had lived before him.

***

“… and that is how the American Civil War ended in eighteen sixty-five with a hard earned victory for the Union soldiers,” stated the teacher as she came to the end of her history lesson.

The teacher was about thirty years old and put her light brown hair up in a bun that looked like a cinnamon roll. She had little brown freckles and cheeks that looked slightly inflated like tiny balloons. She wore a blue dress with a large black belt wrapped around her torso and blue high heels to match the dress. She always walked with a confident upright posture and smiled most of the time unless she was really deep in a discussion. She would change her facial expressions based on the topic of discussion in an extremely animated manner.

“Now for some follow-up questions,” she continued, “What was the main reason the Union soldiers were fighting against the Confederate army?”

A couple of students raised their hands eagerly to be selected to answer.

"Yes." She pointed, "You, in the back left corner."

"To end all of the slavery?" a little fat red haired boy with freckles replied in an unsure tone.

"Yes, that is absolutely correct," the teacher stated proudly and then followed with another question, "And why did the Confederate army fight against the Union soldiers?"

More hands flung up into the air this time. This question seemed a lot easier than the first, given we already knew why the Union was fighting, so it seemed obvious what this answer should be.

"You, in the front," she pointed once again to another student.

"Because they wanted to keep the slavery," a little blonde girl with two pigtails said in a shy nervous tone.

"Yes, that's correct!" the teacher replied in an excited tone.

It was nine in the morning and the loudspeaker blared with a high pitched screech, interrupting the teacher from continuing on with the rest of her follow-up questions. A robotic sounding voice that began to speak,

"Would the following students please report to the office as soon as possible," the voice on the loudspeaker commanded boldly and then read a list of names of classmates and other students that I didn't recognize.

Two students in my classroom whose names had been called got up from their desks and left for the office. They were gone for about fifteen minutes and when they finally returned to the classroom they had fresh tears. The class stared at them confused and concerned at what had happened. The two students slowly grabbed their backpacks and began slowly exiting the classroom. The teacher was speaking quietly in the front of the classroom with the school counselor and the expression on her face showed great concern and disbelief. Once they had finished talking and the two students had left, the teacher slowly walked to the front center of the room hesitantly with her head bowed a little and her hands folded together in front of her waist.

"There has been a terrible attack against America," she started addressing the class hesitantly, "some bad men have stolen a plane and crashed it into the Twin Towers in New York City, causing the buildings to fall down. Thousands of American family members were in those buildings and may not survive. Two of your classmates had family members that were in the towers that collapsed, so right now I would like the class to take out your black composition notebooks and use one of the pages to write a letter to your classmates to let them know that you are there for them if they need you."

The class sat silent and shocked for a moment in disbelief of what she had just said until the silence was broken with eager questions of concern and rummaging through backpacks to retrieve their notebooks.

"Are the men that stole the planes going to go to jail?" a concerned kid with black square framed glasses and dark black hair asked from the back of the room.

The teacher replied, "The men that stole the planes actually died as well when they crashed into the buildings."

"Were the men in the planes Americans?" a little girl asked, squishing her face together and tilting her head to the side.

"The news said that they were terrorists from the Middle East. They are part of a group called Al-Qaeda, but we are waiting for more information," the teacher answered in a calm, steady manner.

"So does that mean we are going to start a war with Al-Qaeda like the civil war?" another little boy asked eagerly.

"I'm not sure. We will get more information later on, for now, why don't we try and focus on writing those letters for your fellow classmates?" the teacher responded cautiously. She was clearly trying to change the subject.

Everyone stayed silent and lowered their hands back to their desks. They picked up their pencils and opened their notebooks. I sat there doing the same, thinking about what we had just been told and how unreal it all seemed. I couldn't think of what to write to them, so I just sat there and pondered the news that was presented.

FIVE

Middle school

I swung my fist forward with raging force in a rapid right hook punch, striking it into a blubbery torso. The blow formed a crater from the impact and created ripples of fat. The feet below the torso stubbled backwards onto a ruffled green patch of grass. The face of the man was desperate and worried from the impact and sweating from the physical effort of his defense. You could see his knees trembling as he stood his ground feebly against my attacks.

We were in a little yard and the grass was surrounded by a stained wooden fence seven feet high that set the boundaries of the conflict. The grass was bordered by neatly arranged little round rocks that came out one foot from the wooden fence. One side didn't have a wooden fence, but instead, the back of a two story house that stood towering above us. It had a cement patio that led to a sliding glass door into the house. The sun shone bright in the sky, beating down on us.

The man, shaking with fright, stumbled his way over the cement patio and struggled to push the sliding glass door to the side as he fumbled into the house. He was clenching the side of his torso where I had struck him, breathing heavily from the pain. I clenched my fists with rage and stood with my chest pushed out like a barbaric warrior. I saw my reflection in the sliding glass door.

If you stepped inside the house from the back sliding glass door, you were introduced to a kitchen area. Beside the kitchen, there was an open room with a TV, couch and entryway that led to a bathroom and two car garage. Directly ahead, you could see the front door of the house in the other more distant room. You would pass a staircase on your way to that room. The last room had a little coffee table in front of a love seat pushed against the wall. The front door led out to a front porch area and a driveway. The street had a neat row of houses similar to this one.

I pursued the man earnestly through the sliding glass door into the house. My eyes were locked on my target and I saw that he was making his way to the front door of the house. I quickly caught up to him and pulled my right leg up to my torso charging the energy of a fierce front kick that I launched into his back. His arms flew back and his knees caved to the ground. He lay face down on his belly with his hands outstretched in front of him. I walked closer to his head. I stepped over his helpless trembling body.

His head lay right next to the corner of the little coffee table in the center of the room. I reached my hand down and gripped the back of his neck tightly in the palm of my right hand. I lifted his head directly above the corner of the coffee table. Adrenaline was shooting through my veins and I could feel my pulse in every one of my limbs. My heart was pounding the inside of my chest like a blood thirsty wolf being held back from a fresh juicy steak. I brought his head up a little bit higher as if I was increasing the tension of a bow in order to shoot the arrow as far as possible. I squeezed his neck even tighter and I could feel every muscle in it tense up. I stared deeply with tunnel vision at the sharp wooden coffee table corner. I tightly held his head in my trembling hand and prepared to smash it into the coffee table. The man had completely submitted to his fate in silence. The top half of his body hung from my grip like a dead animal dangling from the hand of its hunter. My ears slowly started blocking out the noise around me with a high pitched *ring*, until I was almost deaf. I began to deliver his head to the target. Suddenly, I heard the faint shout of a female voice that pierced through what was left of my hearing.

"STOP! STOP! OH GOD, NO! PLEASE STOP!"

***

Jacob, Ruth, my mother and I moved into a brand new house shortly after I finished elementary school. My mother and Jacob were part of the designing process. I had my own room upstairs and so did everyone else. A little shared bathroom separated Ruth's bedroom from mine. Directly across from the bathroom entrance was my mother and Jacob's room. It was large and had its own bathroom inside.

The neighborhood was brand new. There were many houses that were still under construction. When you entered the neighborhood from the main street, it had a fancy framed brick sign that read PINE MEADOWS in white capital letters. The neighborhood had a strict enforcement policy. You could get fined if your grass grew too long or if your front yard wasn't tidy and maintained neatly. It was perfect for a person like Jacob because he was naturally strict and OCD anyways.

There was a little park area on the edge of the neighborhood that had a playground, baseball field, tennis court and a skatepark. The perimeter was fenced off with a stained wooden fence that stood ten feet tall. Surrounding the baseball field and tennis court and tracking through the playground, was a paved hiking pathway that looped in a circle around the park. The skatepark was pushed up against the edge of the park next to the ten foot wooden fence.

It was a fairly quiet neighborhood and definitely the nicest one where I had ever lived. There were always people walking their dogs or jogging while their kids followed them on their bicycles. There was a school bus that would come and pick up all the kids to take them to the public school. Many kids played football at the park all day long during the summer holidays. Every house had a newly planted tree in the front yard.

Jacob enrolled me in a strict fundamental baptist church's school program for sixth grade and my mom agreed to it like she always did with everything that he said now. It was actually the school of the church we attended every Sunday, created as an option for the church attendees. The school had a strict dress code that stated all boys were to have their shirts tucked into their pants and always had to wear collared button down shirts. The girls had to wear skirts that covered down to their ankles and long sleeves that hid their arms. Each class started with an awkward prayer like the one Jacob had given on the mountain before proposing to my mother. The teachers always included Bible verses in every lesson whether the subject had anything to do with the Bible verses or not. There was actually an entire subject dedicated to the sole purpose of learning about the Bible but only the King James version. They taught us that all other versions were secular translations that the Devil was using to deceive the masses. Using profanity was strictly prohibited and all of the literature we read had to be written by Christian authors. Jacob had received a recent promotion at work that provided him with a pay raise. I think that inspired all the changes, like buying a new house and paying for the private church school.

The school shared the same building as the church and actually used many of the same rooms, though a few of the rooms remained vacant on Sundays. When you entered the property of the church there was a three section parking lot that spread throughout the buildings, the other building being the gymnasium that they used during school days. A tall red brick steeple that matched the red brick exterior on the other two buildings marked the entry point into the church. As you made your way to the front entrance of the church you were greeted by two large double doors and a little stained wooden sign with chiseled letters that read WELCOME TO FAITH BAPTIST.

When you entered, there was a large gathering area where everyone would chat. The service would start with the choir singing traditional hymns from a section of three pews behind the preacher. Behind the choir was a clear tank of water and two sets of stairs that lead into the water on both sides. The water tank was used to baptize people during the church services. This church was much smaller than the first church we had originally attended when we lived in the back of the station wagon.

It was shortly after the start of my sixth grade school year at Faith Baptist that I decided it would be easier to get through the school days if I received a baptism. Everyone in the school was extremely committed and overly zealous about being the best Christian they could be in the eyes of their peers, which I thought was ridiculously irritating. I, on the other hand, didn't really care and wasn't into the Bible or being a Christian, but not being baptized meant that I was harassed on a daily basis by the teachers, students and everyone that attended the church on Sundays. I would attempt to tell them that I had already become a Christian and it didn't matter whether I was baptized or not, but they would start reciting numerous Bible verses to convince me that I wasn't truly a Christian yet. This is the reason I finally decided to set up a baptism and get it over with.

I remember it fairly well. I was led into a changing room positioned behind the stage where I was given a white ragged robe to put on. I was then led down the stairs into the water tank in front of all the church attendees. The preacher recited some Bible verses and asked me a couple questions. I could care less what the questions were about, I just said yes to all of them. He then laid me down backwards, fully submerged into the water, and lifted me out quickly. After this, everyone clapped and cheered and the uncomfortable and irritating harassment came to an end. It worked perfectly, because no one ever questioned whether I was a true Christian for most of the school year.

I attended Faith Baptist School, but the public middle school next to our neighborhood was only two miles from our house; about a 20 minute walk away. I had really wished I could just attend a normal public school with normal kids because they seemed to enjoy themselves a lot more than we did at the church school. I would always walk to the middle school on Saturdays because sometimes there were kids doing school projects over the weekend or just hanging out around the school yard.

The middle school was significantly bigger than Faith Baptist. It was extremely tall for only being two stories high and the building was in the shape of a giant T. It had mostly brown painted bricks around the exterior with the exception of three large strips of red bricks splitting the building in half through the center. There were basketball courts on one side of the T and a large parking lot with a bus lane on the other. At the far bottom of the T was the music room. I would hang out just outside the entry door every weekend to see if any of the band members were there practicing.

***

“That will be three-hundred eighty-six dollars and twenty-seven cents. Will that be all for you?” the man asked with a final dramatic push of a button on the cash register.

“Yea, that’s it,” I replied as I reached into my pocket and counted out the amount of money onto the counter.

During the winter halfway through my sixth grade school year at Faith Baptist it snowed at least twice a week, which was great for earning money. I had bought a little snow shovel from the store across the street. I started going from door to door asking the home owners if they wanted me to shovel their driveways so that I could earn some cash. As long as I shoveled Jacob and my mother’s driveway for free, Jacob wouldn’t mind if I walked around the neighborhood and shoveled driveways for cash. I told him I was doing it to save money for a Christian college where I wanted to attend, which of course was a lie, but it made him happy and I knew that was what he wanted to hear. To some people, ignorance really was bliss. I quickly found out that it had to be ignorance against their will for it to really apply, otherwise curiosity would disrupt their bliss.

Living with Jacob was the same as it was in his original house, as far as strict rules and awkward dinner prayers were concerned. The main difference was that now he had more money and we lived in a bigger house. The times that I had to be home for dinner changed slightly, mainly because with his new job he didn’t return home until about six or seven. I was still expected to be home for dinner before those times, and then shortly after to prepare for bed. He added a few rules, as if it was a competition and the ones he had previously made were falling behind. I was strictly only allowed to listen to classical music with an orchestra or a piano. One rule, that was the same as the school, was that any and all books had to be written by Christian authors. He would still grind his teeth together in frustration if anything was not the way he wanted it to be, especially when it came to my behavior or things I would talk about. I adapted fairly well to that though, because I started to learn what triggered him and just avoided using any of those topics, words or phrases when I was around him.

I had a lengthy list of chores that he would attach to the front of my bedroom door, and another copy of the list downstairs attached to the front of the refrigerator. I was expected to deep clean every room and bathroom inside of the house, with the exception of their bedroom which was strictly forbidden for me to enter. That included washing dishes after all meals and mowing the front and back yards during the time of year that it grew. He would tell me that if I couldn't eat my dinner from the toilet bowl, then it wasn't clean enough.

The relationship I used to have with my mother before Jacob slowly started to fade as the years went by. To me, she didn't seem like the same person anymore. The way I remembered my mother was the way I saw her up on that mountain top the day we skipped school and work. She was a risk taker, fearless and resilient, and we used to tackle life together cuddled up underneath those wool blankets in the back of the station wagon. The way she sat freely on the hood of the car with her dirty blonde hair flowing with the direction of the wind. The way she would gaze out at the world below as if she had conquered it and our struggles had ceased to exist. I always thought about whether I was the reason she had changed so much, due to my constant mistakes, or if it had anything to do with Jacob and his overly-structured linear lifestyle. Whatever the reason was, she had clearly changed; for better or worse, I would never know. That was something for her to reconcile with in her own heart.

The cashier scooped up the money I had counted out for him. He entered the amount into the cash register with his index finger. That sparked the sound of a little ding as the cash register drawer flew open and he sorted the money into the draw. Shortly after the ding, while he was sorting the money into the drawer, a receipt started printing out from a little printer next to the cash register. He ripped it off, folded it neatly in half and then handed it to me and thanked me for my purchase. I had bought a black Fender-Stratocaster knock-off guitar in a black case with a cable, some picks, and a little black amplifier. I removed the guitar and amplifier from the counter and proceeded to the exit of the shop.

The store was a little local music shop about a ten mile walk away from my house. It had a glass storefront that displayed drum sets, guitars, bass guitars and a variety of other musical instruments. All of the instruments that Jacob said were "of the Devil". When you walked inside there was a beautiful display of guitars and basses hanging neatly on the wall. As you walked further into the store you would eventually run into a section of drum sets, keyboards, PA speakers and amplifiers. I had only been to the music shop one time before, and that was the last time Jacob had to work on a Saturday.

The music store was located in a small historic town that was also the location of the public high school. There were rows of little stores and restaurants that led to the high school and an older neighborhood surrounding the town. There was a clean symmetrical row of fifteen foot black street lamps that lit up the row of shops at night on both sides of the street. One end of the street ended at the high school and the other at a main road that you could drive straight back to my house. Beside that main road was a paved trail that stretched along the full ten mile walk back to my house as well. I would pass the public T shaped middle school on the way.

Before entering onto my street, I peered around the corner to the driveway to see if Jacob or my mother were outside the house. Once I saw that it was clear, I quickly walked to the front porch of the house, leaving the guitar and accessories I had bought by the front door. I entered the house to scan out the location of everyone inside. I noticed my mother was in the living room watching TV and while I was there I peeked into the garage to see if Jacob's car had arrived yet; it hadn't. It was all clear, so I made some small talk with my mother and proceeded to grab the guitar and equipment from outside and take it quickly up to my room. Once I was in my room, I stored it under my bed with some boxes of clothes positioned in front to hide it. Each night after everyone was asleep, I would pull out the guitar and play it. I played without plugging it into the amplifier, so that only I could hear it. This is how I taught myself how to play guitar.

***

"Yo Gene, let's play it back from the top," shouted John.

John was a tall kid with a large head that sat slightly in front of his shoulders due to his hunchback. His bangs were dyed black and they dangled over his eyes. He constantly flipped them to the side. The back of his hair was cut short. He always wore a large T-shirt with the name or logo of a rock band on it and skinny jeans with holes in the knees. John was a friend, and also a member of my band. I had met him on one of the days when I waited outside of the middle school music room. It was one of those lucky days when I would catch the middle school band practicing on a Saturday. He had seen me watching them play and afterwards came up to ask me why I was there. We exchanged stories and started meeting every Saturday at his house, which was visible from the middle school parking lot. A hop over his backyard fence away. John was in the middle school band as a saxophone player but he also played bass guitar in the rock band we started together.

"Fuck yea!" Blake shouted with excitement as he made little jumps with his feet while seated on a little black leather drum stool.

Blake was also tall. I was the shortest in the band. Blake had blonde bleach-tipped hair that he spiked up with gel. He always wore a hooded sweatshirt and baggy jeans that would fray as they dragged against the pavement when he walked. Blake was another friend I had made, only he wasn't in the middle school band, he just attended school there. I met him through John when we decided we wanted to form a band and needed a drummer.

We were a three man rock band and we would rehearse every Saturday in John's basement. Even though we always practiced new songs, there was one that we made sure to continue practicing religiously. We were planning to play it next year for the middle school seventh grade talent show. The sixth grade talent show had already passed before we met. Since I didn't attend the school I was technically not able to compete in the talent show. However, we managed to sweet talk the school administration into allowing us to sign up for seventh grade. They allowed us to perform under the condition that I got a parental permission paper signed stating that they were allowing me to participate. Jacob would have never allowed me to perform, because he didn't even know I owned an electric guitar, let alone played it in a secret rock band. I simply forged his signature onto the paper. I thought about asking my mother to sign it, but I had learned that no matter what she wanted to do or thought was right in her mind, in the end, she always had to adhere to Jacob's demands. I didn't want to risk it.

I nodded acknowledging John's call to play the song another time and cranked the volume of my knock-off Stratocaster as loud as it would go. I removed the black guitar pick resting in between the guitar strings on the neck of the guitar and raised it proudly in the air like an olympic torch bearer. Blake raised both of his hands up to the sky with a drumstick in each hand. John cranked the volume of his bass guitar and lowered his head so that his hair reached for the ground. He focused his vision on the four strings and his right hand readied at the body of the bass guitar. You could hear the sound of the guitar amplifiers building up a crescendo of feedback from their speaker cones. Blake swung the drum sticks hitting them together to make a loud wooden *click* sound. After four loud *clicks*, a flood of sounds entered my eardrums causing my heart to pound to the beat of the bass drum. It was a rush of music that pulsed through my veins, one of the best feelings I had ever felt. I felt a release. I would sing out loudly allowing all the words I had to hold back whenever I was around Jacob to flow freely without restraint. There, in that basement, I would discard my troubles, my stresses and my worries. The pastor told me that Jesus would discard these things for me, He never did. Music did for me everything that Jesus never could. Music was my sanctuary.

***

"Withhold not correction from the child: for if thou beats him with the rod, he shall not die"

Proverbs 23:13

That Bible verse rang in my ears while the pastor continued to read sternly from his old black King James Bible. It was another long Sunday morning service that felt to have dragged on for twenty hours. I was sitting beside Jacob and my mother in the church pews. I discreetly turned my eyes from left to right attempting not to move my head while I scanned the room and looked around at all the church attendees. They all sat upright with straight heads pointed directly at the pastor. I wondered for a moment if these people took these Bible verses literally or if they thought the verses were simply a figure of speech; like how the expression "I'm going to kill you" really just meant that you were very angry, not that you were actually going to kill that person.

Jacob had been acting very strange today and seemed stressed out about something but I couldn't tell what it was. I tried to engage in as little conversation with him as possible, hoping not to spark his nerves in any way. The drive home was very quiet, not even my mother spoke to Jacob. This was unusual; even though he didn't talk much, he always talked with her. We arrived home and my mother served lunch. I cleaned the kitchen and washed the dishes. My mother and Jacob then went to their room and closed the door while I sat in my room and pulled out a little CD player I had bought from the music store. I listened to my favorite rock bands. I always kept a few classical CDs out on the floor just in case Jacob walked in and asked me what I was listening to; I could show him that it was just classical music.

I no longer kept my guitar under my bed. I left it in John's basement so that I wouldn't have to sneak it out of the house every Saturday. I thought it was much safer that way and when I listened to music, I imagined the guitar parts in my head and played them on an air guitar.

"Gene! Get down here!" Jacob shouted from downstairs in an aggravated tone.

My heart skipped a beat and I quickly took out the rock CD I was listening to and switched it out for the classical one. I then hid the rock CD deep inside the box of clothes under my bed. I wondered how much time had passed since we arrived home from church. I set the CD player down on the floor and quickly started making my way downstairs. Showing up late to Jacob's calls could be brutal. I arrived standing at attention, like a soldier responding to a commanding officer.

"Yes, sir," I said almost hesitant but with forced confidence in an attempt to not sound suspicious, guilty or disrespectful in any way.

"We received your report card from Faith Baptist," Jacob stated firmly as if my mother were standing beside him while he spoke, even though she wasn't present at the time. He continued, "When I was your age, I received straight A's in every class I took because I was thankful for the mind God gave me, but it doesn't seem like you are as thankful as I was. I only see one A on this report card."

He shoved the report card into my face striking my nose and crumbling it to the formation of my face. My nose started to leak a little blood and I wiped it off with the back of my hand promptly. I stood trembling a bit from the adrenaline. I looked down at the floor, not daring to even glance up at Jacob. I tried to sniffle a bit to keep the blood from dripping but it was too strong of a flow. It started dripping to the kitchen floor. I heard the rummaging of kitchen supplies not too far in front of me. I assumed it was Jacob, but I was too frightened to look up and confirm. He returned back closer to me gripping the back of my neck in the palm of his hand tightly. All the muscles in my neck started to tense up and I froze in a shrugged position from the pain. He guided me with his tightened grip on my neck to a little bathroom next to the room with the TV and pushed me up against the toilet seat. He slammed the door shut.

"Take off your pants and put your hands up against the back of the toilet seat!" He yelled in a firm aggressive tone.

My heart sped up even faster and my whole body started to shake profusely like I had been left naked in a fierce winter storm. My nose was still dripping drops of blood as I turned around cautiously and slowly to start removing my pants. When I turned around, I didn't look up high enough to see Jacob's face. I made sure to keep my head bowed to the ground but I caught a glimpse of one of the metal cooking pans tightly held in his right hand.

"Your underwear too!" He shouted boldly.

"No," I responded in a shaken quiet tone, hesitant to say it too loudly.

He lifted the pan high in the air and swung it down harshly, striking my back as I fumbled to my knees and hit my face on the toilet seat. I really didn't want to take off my underwear and was terrified of what he was planning to do. My mind raced with possibilities of what he could be planning to do to me next. That led me to scenarios that I really didn't want to think about at the moment. I just closed my eyes tightly, trying to erase those images from my brain. I slowly and cautiously lifted myself back up onto my feet and started removing my underwear.

"You see, Gene. . . things will go much more smoothly if you just listen to what I tell you to do the first time. Now tell me, Gene, how many do you think you deserve?" he asked with a slight sinister chuckle.

My heart kept pounding on my chest as if it had given up hope on my tired body and attempted to break out and ditch it for a new one. I started to think hard about his question. How many did I deserve? I really didn't know what to say to that question and it was even harder trying to think of an answer while my body shook violently in fear. I started trying to calculate the answer in my head. I thought about how much he would think that I deserved. I was afraid to answer too low of a number, because I'm sure he would give me more for punishment. I was afraid to answer too high, because I'm sure he would give me some I could have avoided.

"Five," I mumbled in a shaken voice.

"Five? All you think you deserve is five?" He questioned as if he couldn't believe what he was hearing and then continued boldly, "I will double that because that is how much you actually deserve."

He raised his right hand gripping the pan tightly at the handle. He pushed me up further against the toilet and swung the pan down striking my bare naked backside. I felt the stinging sensation travel throughout my backside. I clenched my teeth with open lips, breathing in deeply, as if the air I was letting in could provide relief to my burning body. Before I could completely absorb all the pain, I felt the pan strike again. This time I felt it in my tailbone, which reflexed my feet to stand on my tiptoes. I clenched my butt cheeks and swung my left arm around to my backside, attempting to shield myself from the blows. I then felt the pan strike the back of my elbow, causing me to remove it from covering my backside. I pressed my left arm against my chest, while continuing to hold myself up with my right arm. Again, it hit my backside, only this time I was starting to lose feeling in the position that it had struck. Again and again. I felt the pan continue to strike my backside, lower back, and the back of my legs until all of them had become numb. I could no longer support myself on my feet so I had fallen to my knees and held onto the toilet bowl desperately with my right arm for support. Suddenly, it all stopped.

I heard the bathroom door slam shut and turned my head slightly to see that Jacob had left. I tried to move away from the toilet but I could barely move my body properly from the pain. I sank down to the bathroom floor, lying on my side breathing heavily with tears gradually flowing down my face and dripping to the floor.

I lay there silently on my side staring at the wall in front of me for a while. I pondered life. I asked myself questions like why did Jacob do these things to me and why my mother decided to be with someone like him. I thought about how my mother and I used to be so poor. We had nothing except for each other, but now it seemed we had everything except for each other. I thought about that little toy car and how, at the time, I was so excited to have something new that no one else had opened. Now, I thought about how insignificant that little toy car really had been, besides the lasting impact it still had on my life. I wondered if I had never taken that car, if my mother and I still would have ended up moving in with Jacob. I wished they had never met. I wondered if this was still part of my punishment for stealing. If I could go back, I would have never stolen that stupid little toy car.

That beating was the first of many to come. Through those beatings, I had learned that there was never a correct answer to "how many do you think you deserve?", because the pain always felt the same. Thinking back to the Sunday church service, I knew that one thing was for sure. Jacob took that Bible verse (Proverbs 23:13) literally, only his version of "the rod", was a hard metal kitchen frying pan.

***

". . .and on the seventh day God rested and marveled at the perfect world he had created. That everyone, is the history of how the world and the universe came into existence," my sixth grade teacher at Faith Baptist middle school stated in an overly excited tone with an exaggerated smile on her face. She continued, "Now does anyone have any questions regarding this lesson?"

It was nearing the end of sixth grade and I couldn't wait for the year to be finished. The school year at Faith Baptist seemed to have dragged on just like the painfully boring church services each Sunday. To make it even worse, both things happened in the same place so it felt like I never left.

This particular classroom was a small square classroom that had two large windows overlooking the parking lots of the buildings. There were even rows of student desks lined up in a four by four grid facing the front of the classroom. At the front of the classroom was a large green tinted chalkboard that the teacher would use to scribble on during several lessons throughout the year. The teacher had a larger black metal desk placed in the back of the classroom that she would sit at when we were taking tests. Sometimes she would pace up and down the aisles of the student desks and peek down to make sure that we were doing whatever task she had assigned.

A few people raised their hands to her question including myself, though I rarely ever raised my hand. I hated participating. Today was different though. I only had a week left until summer vacation so I finally felt like asking some of the questions I had always kept to myself.

"Yes, Gene. Glad to see you participating for a change," the teacher said in an astonished tone.

The class chuckled at this remark.

"I was talking with someone from my town and they told me that the universe was actually created from the Big Bang and we are all kind of here by mistakc," I stated in a mischievous tone.

"That is the most widely taught lie across the world, Gene. The lie that Satan uses to try to deceive you. They simply do not want to acknowledge the perfect creation of the Lord, our God above in Heaven," she said with shrewd confidence.

"The creation of the Lord, your God, is not perfect. . . if you're talking about this world," I quickly responded back boldly.

A few students in the class gasped in disbelief.

"Gene, I think that is enough from you. . . now you are just being disrespectful," she stated firmly.

I thought about that for a second.

"No, I am not being disrespectful. You simply brush off the idea that you may actually be wrong about a lot of things that you teach," I said with a new found confidence.

"Gene," she said, slightly interrupting in a slow disapproving tone.

"This world is a fucking mess! Look around you and see it for yourself, where is the perfection?" I started getting more passionate with my words and louder as I continued.

This time, even more students gasped in disbelief.

"Gene! You will not use that language in this classroom and you will report to the principal's office immediately!" she shouted. She was becoming increasingly angrier from my unorthodox speech.

I ignored her demands and carried on with my passionate rant, "You teach us these one sided views, while discrediting the opposing argument by saying it is the Devil trying to deceive us. What if they are actually right about the Big Bang and the Bible has been wrong all along? That would make it just a collective set of fictitious stories written throughout history.

What if your God doesn't really exist? Let's say He does. . . even if He does exist, He obviously doesn't give a shit about the people He created because millions are suffering and He does nothing about it."

I had let my rant continue for too long, and that was displayed clearly by the disgusted look on my teacher's face. She glared at me with prominent disapproval. I could tell she had had enough of my outspoken thoughts and questioning of her religious teachings. She stormed towards my desk and grabbed my left bicep tightly, ripping me out of my chair. She started dragging me to the principal's office.

She directed my body to sit down on a wooden chair with a black leather cushion puffed out on the seat and released her grip from my arm. The chair was facing directly at the principal's desk, which had a stack of Bibles. MINISTER DAVE was written in white letters on a black plaque with a thin golden border. I guess the principal of Faith Baptist was also a minister because it was a school created by the church. My teacher started informing minister Dave of what had happened in her classroom in an animated frenzy.

I sat there quietly zoning out and thinking about what had happened. I thought about how I had been in this position before. I remembered when I had to go to the principal's office at the school I was attending when my mother and I lived inside the station wagon. However, this time I didn't feel bad for my actions. Not at all. It was not like before when I had felt regret for my mother having to leave work to come pick me up. This time, that didn't matter to me because she had Jacob. My actions no longer affected her in that way. She seemed to have received everything she wanted. Money and stability. I thought about how tiring it was each and every day pretending to enjoy the things that Jacob did, pretending to be a Christian or to be interested in God, pretending like the relationship between my mother and I hadn't changed and acting as if everything was fine while Jacob beat me on a weekly basis. I couldn't keep holding all of those things inside of me. It was building up pressure and I was ready to explode inside like a carbonated soda bottle that had been thoroughly shaken. I was exhausted from silencing the person I truly was inside my core, simply because of fear of stirring up conflict.

The teacher left the room and quietly closed the door behind her. Minister Dave sat down on a black leather office chair behind his desk setting his elbows gently on his desk with his hands together as if he were about to pray. He centered his head behind his hands and brought them in front of his nose. He stared directly into my eyes with a harsh judgmental gaze.

"Gene, what you did in that classroom was disrespectful to God. The reason you say and do the despicable things that you do is because you don't see your sin as a hard rusty nail entering the hand of Jesus Christ on the cross. You say those things because you are blinded by Satan's deception and you believe that you are wiser and more intelligent than God himself. You say those things because you are a selfish disobedient sinner that should be begging God, on your hands and knees, for forgiveness of your sins. You question the validity of the Bible simply because you have welcomed the dark spirits of the Devil into your helpless soul." minister Dave spoke with conviction.

I pondered what he was saying and tried to make sense of his words while he spoke. I then listened as he continued his speech.

"The Bible teaches that the punishment for sin is death. You deserve death, Gene, that is what you deserve for your sins. Luckily for you, God can forgive your sins if you do as I said and beg him on your hands and knees to deliver you from your evil. Will you beg God for forgiveness today, Gene?" he asked me while raising his right eyebrow and tilting his head slightly.

I thought about his question and whether I should just play the part and pretend to ask God for forgiveness like I always did. Pretend to be sincere. All of the thoughts I had stored silently in my head were becoming too heavy for me to carry anymore. I started deciding that I didn't want to carry them any longer. I wanted them to be free from captivity. I wanted to be free to speak and say whatever I pleased without fear of condemnation.

"No," I replied solemnly.

He lowered his sight to the desk releasing the previously locked stare that he had been holding on me all this time. He then slowly shook his head from left to right, taking a deep breath and exhaling as he did so.

"The Bible also teaches us that unrepentant sinners are to be removed from the church so that they don't infect the rest of the believers. I will have to remove you from Faith Baptist effective immediately. You are banned from attending school here indefinitely. I will be contacting your parents to come get you. May God help your soul," he stated boldly as he rose from his chair and stormed out of the office. The door slammed shut behind him.

***

I was now in seventh grade but I didn't attend Faith Baptist school any longer. I was removed exactly as minister Dave had said I would be. Jacob was not pleased about it at all. He expressed his disapproval with more beatings. He became more creative with the beatings and no longer only used a pan but also used belts, two by fours, baseball bats and other items he would grab in the moment. My mother appeared to be indifferent to the beatings and just avoided being present while it was happening.

The summer had been great for earning money. I started a job twirling signs on a street corner for housing development showrooms. I made ten dollars per hour, which was four dollars more than minimum wage. I opened up a bank account where I would receive my paychecks every two weeks through a direct deposit system. My employer would simply send the money straight to my bank account every pay day. I would have access to it within a few days. I was saving up to buy a car, once I was old enough to apply for my license.

My mother and Jacob were recommended for a self taught homeschooling program after I was banned from Faith Baptist. They decided to try it out for my seventh grade year. It was basically a stack of all the textbooks that they had at all the other schools. I was required to read them and when I finished, take a test. The test was located on a certain page in the test booklet, that was referenced in the textbook. My mother was always distracted by her studies. She was pursuing her college degree. I would sneak over to where she kept the answer booklets and record everything. I would copy the answers to my paper while she wasn't paying attention and finish everything early. With the extra time, I would make it appear as if I was still working hard. Instead, I would simply write songs, poetry, and short stories.

I loved writing because it gave me the release I needed from all the troubles I held inside myself. Any thought, idea or concern I had would be graciously accepted by the paper without condemnation. There was no censorship of my thoughts or words on those pages like at Faith Baptist. My ideas were free to fly like the birds soaring through the wide open skies.

My mother took most of her college classes online at home, but every once in a while she would be required to attend the college campus in Denver. It was usually to take a test.

Curiosity filled my veins one day when my mother had to leave for the college campus. I was at the house alone because Jacob was at work and Ruth had left with her grandparents. I sat at the kitchen table with the school books stacked in front of me. I listened attentively while the garage door shut, confirming my mother had officially left the house. For the next ten minutes, I sat quietly listening carefully for any other sounds. I wanted to feel certain that everyone was completely gone. Once I had confirmed that everyone was completely gone, I stood up from the kitchen table cautiously and made my way up the stairs towards Jacob and my mother's bedroom.

It was strictly forbidden for me to enter. Jacob constantly repeated that. Today, I wanted to enter. I wanted to know what secrets were hidden behind that door and if there was anything that would give me answers to why my mother had changed so drastically. I wanted to know what a person like Jacob did behind closed doors and to uncover his secrets and expose his life. I didn't know what I would find, but I knew that I could find it there.

My heart started to speed up slowly as I pushed my ear to the door to listen if anyone was inside. I knew already that everyone was gone, but I listened closely to reassure myself of that fact. I reached for the little brass doorknob and turned it slowly to the side and pushed the door open.

I looked around the room and slowly surveyed all of its contents. I proceeded deeper into the room with extreme caution. There was a large king sized bed to the right and beside that an entrance to a bathroom. At the foot of the bed was a TV and beside the TV was a dresser full of jewelry. I assumed it was my mother's. Beside the door of the bathroom was a large stained wooden dresser. One of the draws was left slightly open, exposing some clothing. There was a large U shaped computer desk that was cluttered with a lot of different items and a large computer monitor.

I proceeded towards the bathroom and looked inside. It was a larger bathroom with two sinks across from a shower and bathtub, and to the right was a large walk-in closet. I walked into the closet. I scanned it thoroughly for anything that would spark my curiosity. I mostly pushed through a large amount of clothes on hangers lining every wall of the closet. I bent down on the right side of the closet and saw that there were two cardboard boxes sitting on the floor. Both of them had a white paper label taped to the top of them. One label read JACOB GAMES and the other read ANITA OLD STUFF written in black marker. I quickly opened the box that was labeled JACOB GAMES and peered inside. It was full of liquor bottles. There was a variety of half empty bottles of whiskeys, gins, vodkas, and rums stuffed into the box.

I thought for a second. Why would he label this box JACOB GAMES? Then it struck me. Maybe, my mother didn't know about these liquor bottles. Maybe, that was his way of hiding it from her. I then thought back to what the preacher at Faith Baptist had said about alcohol and how it was evil. I remembered how he said they called alcohol "spirits" because when you drank them you were welcoming evil spirits into your body.

I closed the box that contained Jacob's secret liquor stash and moved over to examine the box labeled ANITA OLD STUFF. I opened it and started looking through everything that was inside. An old dusty black leather photo book caught my eye. I lifted it from the box and opened it. It was filled with old photos, mainly of my mother. I noticed a few that must have been me as a baby. I flipped further to the back of the book revealing a small stack of loose photos that I started to flip through. One of the photos was of my mother standing next to a man. There was a large log cabin in the background. Another one had my mother and that same man with a few other people sitting in a jacuzzi. That same log cabin was in the background, but from a different angle. I continued to study and flip through the photos that all appeared to have been taken at this log cabin somewhere in the mountains. In all of the photos my mother was wearing expensive clothes with diamond earrings, a golden necklace and bracelets. After I had finished looking through that stack of loose photos, I slid them back into the book. I closed it and set it back in the box labeled ANITA OLD STUFF.

I quietly made my way out of the closet and back into the bedroom towards the computer desk. I took one more good look around the room. I noticed there was a large stack of books on the computer desk and none of them were written by Christian authors. Jacob was a hypocrite. Besides those books, there were model planes, computer games and random papers scattered throughout. I made my way back to the door and exited. I made sure to close the door on the way out. I quietly went back downstairs to the kitchen table and sat there thinking about everything I had just discovered.

I went into that room looking for answers to my questions but I left with even more questions. Who was that man that was with my mother in the photos? Was that my biological father? Why did my mother and I live so poor, when I saw in those photos that she clearly had money before? What had happened? I then thought about the liquor bottles. Did Jacob have a drinking problem that he was keeping hidden from my mother? Was he an alcoholic? Is that why he beat me? I thought about the books and why he only allowed me to read Christian authors, but in his room sat a heap of secular books. That day, my curiosity for the truth ignited.

***

". . .and in Jesus name, Amen," I said finishing the dinner prayer one Friday evening.

Jacob, my mother and Ruth were all seated at the dinner table and started to eat. Today my mother had made what she referred to as her "special rice and beans recipe". Basically, it was black beans mixed together with white rice served hot, with various herbs sprinkled on top. I enjoyed it because it was simple and tasted good.

"Your mom tells me that you are doing fairly well in the homeschooling program," Jacob said, holding his fork in his hand after he had finished chewing.

That was another one of his rules, always chew with your mouth closed.

"Yea," I replied.

"Yes," he said and continued, "I think the discipline I give to you has worked fairly well. You're starting to shape up your act," he stated proudly while scooping up another bite of rice and beans from his plate.

I couldn't believe that he was crediting his beatings to my success. My success was in my complete control because whatever grade I wanted, I provided for myself. I had all the answer books copied and hidden in my room. I couldn't believe that he thought beating me actually inspired good behavior and better grades. I contemplated whether I was encouraging his behavior by staying silent and keeping the peace.

"I guess so," I replied.

"It's Biblical you know," he said as if there was a feeling of pride in his knowledge, "beat them with the rod it says, and don't hold back correction because it won't kill them."

My mind was on fire. I couldn't believe the deranged reasoning this man held within his brain. He not only beat me on a weekly basis, but he actually thought that it was what God wanted him to do. I had always wondered if he had taken the words of that Bible verse in a literal sense. This was my confirmation. I was no longer able to keep my reactions to myself. I had to let my thoughts flow freely like I did in my writing.

"Is being a hypocrite and an alcoholic also biblical?", I said in a condescending tone.

Jacob slammed his fork onto his plate, releasing it from his hand and glared at me while his anger began to build.

"What did you just say to me?" he said, looking me deep in the eyes.

Allowing that thought to flow freely to Jacob gave me a feeling of release. I almost let go of the fear I had of him. I tried to pretend as if I was calm and unshaken by the threatening tone in his question. I scooped up some rice and beans and casually took a bite. I chewed slowly and then swallowed the bite before looking up to respond to his question.

"I just noticed that you have a number of books written by secular authors and I find it strange that you store a large amount of liquor hidden in a box labeled JACOB GAMES," I responded with a calm and confident tone.

Jacob jumped to his feet knocking the chair he was sitting on into the ground with a loud *smack*. He stormed over towards me and then gripped the back of my neck tightly and yanked me from my chair. He pulled me close and stuck his face right up against mine. He was so close that he was a blur and I could feel the hot air from his breath on my face.

"So you think you can be smart with me now, is that it?" he asked rhetorically while grinding his teeth together the way he always did when things didn't go as he wanted them to.

His breath smelled horrible as he spoke, and I could still feel the hot breath flowing into my face.

"Fuck you," I said boldly, looking him directly in the eyes the way he had done to me.

Those two words felt empowering as I said them and sent chills throughout my body like a therapeutic release. I knew that this wasn't going to end well for me, but for a brief moment I didn't care. I felt free.

Jacob's face was glowing red as he filled with anger and started dragging me to the kitchen sink. He reached over with his free hand and picked up the bar of soap that I used to wash my hands after cleaning the dishes. He started shoving the bar of soap into my mouth. I tried to keep my mouth shut but he noticed. He started using the soap bar as a hammer and beat my mouth with it. My mouth opened slightly, surrendering to the pain as he shoved the entire bar into my mouth. He cupped his hand over my mouth to keep the soap from falling out. He then tightened the grip on the back of my neck and forced me to walk towards the bathroom. He took the pan my mom had used to cook the rice with his other hand.

My mother and Ruth had quietly retreated from the scene and walked upstairs.

He shoved me into the bathroom like a prison guard shoving an inmate into a cell. He didn't ask me to stand up against the toilet this time. Instead, he just started swinging. The blows struck me one after the next with little time in between. He hit every part of my body. The pan struck my back, then my shoulder. I turned around to shield myself with my arms, but the pan struck my wrists. I felt it slam against my stomach as I fell helplessly to the floor. I turned to my side curling myself into a fetal position, cradling my stomach from the pain. I felt the force of the pan drop down again and again until suddenly it all came to a stop. Jacob exited the bathroom and slammed the door behind him. I lay there trembling.

The pain was real and I felt it pulsing throughout my body like a seismic activity radar displaying earthquakes throughout the world. My mouth was sore and tasted of soap suds as it dissolved with my saliva. It dried the insides of my throat. It was hard to tell, in that moment, if those few brief seconds of free thought I had released to Jacob were worth the pain they had caused. I sat and pondered the bittersweet feeling of allowing my thoughts to flow freely, but the pain that it meant for me physically. While I stared at the familiar bathroom wall, I began to wonder if there would ever be an end to these beatings. I wondered if someday, I would be able to make them stop.

***

"That was epic! I think we are ready. This song is gold," John shouted with excitement.

We had just finished practicing a perfect run through of the song we were planning to play for the seventh grade talent show at the public middle school.

"Yo, you guys want a beer?" John asked Blake and me as he walked over to a little fridge in the basement beside the area we would always practice at, "They're my dad's, but he won't mind. I think that was a killer set and we should celebrate a bit."

"Hell yea!" Blake responded enthusiastically.

"Your dad doesn't mind if you drink?" I responded surprised.

"Nah, he doesn't give a shit, as long as I keep it in the house and don't act like an idiot," John said while chuckling a little.

John distributed the beer. He tossed one over to Blake, who was sitting on his drum stool. He stood up to catch it in the air. The other he handed to me. We sat there sipping the beers for a while, just absorbing the energy of the moment. I always felt a rush of adrenaline after we played. I felt the feeling of warm blood traveling through my veins. We had played the song perfectly, and it certainly felt fulfilling.

John looked over at me, scanning me up and down.

"My dad has some workout equipment. We should get you jacked for the show, you know, like Anthony Kiedis," John stated with vision in his eyes.

"Yea?" I responded with interest in my voice.

"Fuck yea, man," John stated confidently as he set his beer on the floor. He started walking towards another section of the basement that had a variety of free weights and workout machines.

I followed John and he proceeded to show me a variety of different workouts. The three of us started curling the different free weights and pushing up the bench press together. He even had a punching bag hanging from the ceiling that we would all take turns punching and kicking. John had told me that his father practiced martial arts and taught him a few things. He showed me some punching exercises and routines that he had learned. That started to become our weekly routine at every band practice. From then on, we would practice music for a couple of hours and then workout and learn fighting techniques for a couple of hours.

I loved the feeling of hitting the punching bag. I would zone out while I hit it and imagine myself as a strong warrior defeating my opponent. I would release all the built up stress that I concealed throughout the week into every kick and punch that I threw at the bag.

John was right, I did start to become a lot stronger. The muscle definition in my body started to become more visible and defined. I was able to run faster and further without losing my breath. I could jump higher than before and my guitar felt like a feather that I could throw around while playing. I was discovering a new found confidence within myself and took the beatings that Jacob would continue to give me with a little more ease. I was growing and I could feel it, both physically and mentally.

***

"Next up, could we have Blake, John and Gene on the stage, please," announced the man.

The man stood in the center of the stage dressed in a red polo shirt that displayed the logo of the public middle school. He spoke into a black microphone that was amplified by a large stack of PA speakers on both sides of the stage.

It was the day of the talent show. The rest of the seventh grade school year had passed since the band started working out in John's basement. The middle school administration had decided to reschedule the talent show for seventh grade. They moved it to the end of the school year to kick off the start of summer break.

There were chairs set up in lined rows that started from the front of the stage and flowed back to the end of the room. All the chairs were filled with students, teachers and even parents. There were groups of people standing because there were not enough chairs to seat everyone. It was a large room with a large wooden stage positioned at the front. On the stage was Blake's drum set, John's bass guitar and my guitar. The instruments were leaned up against the amplifiers. In the center of the stage was the microphone stand holding the microphone the man had announced our names into.

Blake, John and I made our way up to the stand and readied ourselves for the performance. We had practiced every week even after we knew the song perfectly. We were ready to perform. I felt nervous. I lifted my guitar up and swung the strap over my head. John did the same. Blake made his way to the drum set and adjusted a few cymbals and tom drums. I slowly walked center stage so that I could be heard through the microphone. I scanned the crowd below in front of me and felt the butterflies in my stomach. I turned back to look at Blake and then turned over to look at John. We all nodded our heads with a signal of confirmation that we were ready to play. I lifted my guitar pick towards the ceiling. I closed my eyes for a moment to carefully listen for the four *clicks* from Blakes drum sticks. They were our signal to start the song.

Click. Click. Click. Click.

A storm of sound rushed from the stage towards the ears of the crowd below us. Loud cheering came from a group of smiling students as they jumped up and down waving their hands in the air frantically. The rest watched from their seats and listened to the melodies. They started to tap along with their hands and feet.

I felt a rush of adrenaline like a heater blowing hot air on you in an arctic storm. I danced around the stage and strummed my guitar during the parts I wasn't singing. Towards the end of the song, the bass guitar and the guitar went silent as the drums roared throughout the crowd with only my voice as accompaniment. I raised my hands clapping them together above my head while the crowd followed, clapping along. Afterward, the guitar and the bass guitar screeched back into the song until the music came to an abrupt silence with one fierce kick from the bass drum pedal. BOOM! The silence rang for a few moments until the room started to flood with loud screaming, cheering and whistling from the crowd.

The feeling was incredible. We exited the stage after our performance. Many students rushed to us with excitement and congratulated us. A girl in the crowd walked up to me and gave me a little peck on the cheek. She wrapped her arms around me and squeezed me. She then whispered in my ear and told me that I was cute. She believed that I would become famous someday. Nothing felt like that first performance on stage and the energy that followed. It was irreplaceable.

***

I started working at a little restaurant over the summer after seventh grade called “Joe’s Corner Cafe”. It was owned by Joe and his wife Ellen. I would usually work about five days a week after school each night and sometimes on the weekends when it was busy. I worked in a little back area of the restaurant that had a long silver table. Dishes would stack up on it as the waiters brought them back to me. At the end of the table there was a deep sink to scrub the dishes in. There was a machine where I would place the dishes that had a lever to start and stop it.

The lobby of the restaurant was casual dining with wooden tables scattered evenly throughout, capable of seating about fifty people. There was a gray stone wall dividing the restaurant into two spaces. One side had a long bar bench and stools with a large screen TV. The other was the dining area. Behind the bar was an entryway that led to the kitchen. There was an area where the waiters would collect the plates from the kitchen for delivery. Further to the back was the dishwashing station where I worked.

Joe was an ill-tempered man that would grunt under his breath as he paced around the restaurant watching the employees work. He was an older man that had pure white hair with the exception of a large shiny bald patch covering the whole top of his head. He was a little above six feet with a protruding beer belly that was hidden under a blue sweater. He had reading glasses attached to a string that dangled from his neck and a scruffy white beard. He didn't talk much unless there was something he didn't like about the restaurant's process.

I was finally able to convince Jacob to allow me to attend the public middle school. I had received a recommendation from the middle school band teacher because she wanted me to join the orchestra. Since that was the only type of music he allowed me to listen to, he finally agreed that I could attend. I never told him that I played in the talent show and I never planned to. He still didn't know that I owned an electric guitar or had played in a rock band. I planned to keep it that way.

Blake and I found out that John was moving and going to a different school for eighth grade so the band had to break up because of that. I used to keep my guitar at John's house so I had to sneak it back into my house and store it under my bed like before. It was sad for me because band days were the days I looked forward to the most. They kept my spirits up through the most grueling weeks at home.

I had developed a fairly sound routine to keep my mind positive throughout the week without band practice. I would walk to the middle school each morning to attend and afterwards walk to work. I would push through my dishwashing shift at Joe's while singing songs as I worked. Some days that was easier than others depending on how busy it was. When work finished, I would walk home and brace myself for Jacob's beatings. Sometimes I got lucky and he was already in bed. I no longer had to eat dinner with Jacob, Ruth and my mother because I worked through the time they ate at home. That was a relief for me. Once I made it through Jacob's beatings, I would go to my room and listen to my favorite rock bands. I would absorb the lyrics they sang into my soul. I still took precautions and left classical music CD's out because Jacob did burst into my room unexpectedly from time to time. Once it was really late I would pull the guitar out from underneath my bed and write a few songs quietly till I became sleepy. With each song that I wrote, I would release the pain I felt onto the blank white paper through the soothing ink pen. Writing freely and music was the structure that held me together each and every day when I felt weak from the beatings.

On the weekends, I would go for a run around the park and do calisthenic exercises to keep up with the workouts I used to do each week during band practice. Sometimes, I would hang out with Blake next to the middle school and we would throw a football back and forth and grab some pizza from a shop nearby. He would talk about this girl that he liked at school and ask me questions about what he should do as if I had better knowledge than he did on that topic. Anything that I could do on the weekends to keep me from going back home, I did. I tried to avoid home as much as possible.

***

"Hurry the fuck up! We've got fifty fucking people out there," Joe shouted at me scooping his arm up into the air.

"Yes, sir. I'm cleaning as fast as I can," I responded while busy at work.

"It's not fast enough, dammit! Why the the fuck did I even hire you? You are fucking worthless," Joe yelled even louder, attracting a quick glance from the cooks in the kitchen.

It was an extremely busy Saturday afternoon at the restaurant and everyone was working as fast and as hard as they could. The waiters were sprinting with plates in their hands back and forth to the lobby. The cooks were dripping with sweat from the intensity of the grills. Joe had been yelling at everyone and you could see in their faces that they were starting to become irritated with his rants.

I was sending dishes through the machine -and even hand washing- while the machine ran its thirty second cycle. I was running back and forth with stacks of dishes to refill the kitchen's supply but they were using all of the plates on every trip I made. The waiters were running back to me, dropping the dirty dishes off on the dishwashing table that was nearly full. I was racing to keep at least one little space clear for them.

There had been many days like this before with Joe yelling and shouting as the night matured. The whole staff always managed to push through the night and get everything done. I had watched many employees getting yelled at throughout my time working there. Sometimes, they would start crying and not bother to show up the following day. That always pissed Joe off even more. Joe was a hard owner to work for. He was always in a foul mood. He knew the right things to say to get underneath your skin but no one ever challenged his methods. Everyone would always just accept the fact that he yelled and said horrible things and just continued working.

Suddenly I heard a loud *bang* from the dishwashing motor. It chugged to a complete stop. The dishwasher had burnt up from the overuse of the night. I didn't have time during the busy restaurant rush to stop and see if there was anything I could do to fix it, so I started hand washing all the dishes as fast as I could.

"What in the hell was that?" I heard Joe shout from around the corner.

"The dishwasher burnt out," I responded back in a shout so he could hear me through the restaurant noise.

Joe came storming back into the dishwashing area. His eyes were wide open like a lunatic and he had a frustrated look on his face. He went straight to the dishwashing machine and lifted the lever to open it. He looked inside and then tried to get it to start a few times. He smacked the machine with the palm of his hand in anger and then turned around and glared at me.

"What the fuck did you do, Gene? You don't even know how to run a goddamn dishwasher properly," he said with building frustration in his voice.

"I am hand washing the dishes now as fast as I can, Joe," I replied while continuing to scrub a plate vigorously with a dish sponge.

"You're too god damn slow, Gene. These dishes are piling up to the fucking ceiling. You are fucking worthless, Gene, know that, fucking worthless I tell ya," Joe yelled at me while standing right next my ear.

I didn't respond to Joe's rant. I just continued to work as hard as I possibly could- scrubbing, rinsing, stacking and running back and forth from the kitchen to the sink. Scrubbing, rinsing, stacking, running. Scrubbing, rinsing, stacking, running. I ignored the burning in my arms while I scrubbed. I tried to ignore Joe's continuous rant as he followed me around the dishwashing area yelling in my ear. Scrubbing, rinsing, stacking, running. Scrubbing, rinsing, stacking, running.

"I guarantee you're a spoiled rotten piece of shit brat kid and your parents don't fucking beat you enough," Joe said in a disgusted tone and then grunted.

I lost my focus on the continuous routine that I previously had going and froze instantly. I allowed the plate I was scrubbing to sink down into the soapy suds below. I started breathing heavily and stared down at the dishes half sunk into the water and soap suds. I felt anger filling my veins and my body tensed up. I flexed every muscle inside. I placed both hands on the edge of the sink while trying to gain control of this new energy expanding beneath my skin.

"Don't stop washing, Gene, what the fuck are you doing?" Joe shouted at me angrily.

I raised my posture to stand up straight without slouch. I took a step back from the sink and clenched my fists together. I glared at Joe. My arms dangled at my sides like two medieval maces.

“You better get your ass back to work if you want to keep this job, Gene. Do you have a goddamn problem in your brain? You're a fucking idiot,” Joe said glaring at me with mostly anger but a slight bit of confusion.

I didn’t want to accept his yelling and his rants any longer. The blood started to boil beneath my skin. I reached into the sink removing the dirty plate I had previously been washing and lifted it into the air. I swung and released the plate down to the floor right at Joe’s feet. It shattered and sent shards of white ceramic all throughout the dishwashing area.

“Clean the fucking dishes yourself, Joe. I quit,” I said boldly, staring him dead in the eyes as if I was hurting him with my glare.

Joe’s eyes lit up in disbelief but the lunatic-like frustration remained as if he were trying to burn a permanent impression onto his face.

“Get the fuck out of my restaurant, you little shit! You are fired!” he shouted loudly, spewing spit from his mouth as he spoke.

“I’m on my way out, Joe. You can’t fire me because I already quit,” I said in a condescending tone while laughing.

“Get the fuck out of here, you piece of shit! I’m calling the cops!” Joe shouted back at me.

I had already made my way out of the back door of the restaurant. I saw that the kitchen staff was clapping for me on my way out. I guess I had done what every employee there had wanted to do for a very long time. It felt good to be in control of my life and decisions and not accept being disrespected. I felt confident in myself. I knew I could find another job anywhere I wanted to. I walked proudly with perfect posture as I made my way back home. I felt like I could take on anything the world decided to throw at me at that moment. Whatever it was, I was ready for it.

I arrived at my house and opened the front door. I stepped inside and shut the door behind me. I looked up and jumped a bit inside of my skin because Jacob was standing at the front door waiting for me. His arms were crossed and his teeth were grinding.

"You think you can hide things from me, Gene?" he asked in a sinister tone.

"No," I responded with slight confusion in my voice, "Why?"

Jacob turned around and walked to the sliding glass door that led to the back yard. I followed him. He slid the door open and walked over onto the grass. He crossed his arms together and stared at me with a sinister smile. I stepped onto the patio and looked ahead in disbelief.

My guitar was smashed into useless broken chunks in the grass yard. The same guitar I had played in the talent show. The guitar that I played at all the band practices with Blake and John. The guitar that had taken me months of shoveling snowy driveways to buy. Beside my broken guitar were all my rock CDs cracked into little pieces. They were scattered over the guitar like confetti. The CDs I would listen to alone in my room. The CDs that I practiced air guitar with late into the night. The guitar and CD's that had been my therapy after every time I received a beating from him.

I started breathing heavily the way that I had at the restaurant. My veins were burning like molten lava flowing down the sides of an active volcano. My heart started pounding my chest like the sound of a thousand war drums preparing warriors for battle. I moved my head and looked towards Jacob. I was no longer afraid of the man that he was to me. I no longer had fear of his beatings because today, I was going to put an end to it all. I glared into his eyes with intent to kill and to destroy everything he represented to me. I took a step towards him with my fists prepared tightly at my sides. I glared into his eyes again. I made sure that he was aware of my intentions. Just like the employees had been waiting for someone to step up to Joe for a long time, I had been waiting for the confidence to stand up to Jacob my whole life. Today was the day he would suffer for everything he had done to me. Today, I would take my revenge on Jacob by force. Today, I would make him pay for it all.

***

"STOP! STOP! OH GOD, NO! PLEASE STOP!"

The faint shouting of the woman in the background echoed, slightly louder in my mind. I recognized the voice now, it was my mother's. I stopped before Jacob's head reached the sharp corner of the wooden coffee table. I squeezed the back of his neck tighter than before like a stress ball in the palm of my hand. I turned to see the terrified face of my mother staring at the scene unfolding in front of her. She was in disbelief and shaking from the terror. I looked down at Jacob's head helplessly dangling from my grip. I started to regain my hearing as the adrenaline rush through my body came under control. I was surprised by my own rage and what I had been capable of doing to Jacob. I finally released his neck from my grip and stood to my feet. I stared down at Jacob. He was laying on the floor trembling. I saw myself in his position like a hallucination. I remembered all the times I had laid on that cold bathroom floor alone. I started thinking deeply about what I had done to Jacob. I thought about how I didn't want to become the monster he had been to me all of these years. I had finally proved to him that he no longer had power over me. That was enough. I slowly started to take control of my breathing. I inhaled and exhaled deeply. I took a step over Jacob's trembling body towards the front door of the house. I opened it and stepped outside quietly, without saying a word. I closed the door behind me as I left the house.

SIX

High School

It had been awhile since that intense moment when I contemplated killing Jacob. I actually almost did kill him. The ambience at home never really settled from that day on, but Jacob no longer attempted to beat me. While his head dangled above that sharp corner helplessly in my hand, I'm sure that his life flashed before his eyes. I think he might have assumed that I was going to end him right there. I learned a lot from that day, especially about the rise, fall and exchange of power and how quickly one's life could be ripped from the earth. I learned how resilient we are as human beings, but at the same time extremely delicate and only sheer moments from our deaths. I learned the importance of displaying your power, but controlling it as well. I am glad I decided not to smash Jacob's head into the corner of that coffee table, because now I knew he had to live each day knowing he had lost a certain power over me. He had to live with his weakness. If I had killed him in that moment, then he would have died still in-directly holding power over me. His power would have lived on through the prison time I would have served and the lifetime impact that it would have had on my life. I would never give him that satisfaction, he didn't deserve it.

I was going to the public high school in the historic town near the music store. I am in ninth-grade now. The high school was a much older building than the middle school but was still fairly large. It had a football, baseball, and soccer field wrapped around its grass perimeter. It was an old brick building with newly painted blue borders. There was a large student parking lot beside the building because a lot of the students drove to school, including myself.

I bought an old car for one-thousand dollars from a neighbor. I noticed he was selling it while strolling through the neighborhood. It was an old four-door sedan that was painted with a light golden color. It reminded me of when I had held that little toy car in my hands and raced it along the dusty wood floor in my bedroom. I thought this four-door sedan was kind of like that car because it wasn't the car that I had originally wanted (Carlos had taken that car) but I was content with it simply because it was a car. That's exactly how this car felt to me.

About a week after quitting at Joe's Corner Cafe, I applied at the drug store across the street and got hired right away. This was a much better job and the people I worked with were friendly. Every night, after closing, the employees, managers and I would talk in the parking lot for a while. We would laugh and exchange stories. I worked as a cashier in the front of the store and would greet all the customers as they walked in. I made a couple more dollars than the minimum wage, which was excellent pay for a high school student.

***

"Yo Gene, throw me the lighter," Sean said while he lay outstretched on the couch against his bedroom wall the way you would lay down on the grass after finishing a marathon.

Sean played guitar with me in the new music duo that we formed shortly after starting high school. Sean was a wild character and had long shaggy hair that covered most of his face. He was over six feet tall with an extremely skinny frame and always wore an old dirty gray hoodie with faded gray jeans. He was constantly pulling them up as they fell from his waist. He always held a cigarette in his mouth or a rolled joint of marijuana that he would offer to me.

I reached over to the top of the half stack guitar amp next to me and picked up the lighter. I tossed it over to Sean.

Sean's room was in the basement of his parents' house which is where we would practice music and hang out together most of the time. His room had four dark blue painted walls and a large window that opened to the backyard. All our music equipment was cluttered around his room across from a little old cushioned couch that was dirty and stained.

Sean lit the joint resting in between his lips and took in a long inhale that he held for as long as possible. Then, he exhaled in a burst of relief. He let out a few coughs and offered the joint to me with a long outstretched hand. I reached out and took it from his hand and proceeded to do the same as he had done. I inhaled and exhaled the smoke from my lungs. I went and plopped down beside him on the couch and we passed the joint back and forth. We smoked it down to a tiny little roach. We sank into the couch and stared at the ceiling for a while soaking in the high that the joint had given us.

Sean reached his hand into the side of the cushion on the couch and pulled out a little yellow plastic flashlight. He turned it on and off a few times and stared at the light beam it emitted. I looked over as he turned it on and off and observed that there were little particles of dust traveling along the beam of the light.

"What if we could jump onto a beam from a flashlight like this one and travel to a bunch of different worlds all over the galaxy," Sean said deep in thought.

I absorbed the idea for a moment.

"Yea, man, that would be crazy. . . just like those little dust particles," I said, sticking the tip of my index finger into the little beam of light.

We sat there and pondered our new idea for a while, as ridiculous as it sounded. It seemed like anything was a possibility after smoking a joint, of course, until the high wore off. Once we were back to reality, we would just laugh at all the crazy ideas that we had while we were high. Today was the same and many hours passed by while we were in this state.

The high finally wore off and it was time for me to get home and start getting ready for work. Sean and I sprayed ourselves with body spray to cover the smell of the marijuana. I climbed the stairs and started walking back to my house. I didn't drive because Sean lived in the same neighborhood as me.

When I arrived at the front door of the house, I noticed an envelope hidden under the doormat. It was pushed in pretty far and only a tiny corner of it was exposed. I bent over and pulled it from under the mat and turned it over so that I could see the front. In all capital letters it read FOR GENE OLIVER DICKSON. I noticed that it didn't have any postage stamps on it. It had to have been hand delivered. It matched my name perfectly, except that my last name was Nelson, not Dickson.

I thought about the name for a moment. My mother had never told me what our last name had been before Jacob. This letter matched my name perfectly except for the last name so it had to be mine. . . but who brought it here?

I shoved the envelope into my right pocket. Then, I turned around and walked over to my car, which was parked on the side of the street. I got into the driver's seat, started the ignition and drove to the park. It was only walking distance, but I wanted to be inside of my car so that I would have privacy to open the envelope. I parked furthest away from the street, shut off the car and pulled the emergency brake.

I took the envelope out of my right pocket and then looked around to make sure that no one was watching me. I tore it open with my index finger and began to remove the letter that was folded inside. I unfolded it and began to read,

Dear Gene Oliver Dickson

That is your real name, you know? Not Nelson. Your mother and I decided to name you Gene Oliver so that your initials would spell out GOD. That represents what you are to us, a miracle from GOD. I am sorry, Gene, for not being a part of your life until now. I really want to change that. It has always killed me not being able to watch you grow up. I think about you everyday. I live in the country with my brother, out in the middle of nowhere. We live about a three hour drive from you. I included the directions in this letter in hopes that you will come visit one day. Life is crazy, bud. I have so many stories to share with you, if you'll let me.

Your father,

George Dickson

I sat in the car and just stared at the letter for about ten minutes. I was thinking deeply about what was written. I started to connect it to everything in my life. That was the first contact I had ever had with my biological father. George Dickson, I thought. I started to become curious about the type of man he was. Why did he never come and visit me? What had happened to him and my mother? I then thought back to the day I entered Jacob and my mother's bedroom and found those pictures. Maybe the man in those photos was George. I contemplated whether I should follow his directions and go visit him.

I looked up at the time displayed on the stereo in my car and jumped under my skin. I quickly folded the letter and stuffed it back into the envelope. I reached in the back of my car to grab my drugstore work shirt. I threw it over the T-shirt I was wearing. I opened the glove box of my car and slid the envelope in-between the car manual. I turned the ignition and started racing the clock to work.

***

The fire crackled through the night and sent embers that floated to the stars through the towering pine trees above us. Two girls from school, Sean and I, were all huddled around the warm fire. We had pitched two tents and chopped a stack of firewood to keep the fire going throughout the night. There was no one around for miles, just tall pine trees lined up as far as you could see. Sean and I were playing two acoustic guitars and singing improvised lyrics while the girls clapped and danced along. We had a large communal bottle of whiskey that we passed back and forth.

Lisa and Mel were the two girls with us. Lisa had come up with the idea for us to take a camping trip deep into the mountains. I was the only one that had a car at the time. We all piled into my little four door sedan, shoved some camping gear into the trunk and went on our way.

Lisa was a short girl with brown messy hair. Her eyes were bright blue and she had freckles. She wore a jean skirt and a puffy winter coat lined with fur around its hood.

Mel was short as well with dark black hair that she straightened neatly. Her eyes were a light brown with a slight orange glow in them. She wore black yoga pants with a neon orange hoodie and brown winter boots made from fur.

Sean and I stopped playing for a moment and set the guitars down against a long log near the fire. I reached over and grabbed the whiskey bottle, threw my head back and took a large gulp. I coughed as I finished. I passed it to Sean and he did the same. We left the girls by the fire and walked over to my car.

“Dude, I think Lisa is definitely into me, man…” Sean said with a huge smile on his face. He gave me a friendly punch to the side of my arm.

“I think you’re right, man,” I said smiling and then patting him on the back, “but come here real quick. I want to show you this letter I got the other day.”

“Word,” he said with a chuckle as he followed me to the passenger seat.

I opened the car door and pulled out the envelope I had slid inside the drivers manual. I opened the envelope, unraveled the letter and handed it over to Sean. Sean began to read the letter, but paused and looked up at me for a moment.

“Whaaat? Your real name is Dickson?” He said surprised while laughing at the end.

He continued to read the letter. Once he had finished, he handed it back to me.

“Dude, that’s some crazy shit,” he said, “but fuck it, man. You should go. What if your real dad is like some crazy rich inventor or some shit?” he said looking up into the sky as he pondered the thought.

“Right?” I said chuckling a little, “I am actually seriously considering following these directions and heading out there next week. I’ve got the whole weekend off from work,” I said, studying the letter a bit more.

“I say do it, man. What do you have to lose?” Sean said with certainty.

I nodded, smiled a bit and then folded the letter back into the envelope. I placed it back into the driver’s manual. I shut the car door. Sean and I walked back over to the girls who had been gossiping by the fire.

“Guess who’s got some magic mushrooms?” Lisa said loudly and excitedly.

“Shrooms!” Sean shouted with excitement.

Lisa pulled out a plastic sandwich bag full of magic mushrooms and offered them to each one of us. Mel and I didn’t really want to try them, so we just kept passing the bottle of whiskey back and forth instead. We watched as Sean and Lisa stuffed some of them into their mouths. They almost puked as they swallowed. There was still a little bit left.

“You two sure you don’t want some?” Lisa asked as she held out the bag, “Last chance”.

Mel and I both shook our heads.

“Alrighty then. Sean, more for us,” Lisa said excitedly.

Mel and I watched as they ate the last bit of mushrooms. They covered their mouths to keep them from falling out. Mel and I looked at each other and laughed while Lisa and Sean tried to fan out the horrible taste in their mouths. We offered them some whiskey to wash it down.

Everyone was starting to become drunk and it was only a matter of time before Sean and Lisa started their trip on the magic mushrooms. Mel and I sat together on the log near the fire. I picked up the guitar and started to improvise some music in my tipsy state. Sean and Lisa laid on the dirt, hands outstretched and stared at the stars above them.

Mel reached over and gently set her hand on the strings of the guitar to silence them. I stopped playing and looked at her. Her eyes were gazing into mine with a strong display of lust and infatuation. I felt icy chills travel throughout my body as she placed the palm of her hand on my cheek and began to kiss my lips. I leaned the guitar up against the log we were sitting on and then turned back to Mel. She took my hand, standing as she did so and led me over to one of the tents. We both stepped inside and zipped the flap closed. We blocked everything out at that moment. We were driven by passion. We took our clothes off and made love through the night.

***

I was pulled over to the side of a long wide dirt road that went in either direction. There was nothing but trees and bare land for miles. Dried up tumbleweeds blew across the road and leaves swayed with the wind. I had an eerie feeling that sat in my gut brewing as the time passed. I had stopped. This was the place that the directions from the letter had led me to. I looked around to see if there were any houses. I saw none. I looked back down at the directions and traced them back through my memory to see if I had missed anything. I remembered following them perfectly. I kept looking around. My eyes landed on a small square wooden mailbox further ahead. I drove the car in that direction. I found the start of a smaller single lane dirt road that looked like it disappeared over a hill in the distance. This must be it. I started to drive along the small road. Once I made it to the hill, it started descending down to a little white house. I could see a little pink house in the distance that sat on the bottom of another hill opposite of the white house. As I got closer to the white house, I could no longer see the pink house. The view was obstructed by the hill.

I arrived at the little white house. It really was in the middle of nowhere. The letter was right. There were piles of random junk stacked around the perimeter of the house. As I approached the front door, a gray dog started barking fiercely and choked itself with the chain it was tied to. The house was worn out like it had barely survived a few brutal storms. The shingles were peeling off of the roof as the wind blew. It appeared as if the house was abandoned.

I stepped nervously through the junk and made my way to the door. I knocked and stood there quietly waiting for a reply. After I knocked, the dog barked even louder and ran harder against the restraint of the chain. There was a window next to the door that I tried looking into while I waited. I saw the face of a man peer through the window and then disappear. Then, the door opened.

"Oh my God! You must be Gene," the man said in disbelief, "You must have got my letter."

"Yea," I said hesitantly, "Are you George Dickson?"

"Come here, kid!" he shouted loudly, offering his arms out for a hug, "I can't believe it! You actually came. I wasn't so sure if you were going to come. . . being that we'd never met and all."

George Dickson. My biological father. He was a character, that's for sure. He had long brown hair that he combed back and a patchy beard that was showing some gray. One side of his face had a thin scar that ran through his eyebrow. He wore baggy khaki pants and a large black eighties band T-shirt. He spoke with the hint of a New York accent.

"Excuse the mess," he said as he guided me into his house.

The place was truly a mess. There were piles of junk scattered throughout and in some places stacked to the ceiling. There was a brown couch covered in old books and magazines that he started to clear so I could sit.

"Please, take a seat," he said with a hand gesture and guided me to the couch, "Can I get you anything to drink? Beer, juice, water?"

"Sure, I'll take some water," I answered while taking a seat on the couch.

He walked over to a little kitchen sink in the other room and filled a glass with water. He handed it to me and then sat down on an old rocking chair across from the couch. He just stared at me and smiled in disbelief. We sat awkwardly like that for a few minutes.

"So. . . what are you, in high school now?" he asked, breaking the ice.

"Yea, ninth grade," I responded, relieved the silence had been broken.

"What do you do? Like sports or something?" he asked while he lit up a cigarette.

"Not really," I said, "I'm actually more into music and writing."

"Is that so?" he burst out with a bit of excitement, "Like your old man."

He stood up from the rocking chair abruptly. The rocking chair swayed back and forth on its own. He went into a bedroom and returned promptly with an acoustic guitar. It had a black glossy finish. He sat next to me and started strumming a few chords. He then offered it to me.

"Show me what you got, kid," he said and winked.

I took the guitar from him and began to strum a few chords and sing some improvised lyrics. He started singing along and added his own improvised lyrics as well while slapping the arm of the couch to the beat of the rhythm I was playing. We jammed for the next twenty minutes. I strummed one last chord that ended the jam and then leaned the guitar up against the couch.

"So. . . where have you been all this time? Why am I only meeting you now?" I asked eagerly.

His face went from a joyful smile to a despondent frown. He stood up from the couch and walked back slowly to the rocking chair. Next to it was a little side table with an ashtray and a half finished joint that he took and lit. He took a long inhale and then exhaled very slowly. A cloud of smoke exited his mouth. For a moment, he looked down at the floor as he gathered his thoughts.

"Well, God. Where do I start. . ." he said while taking a long anxious breath.

"How about the beginning?" I suggested.

"You really want to hear this shit from the beginning?" he asked wearily, "It's a long story, kid."

"Yes," I said eagerly with confidence while I sat up straight, "I want to know what happened between you and my mother."

He took another long slow inhale from the joint. He held the smoke in his lungs as long as he could before releasing it. He tried to hold back a few coughs that followed by attempting to keep his mouth closed. He sank back into the rocking chair and started telling the story.

"It was the mid eighties in good old New York City. It was a city that moved fast and was unforgiving to anyone that couldn't keep up with it. We had just got through a recession. Unemployment was the highest it had been since the Great Depression. Well, it was over and business was picking up fast at the car dealership I was working at. I was selling cars faster than anyone that worked there. A top seller is what they called me. A couple hundred thousand dollars per year I was making. It really was a great job. I enjoyed it, but the thing about sales that you've got to know is that it gets stressful and everything moves so fucking fast that you can barely keep up. I was tired. Day in and day out I was plowing through sales pitches and working fifteen hour fucking shifts. Cocaine fixed that problem for me, at least for a while.

Your mother was working as a pharmacy tech when I first met her. I was introduced to her by a friend and we hit it off right away. If I remember correctly, not even a couple months went by before we were ringing wedding bells.

Your old man likes to party, kid. I loved throwing down shots of liquor and snorting a little bit of blow. Coke keeps you going while the liquor tends to calm you down. Your mother liked to party too, but in a different way. She would throw down a few glasses of wine but never too much. She liked to dance, god did she like to dance. I could barely keep up with her on the dance floor no matter how much blow I did.

Anyways, we threw the greatest fucking after party for our wedding ever. All of the friends and family were there. We had a live band playing, damn that band was excellent. There was sparkly shit lining the ceilings of the venue like a disco. There was a huge slick hard wood dance floor. Colorful lights were flashing in every fucking direction. I mean, you get the picture. . . it was a full fucking event.

My boss loved me at the dealership because I would get rid of his cars faster than anyone else, and at a substantial price too. He told me he wanted to make sure his top salesman was taken care of, so he lent me a beautiful brand new candy red Porsche for the wedding. That Porsche was pretty fucking quick too.

Your mother is such a strong and resilient woman and it kills me everyday that I am no longer with her. She was right there with me through anything that I did, very loyal. I really fucked up Gene. . . but such is life. I guess I don't deserve her."

He paused his story for a moment in a blank stare of deep sadness.

"So what happened?" I asked with eager curiosity, interrupting his moment.

"Well," he continued, "The night of the after party had dragged on into the morning and it was time for your mother and I to get back to our hotel. I went to grab the keys to the car but your mother took them before I could. She told me I was too drunk to drive and that she thought it would be better if she drove instead. She was right. I was still drunk. I was stubborn and stupid but I jokingly laughed and told her I was fine to drive. I even started walking the straight line the cops would make you walk to check if you were wasted. She watched as I walked the line successfully, but was still hesitant to hand over the keys. I then started telling her that my boss had told me that no one else could drive the Porsche, that he had only allowed me to drive it. She was still not wanting to hand over the keys. I started getting frustrated with her. I went and just ripped the keys from her hands and got into the driver's seat. I told her I was leaving and if she wasn't gonna get into the car then I was gonna leave without her. She reluctantly got in and we started driving to the hotel.

I wasn't driving so bad for being drunk. . . or so I thought. Your mother was seated in the passenger side of the Porsche with a pretty unhappy look on her face. I started looking over to her and making jokes to try and cheer her up. I almost got a few laughs out of her. Suddenly, out of nowhere glass started flying through the air and the front hood of the Porsche started crushing closer to us. It crumpled like a piece of paper. It was horrible, Gene. God awful.

I had drifted to the side of the road while I was turned toward your mother and crashed straight into a concrete highway divider. It was devastating. I had a few bumps and scrapes on me but your mother suffered the most. My god did she suffer.

I was there in the hospital with her every day. I felt terrible about what I had done to her. She must have spent a couple months in that hospital recovering from all her injuries. They had to put metal rods in each one of her legs to put them back together. That's how smashed they were. When she was finally able to leave the hospital she was in a wheelchair and the doctor told her she would never walk again. Never fucking walk again, Gene. I couldn't believe it. All because of your stupid old man's drinking problems. What they told her after that was even more horrifying and unbelievable. They told her that she would never be able to have a child. One goddam drive after the greatest night of our lives, led us to the worst fucking day of our lives. That's why I told you in that letter that life is crazy. It really is. You see, that is why I say that you are a miracle from God. It is because you truly are.

The story doesn't end there though, Gene, there's a whole bunch more. Remember how I told you your mother is a strong and resilient woman?" he looked up to me after asking the question.

"Yea," I nodded.

"Well," he continued, "She really fucking is. Your mother didn't believe that goddamn doctor for one second. She pushed herself harder than I have ever pushed myself in my entire life. I mean, she really pushed herself through some fucking pain, bud. She forced those legs to lift her. In fact, she commanded them and they listened. She didn't stop trying until she was walking normally again.

Now, the story of how you came to life is even more incredible. I mean, the doctor told her confidently, right to her face, that she was never going to be able to have kids. I don't even know if you are going to believe half the shit I'm telling you, kid. It truly is wild.

Anyways, a couple of years had passed since that accident and we were prospering. I apologized to my boss and just paid him for the Porsche I had wrecked. He had no hard feelings towards me as long as I kept selling his cars. Your mother came back swinging even harder than I did. I didn't know how she was doing it, but she was bringing in just as much cash as me. Combined, we were making just over half a million dollars per year.

Living on the East Coast was fast paced. Constantly moving. Your mother and I decided we wanted to buy another property. A place where we could get away and wind down once in a while. You know, from the stressful daily grind. Our hearts were set on Colorado. We found a nice big log cabin in the middle of the mountains. We installed a large Jacuzzi to relax in as well. The place was wonderful. It was perfect.

I invited my brother James, his wife and a couple friends to come party with us to celebrate our new cabin.

I was always getting into shit with my brother James back in the day. The two of us grew up with my mother and we lived in a run down neighborhood in New York when we were kids. There were a bunch of gangs that lived in that neighborhood, but we avoided them for the most part. One day, I remember a few of the gang members surrounded me. They started beating the shit out of me. I shouted as loud as I could in hopes that James or someone would hear me. I guess James heard me, because he came to my rescue swinging a goddamn shovel. He smacked the gang members straight on the head. He knocked out a few of them. He swung me over his little body and carried me all the way back home to safety. That was my brother James, though. He always had my back.

Anyways, back to the cabin. We were all there to celebrate the purchase of the new cabin."

"Wait," I interrupted, "I found some pictures in my mother's closet of a cabin and a few other people in a jacuzzi."

"Did you, now?" he asked, surprised.

"Yea, I did," I said.

"I can't believe she still holds onto those memories," he said with a hopeful gaze.

He took a quick break to roll another joint on the side table beside the rocking chair. He licked the joint to seal the contents inside and then lit it. He took a few rapid puffs and then began casually smoking as he continued the story.

"The cabin was fairly large. I mean, there were five bedrooms, a large beautiful kitchen that overlooked the mountains, a wide open living room area and, of course, the jacuzzi that we added.

I had bought an old four wheel drive vehicle to fit with the rustic feel of being out in nature. I also bought it to keep in the cabin so that we wouldn't have to rent a car every time we visited. I decided to take it for a test drive with two friends while your mother, James and his wife stayed back soaking in the jacuzzi. We brought a couple beers with us and the two of them snorted a few lines of coke as we drove through the mountain roads. The views on those mountains were incredible. . . just incredible.

We were driving up a narrow winding road to get to the highest view. It was fucking steep as we drove along those edges. I took the last turn a little too fast and felt the car tip over the edge. I swear to God I thought that was it for us. There wasn't a doubt in my mind that we were all going to die from that fall. We were getting tossed around that old four wheel drive as it tumbled down about eighty feet. None of us were wearing seatbelts and we suffered hard because of it. That was the last thing I remember from that fall.

Next thing I remember is that I woke up in a hospital bed with a couple of nurses running around me. They hit buttons on a machine next to my bed. I remembered being so confused. I wondered if I was actually alive. I mean, I thought for certain, without a doubt in my mind, that I had died after hitting the bottom of that cliff.

Later, the nurse told me I had been in a coma for about three months. She said that one of my friends was still in a coma. If it wasn't for my third friend surviving the crash and then climbing the mountain to call for help, we would have died down there. Shortly after that, I remember that my friend's mother stood over my bed furious at me and yelled hysterically. She had brought a lawyer. She told me that she was suing me for crashing the car and putting her son in a coma. He eventually woke up from the coma but not for another three months after that. When he did wake up, he was brain damaged and couldn't talk properly. His mind was gone. I mean, like completely fucking gone.

You wouldn't believe how terrible I felt, Gene. The agony. I was ready to end myself right there in that hospital bed. Nurses had to tie me down to keep me from doing it. They categorized me as a threat to myself and others. I had hit rock fucking bottom, or so I thought.

Your mother came to visit me in the hospital, which gave me hope to keep living. She was still supportive through all my horrid mistakes and downfalls. She was there every step of the way," he started shedding some tears. He thought about his story in a moment of silence before he continued.

"My trial for the crash began. They displayed graphic pictures of the accident on a large projector screen in the courtroom as they presented evidence against me. Those pictures were gruesome, Gene. I mean, real fucking gruesome. I lost part of my head, which is why I have this terrible scar. It's proof this shit actually fucking happened. The city had just started a drinking and driving awareness program and they decided to use my case as an example; a warning to everyone that the city would fuck you if you decided to drink and drive. The judge slammed down his hammer and sentenced me to ten years in prison. He also gave me an eight million dollar fine that I needed to pay before I could receive another driver's license. Eight million dollars. Can you fucking believe that?

Prison was horrible, Gene. . . just fucking horrible. I was always looking out for my life there. I was placed in the same cells as serial killers and rapists. I remember every single new cell mate would ask me why I was in prison and they were shocked when I told them that it was because of a drunk driving accident. I mean, they couldn't believe it. Ten years for a drunk driving accident. I couldn't believe it.

Your mother would religiously come and visit me while I was in prison and we would talk for the little time they gave us. My brother James would sometimes come with your mother. He would bring me porno magazines that he told me that he got from his business. I never asked him about that business, but I'm sure he would tell you all about that. He told me to give the magazines to cell mates and people that wanted to harm me in exchange for safety. He was smart. . . it actually worked out pretty damn well.

After two years, I was allowed to have a job outside of prison as long as I returned immediately after work. It was part of a work release program that they were trialing at the time. I had to wear an ankle monitor to track my movement, but besides that I was free. Your mother would pick me up every day and take me to work. We would spend time together during my lunch break but she also had a job that she had to go to. I don't really remember what she was doing for work at the time but she said she was making good money. She said my brother had helped her find some work.

One day, those porno mags didn't work. It was time for lunch in the prison and I was confronted by a very large guy. I remember thinking that he could definitely beat my ass. That is exactly what he did. I don't even remember why but most likely it was just for initiation into one of the prison gangs. He beat me badly. If it wasn't because the guards broke it up, I would have probably died. After that beating, I really didn't want to be in that prison any longer. I hated that place. I had to get out.

See, Gene. . . I don't know if your mother told you this, but she's from the Dominican Republic. Did you know that?" He asked me, taking a break from the story.

"No," I said interested, "I didn't actually know that."

"Well yea, she's from the Dominican Republic," he continued. "I mean, but that's her story, which is crazy as well. She'll have to tell you someday. It's not my story to tell.

Your mother and I were on one of the daily lunch breaks from my work when I told her that I wanted to break out of prison. I told her that with this new work release program it would be simple. A piece of fucking cake. She was hesitant, but I kept pushing the idea. I told her that all we had to do was book the first flight out to her old country, the Dominican Republic. I kept justifying my idea. I told her that even the guards were surprised by the amount of time I got for my offense. They told me that the longest time served for drinking and driving was only a couple of years. Not ten. She eventually agreed.

My plan was simple. Your mother would sell everything, book the flights to the Dominican Republic and rent a car that we would drive to the airport. We would do it during my lunch break at work. We would cut off the ankle bracelet. Then we would take the flight and start a new life in the Dominican Republic with the money we saved. The only problem was that I wasn't too good at speaking Spanish. I figured I could learn when we got there.

My whole plan actually worked. We arrived in the Dominican Republic and rented a little shack by the beach. The island was fucking incredible, Gene. The beaches had crystal clear water and it was warm like taking a bath. It was an island paradise. There was a lot of poverty on the island though. I mean, there were poor little kids with barely any food in their bodies that climbed palm trees for coconuts. It was really insane. We even bought a little moped that we used to drive around the island. It wasn't a bad life at all. It was kind of like a simple retirement.

Your mother and I lived on that island for about a year when we found out that she was pregnant with you. That's right, pregnant. After the doctor had told her it was impossible. Neither of us could believe it. Once we found that out, your mother insisted that she had to go back to The States. She told me that she had grown up in the Dominican Republic and that it was definitely no place to raise a child. I didn't know what to say. I knew that if I went back I would, without a doubt, be thrown back in prison. She suggested that I stay in the Dominican Republic. She told me that she could send me money from The States. I definitely wasn't a fan of that idea. I wanted to see my son's birth and be there while he grew up. I told her there was no way I was staying. I flew back with you mother.

My brother James helped me get back to work by allowing me to use his identity. He said that the business he was in was all cash and no taxes, so the government shouldn't have him in the system anyways. Your mother and I moved back into an apartment just outside of New York City. I worked at a grocery store that didn't pay nearly as much as the car sales job, but hell… it was something. I bought an unregistered gun, because I swore to myself that I was never going back to prison. I told myself that if the FBI ever caught me, I was going to take them all out. If there were too many of them to fight off, then I was going to take myself out. One shot to the head.

We were getting along pretty well like that. I mean, it wasn't as nice as we had lived before, but it was something. We had a nice routine going and everything seemed to be pretty smooth. Your mother and I were excited and looking forward to your birth. We started preparing a room for you and buying little clothes and shit. The whole nine yards.

I would carry that gun everywhere I went. I tucked it into my pants under my shirt. One day, I had left it at the apartment. I went to the grocery store for work like every other day, except I had left the damn gun at home. That was the day that they got me. The FBI stormed into that place and tackled me to the ground. It must have been about five or six guys. The look on my manager's face when that happened, I tell you, was unforgettable. They were shocked beyond belief. I am sure they had never seen anything like that before. The FBI carried me out in hand cuffs like a hog tied to a fucking barbecue stick. I remember screaming out to my manager. I told him to call your mother and tell her what had happened. To this day, I am not sure he did.

That was it for your old man. It was fucking terrible. I wasn't there for your birth and I never got to see you grow up. I got to prison and they told me that I had to serve the whole ten years, no parole. That was the end of any hope I had for being able to see you any time soon. I lost everything, Gene. Everything including you.

My first couple years I had to serve in solitary confinement. I remember one thing about solitary confinement that I will never fucking forget. I was sitting in the cell leaned up against the wall. A little paper dropped through the hole that they would use to uncuff me once I was in the cell. I remember thinking how strange that was that someone just dropped a piece of paper into the cell. I crawled over to read it. It read 'Gene Oliver Dickson was born today. Congratulations, you have a healthy boy'. I remember going completely fucking insane. I was screaming with joy that was mixed with sorrow. I was pounding the door of the cell. I yelled at the top of my lungs that I wanted out to go see my boy. The guards kept telling me to shut up, but I wouldn't stop. I was in agonizing pain. The worst part about it, is that it was all my fault. There was nothing I could do about it. I had lost everything, Gene. Everything.

The days dragged on for what seemed like an eternity after that day. I fell into a deep dark depression. I unsuccessfully tried to kill myself a couple times, so I had to be constantly mentally evaluated. They were always performing tests on me and giving me medication for depression.

The judge went against his previous ruling and allowed me to get out of prison early. It must have been about three years after you were born. As soon as I got out, I looked your mother up in the directory and went to visit. I wanted to meet you and apologize to your mother for everything. I found the house you two were living in. It was a little faded blue house on the outskirts of Denver. I walked right in through the front door without knocking. That was a huge mistake. I don't know what the fuck I was thinking. Your mother was so frightened and then became very angry when she realized it was me. We started yelling back and forth at each other and she told me to leave the house. I told her I wasn't going to leave the house until I saw you. Well, she didn't like that response, because she came at me swinging a goddamn pan in my face. That's the last I remember of that. Next thing I remembered was waking up in another prison cell. That was the last of my second chances from the judges. That was it for me.

Your mother had finally decided to leave me. I mean, I couldn't blame her. She stuck with me through a lot of shit, but everyone has their limits. She placed a restraining order on me. I can't come within a couple hundred feet of her. It kills me every damn day. I shouldn't have even come as close as I did to drop off that letter for you. Thank God you got it before she did.

See kid, I've had my run in with the law. Shit, I've had my run in with life itself. I've been through some pretty hard knock shit. I mean, I've only got myself to blame for it, but still, it gets to you.

Ever since I officially got out of prison I've been keeping it low key. That's why I moved out here in the middle of fucking nowhere. Right beside my brother. You know James, he lives right over the hill in that pink house. I don't know if you saw that on your way here. Did you?" he paused to ask.

"Yea, I did actually see that on the way in. You can't see it from here though, the hill blocks the way," I replied.

"That's right," he responded with a slight grin, "I think it's best that way. You know, to give us our own space. I think he wanted it that way anyways, because he has his own private thing going. I'm not exactly sure what he does, but he brings in a substantial amount of money."

George and I both turned our heads to the front door. Someone had walked up and knocked. George cautiously walked to the front door and peered out the window the same way he had done with me when I arrived.

"Oh, it's your cousin Tiffany. You haven't met her either. She is my brother's daughter, about your age. I think," he told me as he started to open the door.

"Hi, uncle George," Tiffany said in a happy tone.

"Hey, kid. . . what are you up to?" George responded.

"I came to see your son," she laughed a little as if the question held an obvious answer when she replied, "My father wants me to bring him over to our house for dinner."

"What do you think, Gene? You want to go over and meet your uncle James?" George asked me as he turned his head to look at me.

"Sure," I responded and then stood up from the couch.

"Have you ever driven a truck before?" Tiffany looked over and asked me.

I shook my head. I never had.

"Well come on then! You'll drive us over there," she said in an enthusiastic voice.

George stayed at his house as Tiffany and I walked over to an old white truck that was parked in the front. There were a few dents and scratches on the side. The seats were a cloth gray color and there was a pile of cigarette butts stuffed into the ashtray. I got into the driver's seat and Tiffany got into the passenger's seat.

"Head over to that hill in front of you. There is a little dirt road that will take you over," Tiffany said as she pointed to the hill.

I shifted the truck into gear and started driving slowly on the bumpy road up the hill.

"You're not going to make it up the hill going that slow, Gene," she said while looking over and laughing at me, "Step on the gas."

I pushed the gas down quite a bit more and we started to drive up the hill faster. We were bouncing up and down from the bumps in the dirt road. Tiffany and I were both laughing as we bounced. I gradually increased the speed as we continued to climb up the hill. We were almost to the peak.

CRASH!

The truck came to an immediate stop. The windows cracked and the airbag inflated. The airbag punched my face, pushing me into the backrest of the seat. I heard the glass coming down onto various parts of the car like a metallic rain. A cloud of dust engulfed us. I couldn't see anything.

The dust cloud started to dissipate and the airbags deflated. Tiffany and I kicked the doors open and looked in front of us to see what we had hit. Our eyes widened with a look of devastation. A man was sitting in the driver's seat of the car that had been smashed from the impact. We were at the peak of the hill.

The man's face had a large golf ball sized swelling above his right eye and he was covered in blood. There was a pitchfork that had pierced the side of his body from the back to the front. He was moving slightly and moaning in pain.

"Daddy!" Tiffany screamed in agony.

We both ran over to him and Tiffany handed me a cell phone to call the ambulance. She then ripped off her shirt and used it to stop the bleeding. Once I had finished calling the ambulance, we sat next to him for the next thirty minutes, trying to keep him awake. The ambulance arrived and carefully worked to remove the pitchfork from his body and move him into a stretcher. The ambulance started the drive to the hospital with Tiffany in the passenger's seat. That's how I met James.

I stood petrified for a moment. I snapped out of it. I ran as fast as I could back to my father's house to tell him what had happened. We both took my car to the hospital and sat in the waiting room for a few hours while they operated on James.

It was the most frightening thing I had ever experienced. I was shaking inside and out. I could feel the temperature of my bones starting to chill. I couldn't believe what had happened. So many things were going on at once. I was having trouble absorbing all the information. I didn't even get the chance to think about my father's story before this terrible tragedy unfolded. His story had a lot to take in. It was an intense story. I didn't know what to think of my father. I didn't really know him that well. I didn't know anyone that was here that well. I hadn't even met James before crashing into him.

I started to sink to the floor as I leaned up against the wall of the waiting room. What if I never get to meet him? What if this was it? Sitting in that waiting room and not knowing what was going to happen was one of the most gut wrenching feelings I had ever felt. This was all my fault. I shouldn't have driven that truck. I couldn't see anything going over that hill. I didn't have time to react. Why didn't I press the brake? Why didn't I see him coming? Streams of tears started flowing from my eyes.

"Dickson family," a nurse shouted from two large double doors.

Tiffany, George, James' wife and I all got up and followed the nurse into the hospital room that James was in. The nerves in my body were buzzing like a swarm of wasps flying violently out of their nest. My heart was pounding uncontrollably, without rhythm. I started to think about the first impression I had made on James. The first time I met him I crashed into him. I put him in the hospital. What would he think of me now? What did everyone else think of me? How could I possibly make up for this mistake? We arrived at the room.

The room was dead silent, aside from the sound of a subtle beep every few seconds. There was a large window overlooking the parking lot of cars below us near the hospital entrance. The bed was propped up and James was laying there looking at us as we came in. He had an IV stuck into his arm and a large white bandage wrapped around his head. He smiled a bit as we all entered the room.

"Who the fuck are you?" James said in a deep raspy voice while looking at me.

"I'm Gene, George's son," I said quietly with instability in my voice.

"Who?" he barked back in a higher raspy tone.

"George's son," I said a little louder.

"Come here," he said roughly.

I cautiously walked closer to him. I stood right beside the hospital bed. I was scared of how he was going to react to what I had done to him. I was afraid he was going to hate me. He grabbed my arm and pulled me closer to his face.

"It's gonna take a lot more than that to kill me, kid!" he said and then broke into an airy, coughing laugh.

I looked around the room and everyone was smiling along with him.

"Welcome to the family, kid," James shouted to me while continuing to laugh.

A sense of relief came over me after James had said that, but I still felt terrible inside.

"Listen to me, kid," James said while looking at me with a serious face, "Forget about this shit. It's in the past. What happened, happened, so just fucking scrap it. I'll be fine. You can't tell your mother about this shit either, because then she's going to know you came over here. Trust me, we don't want that drama. She has a restraining order on your father and you're not eighteen yet, so I think it goes for you as well. We don't want police over here and shit. Your father really wanted to meet you and he got to do that, so we're good. No hard feelings. Do you understand what I'm telling you?"

"Yea, I understand," I said, tilting my head and looking down to the ground.

The nurse entered the room with a clipboard and a piece of paper and walked over to James. She asked him who his insurance provider was so that she could run the hospital bill through his insurance company. He said he didn't have one. She told him the bill was going to be pretty expensive. He told her not to worry about it. He said he was going to pay with cash. She seemed unconvinced that he was going to be able to pay with cash but she wrote it down anyway. Then, she walked out of the room. James stared at the wall with a worried look on his face after she had left. When he noticed I was looking at him, he turned to me and smiled. He gave me a thumbs up. I smiled back at him, but I was starting to worry about how he was going to pay for the hospital bill.

***

"I'm telling you. . . easy money, Gene. We can do this," Sean said as we walked down the high school hallway together.

"I don't know, man. It's a little risky. . . don't you think?" I replied hesitantly.

"What's not risky, Gene? Anything you do in life is a risk. This is no different. Think about it and let me know after school," he answered me before running to catch his class.

It had been a couple weeks since the accident. I was having nightmares about it and I constantly played it back in my mind. It was hard to focus in my classes because I was thinking about it. I was thinking about the nurse talking to James at the hospital. I felt like it really was my fault, and I wished there was something I could do to fix it. I also thought about my father's story. I thought about the circumstances of my birth and what my mother had been through. I had always wondered why she had a stiffened walk. I had so many questions in my mind. What happened to my mother after my father went to prison? How did my mother make it to the United States if she grew up in the Dominican Republic? Was the dream that I had in the Volvo station wagon actually a memory? It was so similar to the part of the story my father had told when he went to visit my mother and me in the faded blue house. Was everything my father said even true?

Ever since the night up in the mountains with Sean, Mel and Lisa, Sean had been doing a lot more drugs than just those magic mushrooms. He was trying everything. He was a very observant kid and would take advantage of every opportunity that landed in front of him. This opportunity happened to be a jar of one hundred ecstasy pills.

There was a kid at school that everyone called 'Sticks’, because he was tall and skinny. I never heard anyone call him anything else. I didn’t even know his real name. Sticks had a reputation of always trying to be cool and fit in with everyone. Even when he was rejected, he stayed persistent. He would talk shit to the other kids in an attempt to fit in. He was extremely smart when it came to school but he lacked common sense and street wisdom. He made the mistake of telling a few people that he kept a jar of Ecstasy pills hidden in his truck. Sean wanted to take advantage of that.

The bell rang signaling the end of school. I lifted my backpack from the floor beside my desk and started to head out of the classroom. All the kids in the class piled out quickly. I stayed back and waited for everyone to pass. My teacher noticed I was taking my time and decided to take advantage of that moment.

"Hey, Gene. . . come here real quick," she said, tilting her head and waving her hand.

Her name was Miss Bach. She had dark black curly hair and a smooth pale white face. She wore a hand knit white sweater with black jeans and high heel boots. She was a younger teacher, around her mid-twenties. She was sitting on top of her desk with her legs kicking back and forth in front of her.

I walked towards her and set my backpack down on one of the student desks near her.

"So. . . what's up?" she asked with a slight bit of concern, "I notice you look a little down these last few days."

I didn't really want to talk about everything that had happened when I met my father and crashed into my uncle. That was my business. So I pushed those thoughts aside.

"No, I'm good," I said, adding a bit of a forced grin, "maybe I'm just stressed about tests and school work, that's all."

"Well, you are an extremely smart kid and I see a bright college future ahead of you. I am here, if you need anything, just let me know. I want to see you succeed."

"Thanks," I nodded with an awkward closed mouth smile.

I then turned and left the classroom. Sean was waiting right outside the door for me.

"So listen, Gene, before you say anything," Sean started talking to me quietly, but with enthusiasm, "Sticks is an idiot. He is an asshole to everyone anyways. He is a prick who is always trying to become popular. He's pathetic. He was the idiot that told someone where he hid his pills anyways, so he is practically asking us to steal them. A jar like that could make us each one thousand dollars cash, easy. I already have a buyer and he wants to buy them all. We take the jar and we go to the buyer. Done. Easy money. Before you say no, think about how often an opportunity like this comes around."

I listened to him. This time, I was really thinking about the idea. He didn't realize it, but his words were actually speaking to me at that moment. I never told him about the car accident with my uncle. I started contemplating his offer. One thousand dollars could be good money to give to my uncle. I know that James would probably say he is fine, that he doesn't need it, but I was starting to think that was simply his pride. I think he hides it, but he really does need help.

Sean was starting to get anxious with my silent thoughts as we walked.

"And Gene, who is he going to call? The police? It's illegal. He can't do shit about it once it's done," Sean added with the most convincing tone he could deliver.

I started to think about that part as well. Having only two Ecstasy pills in your possession could give you life in prison. We were going to have one hundred. That was a shit ton of pills. That was a lot of prison time. That part made me really nervous but I thought about what Sean had said. Everything you do in life is a risk. I thought about my uncle's bloody face in that smashed car. I thought about the worried look he had when he stared at that wall. I had to do something about that. I felt terrible for what I had done to James. That was the first day I met him. I just showed up and wrecked his life. Then, I had to leave without talking to anyone about it, as if it had never happened. It did happen, and I had to make it right.

"Alright. Fuck it. I'm in," I said with a sudden jolt of confidence.

Sean jumped in the air and swung his fists around in celebration of his excitement. He turned to me and gave me a hug followed by a few taps on the back. He was filled with so much excitement that his smile was almost too big to fit his face.

In that moment of watching his celebration, I thought back to the little toy car I had stolen with Carlos when I was a child. I thought about how much the consequences of that action had affected the rest of my life. That made me very nervous and I wanted to change my mind about stealing the Ecstasy pills, but I couldn't go back on it now. Sean was already too excited. I had already made up my mind that I was doing it for James. I thought that maybe stealing the little toy car had ended badly because I was doing it for myself. This was different. I was doing this for James. I wasn't doing this for me. I was doing this to fix my mistake. The heist was on.

***

Sean and I were sprinting down the street as fast as we could. We rounded the street corner where my car was parked and jumped in. We drove to the location the buyer had texted to Sean earlier and sat parked on the side of the street. We caught our breath for a few minutes. Sean pulled out the jar of Ecstasy pills from his pants with a huge grin on his face.

"We fucking did it, Gene," he said proudly while holding his smile.

"It was actually way easier than I thought it would be," I responded with a slight grin. "Sticks didn't even lock his car."

Sean pulled out his cell phone from his pocket. He read a text that the buyer had sent him earlier. He read the location again to make sure we were at the right place.

"Ready to do this shit?" Sean said, looking up at me.

"Let's get it over with," I said as my smile disappeared and my face became more serious.

The nerves started pumping through my veins at that moment. Stealing the pills wasn't so nerve-racking, but now, I felt the adrenaline. My chest felt as if a giant black hole had appeared in its center and I became very cold. My stomach was wringing itself out like a drenched towel.

It was dark outside and late in the night. There was a cold chill that would blow every few minutes. The hairs on my arms would rise and fall with the chilling wind. There was nothing but an empty street where we had parked with a flickering street lamp.

Sean and I waited for a few moments. A black four door sedan with heavily tinted windows pulled up behind us. The headlights flashed at us and then turned off completely. Sean's phone vibrated and we both looked down at the text message. The text instructed us to get out and walk slowly to the car parked behind us and sit in the back seats.

We slowly stepped out of my car, walked to the car behind us and got into the back seats. A younger guy in his mid twenties turned around and looked at us. He wore sunglasses and a black hood covering his head.

"Let me see them," the man said.

"Why don't you show us the money first," Sean said confidently back to him.

The man turned around and faced forward in the driver's seat. He pressed the lock button to lock all the doors in the car before reaching over into the glove box. He pulled out a black nine millimeter pistol and aimed it at us. We flinched a bit and pushed our backs into the seat rests. We raised our hands to the top of the car above our heads.

My heart sped up faster than ever before. I could feel each heart beat pushing all the way up into my throat. I was cold, but my body started producing little drops of sweat.

"Why don't you two stop fucking around and show me the pills," the man said with an irritated look on his face.

"Seriously, you're going to pull a gun out on us," Sean said with his hands still raised in the air.

I couldn't believe that Sean was questioning this guy. He had a gun pointed at our faces. He obviously had the upper hand.

The man turned around and reached to the back seat. He grabbed Sean by the shirt and shoved the gun into his mouth.

"I don't have time for your childish attitude. What are you, in fucking high school?" the man said boldly.

Sean looked at me and moved his eyes down towards his pants as a signal for me to grab the jar of pills. I reached over and took the pills from his pants and showed them to the man. He took the gun out from Sean's mouth, took the pills from me and then went back to the driver's seat. He started to examine the pills to make sure they were all legitimate. Once he was satisfied, he tossed a rolled wad of cash to us.

"Good. Now get the fuck out of my car," the man said as he pressed a button unlocking all the doors.

Sean and I got out of the man's car and returned back to mine. I started it right away and drove to Sean's house. I decided to stay there for the night. I had told Jacob and my mother earlier that we had to stay up late to work on a school project together and that I didn't want to disturb them. They told me it would be better if we worked at Sean's house. They approved of me staying the night. I knew they would because Jacob hated visitors.

Once in Sean's room, we counted the money. The buyer had shorted us. There was only five hundred dollars to split. I knew James would need more than that for all of his medical bills. Two hundred and fifty dollars was nothing. I was so disappointed that my face tensed up and my throat strained.

"Bastard," Sean said angrily, tossing his portion of the money on the ground, "We got stiffed."

"We almost fucking died, Sean," I added.

"Nah, he wouldn't have shot us. He was just a little bitch trying to scare some high school kids," he said as he lit a joint in his mouth.

"What are you talking about, man? He shoved that gun into your mouth," I replied, not convinced with his interpretation of the situation.

Sean was silent and didn't respond to that. He just kept smoking the joint quietly and stared at the wall. Right then, I decided that I never wanted to get money like that again. That was way too close. Sean had a loaded gun in his mouth. I thought he was going to die. Sean seemed to brush it off like it wasn't a big deal, but to me, it was insane.

***

Months went by since we had stolen those Ecstasy pills. It was the start of summer break. I had mailed the two hundred and fifty dollars for James to the address my father had written in his letter. I figured that if I put a name on it then James might not accept it, so I sent it anonymously. It helped, but it didn't really make me feel any better about what I had done.

I was relieved to be out of school for the next couple of months. It was nice to have some extra free time however, I kept working through the summer at the drugstore. A car and a job made life way easier and gave me the freedom I needed from Jacob.

Sean and I didn't practice music as much as we used to, but that was fine because I was doing my own thing with it. Sean was still taking a bunch of drugs and seizing every opportunity that presented him. That was Sean. He would invite me to a lot of parties or bonfires, but I turned him down most of the time. He finally suggested something that I was interested in. Going to the movies. Nice and chill, just us and another friend.

The third person was Jake. He was a shorter kid, about my height, wore skinny fitted jeans with an old purple hoodie. He had long brown hair that he was constantly flipping out of his face, similar to Sean.

I had left my car at home. We rode to the mall where the movie was showing with Jake's mother. She dropped us off and told us she would pick us up later. Sean had snuck in some rum and cola, so we decided to drink a little bit before the movie. We mixed the rum and cola together fairly strong and started sipping while we waited.

"Gene, you've never tried Ecstasy right?" Sean asked while pulling out a little bag of orange pills.

"Nah man, I think I'm good with just smoking a little weed every once in a while," I responded.

"You really should try it. It's the best feeling in the world," he said while throwing a pill in his mouth.

He handed another pill to Jake, who did the same. They both chased the pills down with the rum and cola.

"I've got one more, Gene. Your name is written all over it," Sean said with a convincing tone.

"I don't know, man. . . the trip lasts like eight hours, doesn't it?" I asked. I was still unconvinced it was a good idea.

Sean grabbed my drink and tossed the last pill into the can.

"Just chug it, man. . . you won't even notice it. It's dissolving in your drink now, you're not going to let that pill go to waste, are you?" Sean said while holding the drink out to me.

I took the drink from Sean's hand and stared down into the open can. I felt an empty feeling in my stomach that moved around like a bubble. I was nervous and felt a little sick when I thought about taking the pill. I really didn't want to do it, but the pressure from Sean and Jake overtook my feeling of nervousness. I started to convince myself it wasn't so bad. I swirled the drink around. I looked back down into the can. I looked up to Sean, who had a giant smile on his face. I looked back at the can and then swung my head back and finished the drink.

"Was that so bad?" Sean said while laughing a bit.

"I guess we'll see," I said uneasily.

"You'll be fine," Jake added.

We tossed the cans in the trash and then entered the movie. I didn't really feel any effects throughout the movie. We walked out of the theater and waited for Jake's mother.

It hit me hard. I felt my eyes widen and my body became extremely sensitive. I wanted to touch everything. I felt as if millions of fuzzy caterpillars were crawling all over my body.

Jake's mother pulled up to the curb and we all got into the back of the car. She asked us how the movie had been and I broke out laughing uncontrollably. I just couldn't stop. I was laughing at nothing but I couldn't stop. Sean started laughing along with me really loudly and Jake joined in as well. They told Jake's mom that it was an inside joke that we had from a part in the movie that we were laughing at. Eventually, my laughing came to a stop and I sat there quietly. I smiled while squeezing my legs with my hands.

We arrived at Jake's house and pulled into the garage. I noticed Jake lived in the same neighborhood as Sean and me. He lived a little closer to the park. It was getting pretty late so Jake's mom suggested that we stay the night at her house. Sean had already told his parents that he was going to stay the night at Jake's. They had already planned to take Ecstasy before I arrived. I hadn't told Jacob or my mother that I was going to be out all night but it was too late to tell them now. I couldn't speak to them in the state I was in. I just let it be.

"What the fuck!" Jake's mother shouted loudly as she stared at the three of us under the light in the garage, "Get the fuck out of my house, the three you! There will not be any drug addicts sleeping under my roof tonight."

She had noticed that our pupils were largely dilated and that we were obviously on a high from the drugs.

We didn't say a word. We didn't even try to argue. She was right. We were on drugs. We just walked out onto the street and started heading towards the park. Jake's mother had been serious, because we noticed she locked the doors and closed the garage. We had no place to stay that night.

Once we arrived at the park, Sean led us to the edge where the fence which marked the border of the neighborhood was. We all ran to it and climbed up enough to see over the top. It was really dark, but the stars and the moon provided enough light to see fairly well. There was a large open field with patches of grass scattered unevenly throughout the land. The field was split by a little stream that flowed through the land. A reflection of the stars twinkled in the stream. A large lonely tree stood right beside the stream with many climbable branches stretching out in every direction.

"Let's go," Sean said smiling, "that looks awesome."

I agreed. It did look pretty awesome. I couldn't tell if it was the drug enhancing my vision or if it was actually beautiful. Either way, it was perfect for the time. Sean and I leaped over the fence and started walking to the tree while Jake had run over to the portable toilet near the skatepark. He said he would meet us there.

Sean and I leaned our backs up against the tree with our legs outstretched in front of us. The stars were amazing and brighter than normal. You could see hundreds of constellations in the sky. The star's light was brighter than normal. We saw a few shooting stars and comets pierce through the black sky as we laid there. There was a gentle sound of water flowing from the stream behind us. It was relaxing. It was impossible to sleep because of the Ecstasy, but laying there was close enough.

Sean and I turned our heads to a sound that came from the fence. It must have been Jake. He had just leaped over the fence. We started feeling vibrations on the ground and looked a little closer to where Jake was coming from. Jake was sprinting. He was moving faster than I had ever seen a human run in my life. He was waving his hands frantically forward, signaling for us to move. He was approaching us fast. We looked further to see what was causing the commotion and that is when we saw it. There was a bull charging at him. A fucking bull. Sean and I jumped to our feet and took a quick look around. Then, we jumped and grabbed onto the tree branches above us. We climbed a bit and then held tightly to the branch we were on while offering our arms out for Jake. He continued running frantically towards the tree. He leaped into it as we grabbed his arms and pulled him up close to us. The bull charged into the tree striking it with its horns. The tree shook and a rain of leaves fell to the ground. Jake didn't have a tight grip and almost fell out of the tree when it shook, but we pulled him back up from falling. We sat in the tree for the next five hours, shaking from the adrenaline.

The sun was starting to rise and the bull had moved far from the tree closer to a large house that we saw in the distance. It seemed safe, so we climbed down slowly and quietly. Once down, we leaned our backs against the tree like we had before.

We sat there in silence for a while. The effects from the Ecstasy were slowly starting to wear off. A woman started walking towards us. She was wearing a cowboy hat, jeans, cowboy chaps and a black western collared shirt. She held a twelve gauge shotgun in her hands readied to shoot as she approached us.

"What the hell are you doing on my property?" she yelled with the shotgun aimed directly at our faces.

We slowly stood up with our hands raised above our heads.

“Are you fucking with my bull? You know he could have killed you, right?” she continued shouting out reproaching questions.

She approached us until she was only a gun's length away, still aiming and ready to shoot. We stood silently, dazed and confused from the situation.

“Well, are any of you going to speak up with an explanation?” she asked, swaying the barrel of the gun back and forth between our faces.

“Just exploring. We got lost, ma’am. We’re leaving now,” I replied, barely managing to put a few words together.

“Bullshit,” she snapped angrily but continued, “I’m going to escort you back over that fence, but next time I see you on my property, there will be less questioning and more shooting.”

We walked in front of her. She kept the shotgun aimed at our backs. We carefully started climbing over the fence. Once we made it over, we ran to the grassy area by the playground. We collapsed in relief and laid on the grass. We caught our breath and stared straight up into the sky. We sat there in silence for a moment and allowed our heartbeats to slow down back to normal.

“What the fuck?” Sean said and then started breaking into an uncontrolled laugh.

"That's two fucking times, Sean! Two times that we've almost been shot," I said in a serious tone covering my face with my hands, "Not cool."

Jake just laughed along with everything. The three of us just laid in the grass as the sun rose higher into the sky.

I finally started getting tired. The Ecstasy refused to allow me to rest all night because it kept my eyes wide open. It was a relief to lay down and give my heart a break from pumping extra blood through my veins. I started to go deep into thought. I thought about the story my father had told me. I thought about the two near death experiences he had in those car accidents. I related them to the two times Sean and I almost got shot. I didn't want to end up like my father. His life seemed miserable. He never got to watch his kid grow up. He spent about ten years of his life in prison. He tried to kill himself multiple times. He did a bunch of drugs. That wasn't going to be me. I didn't want that for my life. I didn't want to be like Jacob either. He needed to beat someone inferior to him to feel powerful. He was incarcerated by his OCD. He was boring. I couldn't think of a role model to look up to, so I decided I was going to become my own person. I was going to be my own role model. That day had been a frightening experience, but I was thankful that it had happened. It made me never want to go through that ever again. I wasn't going to become addicted to drugs like Sean. He had lost control of himself. I was starting to realize that. He lived his life from trip to trip, drug to drug. Drugs directed his life. I wasn't going to live like that. Laying on that grass field that morning, dirty, tired and shaken, forced me to make a lot of decisions for my future. From then on, I was going to take full control of my life.

I suddenly jumped to my feet after trailing off into those thoughts. I began to walk back to my house. Jake and Sean had fallen asleep on the grass, so they didn’t notice me leaving. I walked with a new found confidence, determined that life was going to be different. I rounded the corner to my house but realized that it was still very early. It would be too early to try and return home. I decided to get into my car instead. I sat there and stared out the window until eventually I drifted to sleep.

***

“I really think you are making a huge mistake, Gene. Why don’t you think about it for a few days before coming to a final decision?” Mr. Knowles said with a desperate tone.

Mr. Knowles was a man in his mid-thirties that worked as the high school counselor. He was a friendly man and had a smiling face to match his personality. He always peered over the top of his square framed reading glasses when he spoke with you. He had a thick curly black ‘fro that bounced around when he walked.

“Mr. Knowles. Did you not just say that I have more than enough credits to graduate a year early because of the advanced courses I took?” I asked.

"Yes. You technically do, Gene, but listen, you're a smart kid. You could apply to some great colleges," he said while showing me a pile of college brochures.

"I just think it's a waste of money. I really need to get out of this town. I can't live here anymore. I need to see what else the world has to offer," I responded.

"I understand, Gene. How about this? Take some of these brochures home with you. Think about it for the next week. If you still feel the same way, then I will sign the approval for your early graduation," he said with a little bit of hope left.

"Alright," I said. I took the brochure from his hand and walked out of the office.

***

I pulled up to my house and parked the car on the side of the street. I turned off the engine and sat there for a moment just thinking about life. I really wanted to leave. I wanted to start my own life somewhere else. I felt there was nothing of value in this place for me. I had stopped hanging out with Sean. Tell me who you hang out with, and I'll tell you who you are. That is not who I wanted to become.

I opened the trunk and walked to the back to lift it up fully. This is where I kept the new acoustic guitar I had bought, since Jacob had wrecked my electric guitar. I kept it in the trunk so that Jacob wouldn't find out about it. Even though I could beat him in a fight, it was better not to do things to make him mad. I pulled it out and closed the trunk. I opened the back door and got in. I started playing some chords in the back seat and improvising some lyrics into a melody to go along with them. The chords started formulating into a song. I thought of some lyrics for the chorus and started to sing them in a melody. I started working on the verses. I spent hours singing, playing and writing a new song in the back seat.

Suddenly, I heard a *knock* on the window that made me jump. It made me smack my head on the top of the car. Jacob was standing outside with his fists clenched against his sides. He was looking in through the window. I could tell that he was angry. He signaled for me to get out of the car. I did so on the opposite side that he was standing on. I left the guitar inside and locked the door once I was out. I stood on the opposite side of the car and looked over at him.

"You think you are above my rules now that you have a car?" he said in a snappy tone.

"Look, Jacob," I said and continued, "I bought this car with my own money. I keep my guitar in here because it is my property. I will respect your rules when I'm in your house, but this isn't your house."

"While you are living under my roof, you listen to my rules. You can not have that guitar and you can't play it. Give it to me," he ordered boldly.

"I'm not giving you my guitar. I will be moving out of your house soon anyways," I responded.

He glared at me in disgust and then turned around and walked into the house without saying another word. I thought that it was strange that he had given up so easily. I unlocked the car. I took my guitar from the backseat and placed it back into the trunk. I locked the door and walked up to my room. It was time for me to get ready for work.

I took a quick shower and threw my work shirt on. I walked down the stairs back to the front door and headed to my car. I stopped halfway. Every tire had been slashed flat. I knew that there had to have been a reason Jacob had given up so easily. He knew I could beat him physically, so he just damaged my car instead. I was pissed. I didn't have time to confront him about it. I started jogging to work so that I wouldn't be late.

After work, I hung out with everyone as usual in the parking lot of the drug store. My manager was smoking a cigarette and my co-worker was leaning up against the manager's car. We had a short staff that day.

My manager was a short lady with red hair that flowed down her back. She was in her late twenties and had a tattoo sleeve on her left arm.

I was standing around while the two of them chatted, but I had zoned out. I was staring at the tire on my manager's car.

"What's up, Gene? You've been staring at my tire for like ten minutes. You haven't said a word," my manager said as she dropped her cigarette to the ground and smashed it with the bottom of her shoe.

I shook out of my stare and rejoined the conversation. I hadn't really been thinking about anything. I was simply just absent from my thoughts.

"Oh sorry," I said looking back at her.

"I've seen that face before. What you need is a drink," she laughed as she said it.

"I don't know, maybe," I said with a half smile and a chuckle.

"Get in," she tilted her head and started to get into her car.

"Where are we going?" I said curiously as I got into the front seat.

"I'll catch you guys at work tomorrow. Goodnight," my co-worker shouted as she walked to her car.

"Well," my manager continued once we got into the car, "due to the fact that you're under age and we can't go to the bar, I was just going to buy you a bottle of vodka to take home with you".

"Oh. . . ok," I said laughing, "Thanks."

We drove to the drive-thru liquor store across the street. She ordered a box full of different types of liquor including a little bottle of vodka for me.

She then insisted on driving me home. I gave her directions to my house. She dropped me off where my car was. I sat there miserably on the side of the street. I stared at my slashed tires for a while. I walked around to check if there was any other damage. . . there wasn't.

I walked to the front door of the house but it had been locked. I peered into the window. All of the lights were off. I walked back to the street and looked up at the other windows. They were all off.

I pulled my car key out of my pocket and unlocked the door. I got into the back seat and curled up on my side. After a few minutes, I sat up and opened the bottle of vodka. I looked inside the neck of the bottle and then looked out the window. I thought about what a shitty couple of days it had been. I was exhausted. Maybe she was right. I just needed a drink. I tipped the bottle up, taking a mouth full of vodka and swallowing it. My eyes closed tightly as I focused on pushing the alcohol down my throat. What a horrible taste, just awful. It burned as it went down my throat. I took a couple more mouthfuls and then sat the bottle down underneath the front seat of the car. I leaned over and grabbed the notebook that I kept in the car to write songs. It was a black spiral notebook with college ruled lined paper. I sat there and stared at a blank page with a pen in my hand ready to write. I started writing a poem, but the words began to blur. I reached under the front seat and grabbed the vodka bottle. I drank some more and put it back underneath the seat. I took the pen and notebook and slid them under the seat as well. I curled up like before and laid down on my side. My eyes were trying to keep up with everything that was spinning around me until I fell asleep.

SEVEN

2010

I clicked my motorbike into sixth gear and took a quick glance at the flashing blue and red lights behind me through my side view mirror. There was a strong force of wind pushing against the windshield on my black tinted helmet. I was hunched over with my chest resting on the fuel tank of my motorbike. My legs were squeezed against the seat tightly. Cars blurred as I passed them through the middle lane of the highway. It was the same highway I had driven before with my mother up to the mountains.

Adrenaline pumped through my veins the same way the fuel pumped through the engine in my motorbike. I was in sync with my machine. I was unstoppable. I was challenging the law just like I had challenged Jacob's authority. It felt amazing. There was nothing the police could do to catch me as I swerved in and out of the traffic. I checked back in my sideview mirror and the red and blue lights had disappeared. I had defeated them. I had won. I was free.

I climbed the mountain all the way to the top. The vanilla scent of the Ponderosa pines was stronger than before. I was with them, in the outdoors, outside the comfort of the car's frame. I reached the top of the mountain and drifted to a stop on the gravel road. I set my feet down on both sides of the motorbike to balance myself. I removed my helmet and set it on the fuel tank in front of me. I took a deep inhale of the crisp mountain air and closed my eyes as I did so. I opened my eyes and gazed down at the world below. A gust of nostalgia blew upon me and I saw my mother sitting there with her legs dangling carelessly over the edge of the car. I released my worries on that mountain top like the trees released their leaves every fall.

It had been about a year since I moved out of my parents house and graduated high school early. Jacob slashing my tires was all the confirmation that I needed to make my final decision. Mr. Knowles wasn't very happy with my choice at the end of the week, but a deal is a deal. He had to sign the approval. I didn't feel anything when I left home. I didn't even consider it my home. I had nothing keeping me there.

I moved into a two bedroom apartment with Blake, my old drummer from middle school. We were still underage, but his mother co-signed the rental agreement for us. It was a simple apartment. Beige carpet throughout the whole floor with the exception of white tile on both the kitchen and bathroom floors. There was a little wooden patio outside of the front living room. There was a set of stairs just outside of the apartment that led to a parking lot.

Blake taught me a fair amount about motorbikes, a hobby he had picked up since I had last seen him. He had one as well, so we would ride together all the time. After moving in with him, I found a practically brand new motorbike for sale from a rich kid downtown. Blake and I went to check it out. It wouldn't start when the kid showed it to us so we lowballed him on the price. We practically stole it from him. He wasn't too smart because all it needed was a battery charge since it had been sitting in his garage for a couple of years. We told him that there was a lot of work that had to be done before we could get it to run again.

I played shows around the city with my acoustic guitar and recorded a small three song demo. I submitted the songs to a local radio station and the DJ selected one of them for airplay. That was a great feeling. I remember Blake and I cracked open a few beers and waited for my song to play on the radio at the apartment. We blasted it until the neighbors underneath us started pounding a broom stick to the floor. We got wasted that night.

I started a new job at a nice hotel. It was only a twenty minute drive from the apartment. It paid way more than the drug store and I was naturally good at it. I walked into that hotel to apply for the job not knowing anything about hotels. I simply wore a suit I had bought at a local thrift store and told the general manager that, one day, I was going to take his position. I guess he was so impressed by my confidence that he hired me right on the spot.

Life was the best it had ever been. I had a new job, new motorbike, an apartment with Blake and freedom. Freedom was the most important part. I could play guitar and write songs whenever I wanted without fear of Jacob interfering. I could come and go as I pleased and I didn't have to pretend to be interested in things I didn't like. I could do anything.

I leaned my motorbike on the kickstand and walked closer to the edge of the mountain. I sat on a large rock and wrapped my arms around my knees to keep them in place. I continued to gaze out at the view of everything below. I heard the faint sound of a motorbike climbing the mountain. It became louder as time passed. The sound was behind me. It was Blake.

I smiled and watched as he leaned his motorbike over on the kickstand and removed his helmet. He hung it from the steering handle. He had my guitar in a black cloth case strapped to his back and a few beers that he pulled out of his riding jacket. He walked over to the rock I was on.

"I thought your ass might be up here," he said as he leaned up against the rock.

He opened the two beers and handed one over to me. We tapped the beers together and raised them up to the sky before taking a sip.

"You know me too well," I replied with a grin.

"It's fucking beautiful out there," he said pointing his beer to the view.

I nodded in agreement. We sat for a while and just gazed down at the view. The sun was already behind the mountains. I realized that there were a lot more buildings and houses than before, when I was a kid. The lights below began to flicker like the stars and became brighter as the sun disappeared. The car lights looked like lasers shooting through streets. Every once in a while, you would see the red and blue flashing lights from the police cars move past the rest of the car lights. You could hear the faint wailing of the sirens as well. It was quite a sight. It had grown and changed so much since I had last seen it with my mother.

Blake removed my guitar from his back and set it down by the rock. He took out my guitar and offered it over to me with an outstretched hand.

"It's not going to play itself," he said with a smile.

I laughed with a bit of embarrassment and then took the guitar from his hand. I started to strum a variety of chord progressions. I played a few covers from some bands that we liked and we sang out to the city below us. The city lights fought with the stars as the night progressed. I stopped playing and looked over to Blake.

"You ever thought of leaving Colorado? Going out and seeing the world?" I asked him.

"Maybe to visit, but I like it here," he replied.

“There are so many more places though, like don’t you want to see the ocean?”

Blake paused and thought about that for a moment.

“The ocean would be pretty cool, like California,” he said.

“Yeah, like California,” I agreed and then turned back to the view of the city lights.

We stayed up late into the night and stared at the stars. I played a few more songs and we finished the beers Blake had brought for us.

***

Knock, knock, knock!

I slowly started to force my eyes open after I heard the *knock* on the apartment door. I was stretched out on a double mattress that lay on my empty bedroom floor. It was my day off from work. I leaned over to grab my cell phone that was plugged into the wall and laying on the floor of my bedroom. It was still early, only six in the morning. Who could possibly be at the door at six in the morning? I really didn’t care, I started to drift back to sleep.

Knock, knock, knock, knock, knock!

The knocking was a little louder and more aggressive. I yelled out to Blake to see if he was home, but I didn’t receive a reply. He must have been at work. Blake worked at the grocery store and had to work overnight shifts until eight in the morning. It was too early for that, so I just continued to lay on my back.

Knock, knock, knock, knock!

It wasn't going to stop. I figured if I wanted to get any more sleep then I had better just go and see who it was. I slowly stood to my feet. I was in my underwear and thought for a second about putting some clothes on. I decided not to. I walked to the front door. I cracked it open a bit and looked outside.

"Gene!" John shouted.

I shushed him because I was sure all the neighbors were still sleeping. I was surprised. I couldn't believe it. It was John from our middle school rock band.

"Come in, man," I said quietly.

He entered our almost empty living room. There was only an old beaten up couch in the center of the room. He walked over and sat on it as I closed the door.

"What the hell, man?" I said in a surprised voice, "It's been a while. I haven't seen you since middle school. What's going on with you?"

I noticed he had a backpack full of things with him and a bass guitar case that he set next to the couch.

"I got kicked out of my parent's house," he said in a worried laugh.

"What happened?" I was concerned.

"I told them I wanted to move to Hollywood, California and pursue a music career. They didn't like that. They would rather have me go to a business school or study law," he explained.

"Oh, I see," I said with understanding in my voice and then continued, "Well. . . fuck it. Why don't you just do what you want to do with your life?"

"Yeah, that's what I want to do"

"Then do it," I smiled and laughed a bit.

"The problem is I spent most of my money on the plane ticket so I don't have enough for a place to stay while I wait," he said ashamed and looked to the ground.

I caught his subtle hint.

"Well, when is your flight?" I asked.

"In only two weeks," he said, lifting his head with a slight grin.

I knew he was waiting for it.

"Why don't you just stay with us until your flight?" I said, giving him the much anticipated suggestion that I knew he was looking for.

He jumped to his feet with a huge smile on his face and gave me a tight hug.

"Yes, thank you so much, Gene," he said, overly grateful.

I smiled and laughed at the whole thing. His intentions were obvious the whole time, but it was fun to humor him. I didn't mind if he stayed with us for a couple weeks. I actually thought it was really cool that he was flying to California to pursue a music career. I thought about what Blake and I had talked about on the mountain top a few weeks back. I told him I wanted to go out and see more of the world. John was doing that, and I wanted to help him succeed.

Blake told me that he didn't mind either when he got home. John didn't really need much and we were happy to help. John just slept on the old beaten up couch in the living room. He took the bus into the city a few times to play some Jazz gigs. He got paid for them and always offered to give us some of that money, but we refused.

Blake and I decided to throw a party for John a couple of days before he left. We purposefully scheduled it early so that he would have time to recover from the hangover. We invited some old friends. We set up a beer pong table and we played the whole night. John was uncertain about his move during the party, but after a few drinks, he talked himself back into it. He said he knew that it was his passion and that it was what he really wanted to do with his life. I admired that. He told us that he was going to party hard in Hollywood and that we should fly out to come visit him sometime. I thought about it a lot more than Blake did. I even discussed moving there. He liked the idea, but never took it seriously.

I remembered when the local radio station played my song. That gave me some inspiration. I thought that maybe I wanted to do the same thing as John and move to California. I dreamt of playing shows in gigantic stadiums. I imagined meeting big rockstars in Hollywood. It was a nice day dream. I wondered if something like that could actually be possible. Maybe, I could go to California and meet the right person at the right time and become famous. I continued to ponder these thoughts.

***

Bzzzt! Bzzzt! Bzzzt!

My phone was vibrating on the kitchen counter as some eggs sizzled in the background. I got up from the couch in the living room and walked over to my cell phone. I noticed the eggs had cooked long enough so I turned off the burner before answering the phone.

"Hello," I said while tapping the speakerphone button. I held it in front of my face.

"Gene!" a voice shouted. There was a crackly connection.

I knew that voice pretty well.

"How's California?" I asked.

"It's great, man, you wouldn't believe it! I've been to a Hollywood party every single night. They are crazy! There are huge swimming pools and girls everywhere," John said ecstatically.

"That's great to hear, man! I'm jealous," I said with a laugh at the end.

"That's why I'm calling, Gene. You've got to come move out here with me, it's insane! You are a great songwriter and musician. You would do so well here. Trust me. You would love it," he said in a convincing manner.

"You think so?" I asked with excitement.

"I know so," he responded confidently.

"What about my new job, the apartment and all my stuff?" I asked unconvinced that it was as easy as he made it sound.

"You don't need anything, just bring some clothes and your guitar. You can come live with me for free. I owe you one, for allowing me to stay at your place," he said and then added, "Just think about it and call me back. Let me know by tomorrow so I can make arrangements for you."

He said that last part and then hung up.

I set my phone back down on the kitchen counter. I took the eggs and started eating them out of the pan. They were starting to get cold, but I didn't feel like heating them up. We never bought a kitchen table so there was no place to sit and eat besides the couch. I walked over to the porch area and stood outside with my breakfast. I stared at my motorbike in the parking area.

I started to seriously consider what John had said. I always wanted to get out and see the world, but I kept finding excuses. He made it sound so simple. I could just get rid of everything and go. The apartment was no longer a valid excuse. Blake told me he was saving up for a house that he wanted to buy, so he was thinking about moving back in with his mother. He could save more money that way. Maybe, it really was as easy as John had made it sound. After all, he had done it. I wouldn't have to worry about a place to stay, because he said I could stay with him. That would give me enough time to find a job out there. I could ride to California on my motorbike with my guitar strapped to my back. I heard people say that traffic was horrible, anyways. My motorbike would be perfect to get through it. The idea of going was growing stronger and stronger in my head.

I walked back into the apartment and sat down on the couch. I picked up my guitar that was leaned up against the arm rest and began to play. I closed my eyes and imagined that I was strumming each chord on a beach in California. I switched the scene in my mind. I was on a massive stage performing for thousands of cheering fans. I imagined John jamming along with me in an expensive Hollywood recording studio. The dream was starting to come alive. I could feel it. It felt so close to reality in my mind. I stopped dreaming. I was interrupted by a sudden *knock* on the front door.

I set the guitar back up against the armrest of the couch and walked over to the door. I cracked the door open a little bit and peered outside. It was my mother. She was in tears. I placed my arm around her and guided her into the apartment. We both sat down on the couch quietly until she finished crying.

I was shocked that she came to my apartment. I couldn't believe that she was there. I couldn't figure out why she would come. I was confused and curious about what had happened.

"What's going on?" I said softly while rubbing my hand against her back.

"It's just hard, Gene," she said, wiping some of the tears from her face.

"What is?" I asked.

"Jacob," she said as she bowed a little in grief.

I nodded and continued rubbing her back.

"He is so stubborn and only allows things to go his way. I thought he would be good for us, Gene, we were struggling. He is just so hard to deal with," she said as her tears started to drip again. She continued, "but I have

Ruth with him now. I really love Ruth, I do, but she is so similar to Jacob. That makes it difficult for me. I just need a break from him every once in a while."

I continued to rub her back and nod my head to acknowledge that I was hearing what she was saying but I truly didn't know what to say. She had arrived so suddenly and unexpectedly.

"I never really told you my story, Gene. I thought you were too young to understand before, but you have grown so much now. You're out here on your own. You are doing so well for yourself and I'm so proud of you," she said with a slight smile showing through the tears.

"Thanks, mom," I said humbly.

"When I was a little girl," my mother began to tell her story, "I lived on a very poor island. It was a beautiful island, but poor. I was born in the Dominican Republic. Life was really hard in the Dominican. My family had trouble supporting all my brothers, sisters and me when we were young. Food and fresh water was expensive.

As soon as we started doing a little better, a hurricane blew right through the island and destroyed everything. I remember holding my head up, just barely above the water, as the hurricane's fierce winds cut into my face. It was terrible. I was scared. I was just a little girl.

My family eventually gave up on all of us, so we were on our own. I remember chasing after wild chickens for food. I snatched them by the neck and swung them around until I heard the neck snap. It was on good days that I caught one. That allowed me a decent meal for the next couple of days. I would also climb tall trees to drink the water from the coconuts.

I was found by a Catholic orphanage on the island and they took me in. They gave me food to eat, but it was horrible living with the nuns. They would beat my knuckles until they would bleed and pack us into a small room to sleep in. It was hard to sleep there.

I hadn't heard from my parents in a while. I wasn't sure where all of my brothers and sisters had ended up. I felt so alone.

One day, one of the nuns told me that my mother had petitioned for me to get my green card in the United States. I had no idea she had gone there. I started learning English as fast as I could before I arrived in the US.

When I arrived, I didn't see much of my mother. She had gone on to do her own thing. I was eighteen years old in a brand new country I had never been to before. I was doing well with learning English, which helped me a lot, but it was still difficult to adjust.

I was in New York and I worked at a little pharmacy when I met your biological father George. He was a really nice guy, but he had a lot of issues with drugs and alcohol. Despite those issues, I fell in love with him and we decided to get married.

We were doing well with money and your father had a really good car sales job. His boss had let him take one of the Porches that he sold at the dealership for our wedding. Your father was way too drunk to drive that day. I tried to stop him. I took his keys from him but he overpowered me and ripped them from my hands. He became an asshole when he drank. He told me he would leave me if I didn't get in the car with him. I finally decided to just get in the car, and that was one of the worst mistakes of my life.

He crashed and both of my legs were crushed from the impact. The doctor had to put metal rods in both of my legs and told me that I wouldn't be able to walk again. He also told me that I would never be able to have kids either. I was very hopeful ever since arriving in the United States. I believed that if I was able to go from starving and losing all of my family in a hurricane to becoming rich and starting a new life in the United States, then anything was possible. I was right. Within a year, I was walking again.

I tried to give your father a second chance even though he had hurt me. I truly did love him and I wanted to see him do great in life. We even bought a brand new log cabin in the mountains of Colorado. It was my favorite place, surrounded by mountains.

Your father let me down. Thankfully, I didn't go with him this time. He took some of his friends with him. They drove over a tall cliff. The accident paralyzed his friend for a long time. He himself was in a coma for three months. I thought long and hard about leaving your father at that point because I didn't think he was capable of learning from his mistakes. I didn't think he could change. I decided against it, because I loved him too much.

They threw him in prison for what he had done. I went a long time without seeing him. That was really hard on me. It was really difficult for me paying for everything that he had left me to take care of with my own income. Your father's brother James helped me out with that.

James owned some stripclubs around the city. He made a lot of money. It was mostly in cash but he liked it better that way, since he didn't want to pay taxes. It wasn't the type of work I wanted to do but it paid way better than anything else I was doing at the time. I had my own booth and I was making thousands of dollars each week. Sometimes, I would make a week's worth in one night.

I never told your father about that because I thought it would make him angry or jealous. I did what I had to do to survive. I was finally able to start visiting him in prison. I stayed loyal to him the whole time. Sometimes, James would give me a ride and we would go visit him together.

Your father told me stories of how prison was hard on him and that there was a man that had beaten him up pretty badly. He was worried that he might die in prison and suggested that he should escape. He was out on a work release program, so we took advantage of that time to fly back to my home country.

I was indifferent about the idea of living in the Dominican Republic because it brought back a lot of bad memories from my childhood. I set that feeling aside, because I saw it as the only option for your father. I thought that it might be good for him to see how life was outside of the United States. I thought it might be a sobering experience for him.

To my surprise, I became pregnant with you. The doctor told me that it was impossible, but it happened. It was a miracle. Once I was pregnant, I thought about all the struggles and hard times I had endured on that island. I didn't want that for you. I wanted you to have a better life. I told your father that I had to go back to the United States to raise you and that it would be safer if he stayed on the island. He didn't listen, he came with me anyways.

For a while it actually worked out for us. He was employed under his brother's name. I continued working for his brother without letting your father know. We lived in a more modest apartment and George tried to keep under the radar.

I was nine months pregnant with you when the FBI raided the apartment. I was all alone because your father was at work. I was so frightened when they kicked down the door and stormed inside. I remember holding tightly to my belly to shield you from whatever was about to happen. The FBI agents told me that I was being arrested for aiding and abetting the escape of your father. They told me that my baby would be held up for adoption after birth.

My mind became scattered. I flashed back to the time I had spent in the Catholic orphanage. I remembered the times I was beaten on the hands with those rulers. The times that the hurricanes destroyed everything. The times I chased and killed chickens with my bare hands to survive. I didn't want that for you. I was so afraid.

There was one FBI agent that I will never forget. He looked like he was from the Dominican Republic as well. He walked over to me and looked down at my pregnant belly. Then, he looked up into my eyes. He placed his hand on my shoulder and told me to leave. He would say that he had never seen me. He said that this was no way of starting the life of a child. He announced to the rest of the men that they hadn't seen me and allowed me to walk out of the front door.

The FBI still had to seize everything that had George's name on it. I was left with nothing. I didn't mind too much because at least I wasn't going to prison. I wouldn't have to send you to an orphanage. I did have an old Volvo station wagon that was under my name. I drove it to the hospital and camped out there until my delivery date. I didn't think it was a good idea to stay with James, since his name had been involved with your father's case.

I went to the hospital alone when my water broke and delivered you by myself. I remembered discussing names with George and that we had decided on Gene Oliver Dickson because those initials spelt GOD. It really was a miracle that you were born and a miracle that I was able to keep you and not go to prison.

Once I recovered from the hospital, you and I drove cross country, from state to state, living in the back of the old Volvo station wagon. I decided to drive us to Colorado because I loved the mountains.

I picked up some house cleaning jobs, that way you could crawl around on the floor while I worked. I saved up enough money to rent out a little faded blue house. I planned to raise you there. I thought it was really nice for the price.

You were a difficult child to raise. You were always getting into trouble. I remember one time, I was searching everywhere for you and became sick from worrying. I couldn't find you anywhere. Eventually, I found you curled up in the oven. You had opened the door to the oven and jumped right inside. I closed it shut on you. Another time, I ran inside the house for a few minutes to grab some things. I left you inside the station wagon. You climbed into the driver's seat and let down the emergency brake. The car rolled across the street and crashed into the neighbor's car. Luckily, it only caused a tiny bit of damage and the owner didn't charge me for it.

I finally decided that it was best to move on without your father. He wasn't going to be a good role model for you and I didn't want to risk losing you. He constantly reacted in an unstable manner towards me because of that decision. I decided to place a restraining order on him once he got out of prison. I didn't want to deal with the drama any longer.

When he got out of prison, he found us at the faded blue house. He walked in through the front door without knocking. He became aggressive with me and demanded that I let him visit you. He was shaking his finger at me and poked me in the eye. I reached over, grabbed a pan and started to chase him out of the house with it. I swung that pan so hard that I knocked him out. I hit him right on the temple and he dropped to the floor. I was terrified. I thought I had killed him. The police came and told me that he would be fine and apologized for the experience. Since that day, I never wanted you to meet your father.

Life is crazy, but I never lose hope. I have always believed that everything in life eventually gets better with time. We all have to make tough decisions. You just have to be patient with life. We all breakdown at some point. As long as we get up and keep moving forward then we'll never stay down for long."

I sat silently and absorbed my mother's story. I guess there are always a couple different perspectives in any situation. I didn't really know what to say to her, but I was glad that she had told me everything. It was something I had always been curious about. I noticed that she seemed to feel better after she told me her story. It was as if she had removed a heavy weight from her shoulders and was lighter again. I didn't really have to do anything. I just sat there and listened.

My mother and I didn't say a word after her story. We just sat there for a while and then she left. Our relationship had changed significantly since the station wagon days. I was closed off to her emotionally and felt like a shy guest in her presence. There were a lot of emotions that I had bottled so deep that I couldn't feel any longer. There were many things left unspoken between us. I didn't even feel the urge to ask her why she did nothing when Jacob would beat me. I really didn't care anymore. I had heard her story. I had listened to her struggles. I came to realize that we all have some.

I walked over to the kitchen table, picked up my cell phone and dialed John's number. I walked to the porch and took in a deep breath of fresh air. I stared up into the sky while the phone rang, until he answered.

"I'll be there in a month," I said boldly.

***

I tossed my backpack onto the back seat of my motorbike and fastened it down with some bungee cords. I leaned my guitar up against the seat of my bike. I turned around and gave Blake a big hug.

"Best of luck out there in California, Gene," he said, patting me on the back, "and don't forget about us little guys when you make it big."

I laughed and squeezed the top of his shoulder. I lifted the guitar up and swung the strap over my head, fastening it to my back. I swung my leg over the seat and started the motorbike. I revved the engine a few times and then turned to Blake with a bittersweet grin on my face. I placed the helmet on, over my head and then drove off. My journey to California had begun.

I planned the drive out pretty well. In my pocket, I had directions I had drawn out on a piece of paper. John sent me the address he was staying at through a text message. It was too long of a drive for one trip, so I planned a stop in Las Vegas for the night. I wanted to see The Strip anyways. I condensed everything I owned down to a school sized backpack. The rest was in my guitar case.

The route took me through the Rocky Mountains first. It was a beautiful drive. There was a river that crashed against the rocks on the side of the road that I followed deep into the mountains; further than I had ever been before. There were birds that flew alongside me as I leaned side to side through the winding roads. The air became thin and crisp as I climbed. There was a slight chill against my knuckles.

I had hours to think and ponder life as I drove. It was a fourteen hour drive to Las Vegas, including stops to use the restroom and eat. I started to dream about California. I dreamed that I was walking down Hollywood Boulevard with my guitar strapped to my back. I met a famous producer that wanted to record an album with me. I pictured John and I jamming by the beachside as the waves crashed against the sand. I pictured people gathering around a massive bonfire. They were jumping around and dancing to the music. It seemed like that reality was getting closer as I drove.

The landscape started to change to a reddish color. There was dessert stretching for miles with spiky green shrubs scattered throughout the hardened soil. The air was easier to breathe after leaving the mountains. There were rocky plateaus in the distance and some positioned right alongside the road. I passed an area that had large natural arches that formed from on the cliff sides. The landscape changed to a fiery bright red color as the sun started to set.

After the sunset, I drove through an empty desert of stars. There were billions of them lighting the way. I could see the faint white clouds that formed the Milky Way. I saw comets leave a long white trail as they burned through the night sky.

I drove over a dark black hill. On the other side, there was a whole city of colorful lights. I drove past hotels that looked like different cultural landmarks from around the world. There were floods of people crossing the streets in every direction. Some men were wearing fancy suits and some women were wearing long sparkly dresses. There were street performers that threw swords and juggled fire sticks. People drank beer as they walked along the streets. Limousines of every type and color drove through the streets. I passed a fountain that shot ropes of water into the air. The water danced to the music that played in the background. The city was alive.

I pulled up to the hotel I was staying at. I received a free night from when I worked at the hotel in Colorado. I decided tonight would be the perfect night to use it. The hotel was fancy. In my room, there was a bathtub the size of a jacuzzi and a king size bed that could fit four people. It overlooked the busy streets below with a large wide window. I left my guitar and backpack there and went out to explore Las Vegas.

I realized that there were a lot of things that I couldn't do since I was underage. I still walked around anyway. I walked into one of the Casinos and sat down at a slot machine. I wanted to look at it. A waitress in a short skirt and high heels walked up from behind me and placed a drink down beside me. It was strange to me, because I hadn't ordered anything and I was too young to drink alcohol legally. She told me it was 'on the house'. I sat and relaxed for a while. I sipped away at the drink.

I started to head back to the hotel, so that I could get some sleep before driving the rest of the way. On my way back, I saw a drunk half naked lady being dragged from her outstretched arms by a man on the sidewalk. There was a younger man in a suit that puked on the side of the road. There was a large group of drunk girls shouting in an unsuccessful attempt to form some words. Las Vegas was wild. I had heard the famous saying ‘what happens in Vegas, stays in Vegas’, and from then on, I understood why.

The next morning I woke up refreshed and excited for the rest of the drive. I couldn’t wait to get to California. I wanted to play music with John and go to Hollywood. I fastened my backpack onto the back seat of my motorbike and continued the journey.

I felt tingles of excitement as the warm breeze blew against me on the highway. I noticed that more cars started to fill the roads and more buildings were scattered throughout the land. Poking out from all of the buildings were tall palm trees that swayed with the wind. I pulled off at the final exit that was listed in the directions. I drove the last couple of streets before I arrived at John's place.

The neighborhood was really dry and felt like a desert. It was full of small apartments that had barred gates surrounding them. There were tall palm trees positioned on the sides of the roads. A large university campus was across the street from the apartment buildings, along with a few shops. The sun shone brightly. Not a single cloud passed over.

I turned off my bike and propped it up on the side of the street. I reached into my pocket to grab my cell phone and called John. He didn't answer. I tried to call again but while it was ringing I noticed a large group of guys walking towards me. John was with them. John had a big smile on his face but looked a lot different from when I had last seen him a month ago. He had shaved his head completely and was wearing bright clothes.

"Welcome brother," John said and then gave me a hug.

I noticed he spoke differently. He had never called me 'brother' before, which I thought was strange. He introduced me to the bulk of guys that were with him and they all smiled and greeted me the same. They helped me grab my backpack and guitar and we walked to the apartment.

The apartment was upstairs on the second floor and we used an outdoor staircase to get there. Inside was a small living room area with two couches. There was also a coffee table in the middle of the couches. Straight ahead was a little kitchen area with a window that looked out towards the university across the street. The apartment had two bedrooms. They led me to one of them, and placed my backpack and guitar inside. The room was empty besides a bunk bed against the wall and a small closet that had some clothes and shoes inside.

"You will stay here with me and the brothers," John said cheerfully.

The brothers? I thought. Why was he talking like that? What was he talking about? I just went with it and nodded. I looked around the room again but I didn't see John's bass guitar. I was excited to play some music with him.

"Where's your bass guitar?" I asked.

He looked over to the group of guys. They all knew something that I didn't.

"That's actually a long story," he laughed a little, and the other guys smiled, "I'll show you around the neighborhood and tell you about everything."

I felt a little nervousness come over me and I was beginning to feel awkward, like I didn't belong. I followed John out of the apartment. The others stayed in the living room. We started to walk towards the university. He began to explain.

"These guys are great, Gene," he broke the awkward silence, "I think you're going to love it here in California."

"The weather is great," I said in an attempt to keep the nervousness inside of me positive, "but who are those people?"

"They are the brothers in the church," he said as he began to tell his story, "When I first arrived in California, I started to attend the music institute right away. In my first week there, I started to hang out with some of my classmates. We went out and partied every night. I took cocaine, acid and other drugs with them.

I got lost in the city one night. I was scared. I was somewhere in Los Angeles, but I had no idea where. I hired a prostitute so that I would have someone to stay with. It wasn't my intention to have sex with her, but I did. I was out of control. She left with my money and I was alone again. I went to a little store and bought some alcohol. I drank until I passed out on the side of the street.

The next morning I stumbled through the city trying to figure out where I was. Someone had stolen my bass guitar while I was sleeping on the street. The only thing I had come to California to do, was taken from me, just like that. I was devastated. I had hit rock bottom. I didn't know what I was going to do.

I found a college university campus and decided to sit on a bench inside the campus for a while. I was exhausted. That's where I met Colton.

Colton came to me with a big smile on his face and started to ask me about my day and how I was doing. I told him everything. He asked me if he could show me some scriptures in the Bible. He thought that they would relate to my life and would help me. I agreed.

I realized that God gave me a desire to move to California for a purpose. I thought that the reason I came here was to go to school and become a professional musician, but God had a different plan for my life. His plan was so much better than mine. I am happier than I have ever been before. I asked God for forgiveness from all of my sins. I was alone and lost before I met Him.

Colton studied the Bible with me. I got baptized and then became a disciple of Christ. It was the best decision I ever made in my whole life."

My eyes were wide open. I was shocked. I couldn't believe that only a month ago I was drinking beer with John and now he was a Christian, or a 'disciple' as he called it. He was part of a church. I didn't even know what to say to him. I suppose it was a good thing, if that was what he wanted for his life. I wondered why he never told me about his drastic lifestyle change on the phone. I expected to arrive in California and play music and party with him. I guess it didn't matter.

"Well. . . fuck yeah, man! Good for you," I said, congratulating him on his transformation. I gave him a pat on the back.

He half smiled in an awkward way.

"I think it's better not to use profanity, Gene, if you don't mind?" he asked with a little hesitation. He appeared to have a sense of hope that I would listen to him.

"Oh. Yeah. Sorry, man. . . no problem," I said awkwardly.

"Thanks, Gene," he said with appreciation and a smile, "We are having a mid-week church service tonight at the apartment. I think you are going to love it. We sing songs and have a great time. I know how much you love music."

"Yeah, cool. Sounds good," I said with an uncomfortable grin.

So far, California was nothing like I had imagined it would be. I thought I was going to arrive and John and I were going to go to the beach with our instruments. I thought we were going to walk up and down Hollywood Boulevard and pass out demos of music we recorded together.

I started to become nervous about everything. I started to wonder if I had made the right move. I had quit a nice job and left my apartment with Blake for this place. Before, I had so much control over my life. I felt like I could do anything. I had freedom. Now, that feeling was beginning to fade. I had placed myself in a predicament. John wasn't the same person. California was nothing like I thought it would be. I never figured out what I would do if I didn't like it here. I was positive that I would. I didn't know anyone in California other than John. Apartments and housing were extremely expensive. I had no job, no connections. I realized that I had taken a one way trip to California. For better or for worse. That unsettling reality hit me in my chest, like a punch to the spleen.

EIGHT

Wade in the water

Wade in the water children

Wade in the water, woh

God's gonna trouble the water

The whole room sang those words loudly while clapping, with passion, to the beat. Everyone was stomping their feet while they sang. Smiles were overstretched on their faces. I hesitantly clapped along. Twenty people were crammed into the living room of the apartment John had brought me to when I had first arrived in California. It was another mid-week church service as they called it.

I had been sleeping on the floor of the room in the apartment. I used my jacket as a pillow. Every night, they would pray and read their Bibles for an hour or more before going to bed. They would wake me up early in the morning, before the sun came out, to go on 'prayer walks'. They considered it essential for a productive and functional day. They talked to God during those walks.

I had met Colton from John's story. He lived in the apartment with his wife in the other room. He had given me a Bible to read. Colton was a tall skinny man, with a little scruffy black beard. His hair was cut short on the sides, but held a little length on the top. He couldn't have been older than twenty five years. He was the 'lead minister', as they called him, for the Riverside section of the church.

I learned that the church believed that physical buildings weren't necessary. They believed that the people were the church, or the 'body' as they called it. They had small groups spread throughout the world because they were attempting to create the one world church. They believed there could only be one true church and that all the others taught false doctrine.

I quickly started to realize that Riverside wasn't really the California that I had dreamed about. There were no parties or music on the beach. I wasn't walking up and down Hollywood Boulevard passing out music demos. I was living in a small apartment with John and a ministry leader from a cult-like church in the desert.

Colton asked me if I was interested in studying the Bible multiple times throughout the week, but I told him I really wasn't interested. I told him that I had come to California to play music and party with John. I added that I didn't mind that the church was around me all the time, that I could just go off and do my own thing while everyone met together. I needed to look for a job anyway so that I could start paying rent. John told me he owed me a place to stay when I arrived in California, but he only stayed at my place for a couple of weeks. I wanted to become independent as quickly as possible so that I could move out and start my own life in California. Church was not for me.

The mid-week service came to an end and everyone started piling out of the apartment building. I went to the room that I was staying at and opened my guitar case to look at my guitar. I wanted to write more music and explore Los Angeles. I overheard John and Colton talking in the other room. I closed my guitar case and peered around the corner so that I could hear them better. They were whispering in the kitchen while looking out the window.

"I understand that he is your friend, John, but unless he shows an interest in studying the Bible with me, he is going to have to find another place to live. This household is for the brothers of the church. You are a new disciple. It would be too much temptation for you. I can not allow him to stay here without becoming a sold out disciple for Christ," Colton whispered in an authoritative tone.

"You're right. I understand," John replied obediently.

I turned back into the room and laid on the floor. I made it appear as if I had been there the whole time and that I hadn't heard anything. I was starting to panic. I thought that I at least had a place to stay while I figured everything out. I didn't think that I would have to worry about being kicked out. Now, that seemed closer to my reality. I didn't expect to arrive in this situation. I had no idea how to maneuver this obstacle. I couldn't talk to John about anything. He was a completely different person. His mind belonged to the church now.

John and the other guy that stayed in the room with me walked in. They both had a Bible in their hands. Everyone in the church carried a Bible wherever they went; school, work, grocery store, gym. It didn't matter where. They always had a Bible with them.

I started to think about what options I had. I didn't have a car where I could sleep, only my motorbike. I thought that maybe I could find some place to sleep beside it. I then thought about how John's bass guitar was stolen when he slept on the street. I couldn't risk losing my guitar. That was the only thing I still had, besides my clothes. I didn't have time to think of a plan. Everything was happening too quickly. I remembered when I was a kid and I attended Faith Baptist. I remembered how I just pretended to agree with everything that they said and taught. I remembered the baptism I had received and how well it worked to make them believe I was a Christian. Maybe, that would work in this situation.

"How did you like mid week service today, Gene?" John asked while he lay in his bed with his Bible open.

"It was great. I had a lot of fun," I responded, hiding how I really felt about it.

"That's awesome, man. I am so glad to hear that. I think you would love the Bible if you just gave it a chance," he suggested.

My option started to become more clear with John's statement. I realized that my only option was to fake it. I would have to pretend to be interested in something I wasn't, just like I had done with Jacob and the church school. I felt that my life was moving backwards. I had conquered my life and risen above the authority of Jacob. I had questioned the teachings of the church school. I had become independent enough to help out my mother and John when they needed it. I had a freedom in my life that I had never felt before… but now, I was right back to the beginning. I had no freedom. I had to pretend to enjoy the things I didn't. I was dependent on that, once again.

"You know, John, I've actually been thinking about that a lot lately. I really want to set up a Bible study with Colton," I said.

John smiled with excitement and surprise. He turned his head over to me and then looked up towards the ceiling.

"God works in mysterious ways, Gene, he really does," he said through his smile, "I am so happy and relieved to hear that. You have no idea."

I turned to him and put together a little smile. Then, I stared up at the ceiling. Everyone fell asleep shortly after. I couldn't sleep for a while. There was too much to think about. I had to reconstruct the way I thought. I had to figure out how I was going to get out of this situation.

***

"2 Timothy 3:16-17 is telling us that all Scripture in the Bible can be used for teaching, rebuking, correcting and training. It tells us that all Scripture is from God. Not only that, when we look over to 2 Peter 1:19-21, it tells us that none of the Scriptures in the Bible were of the prophet's own interpretation. That means every single word in this Bible is exactly how God meant it to be," Colton said as we began the Bible study.

We were sitting on the floor of the apartment and he had given me a little black Bible to use. We had the Bibles open on the coffee table. Everyone else in the house had left for the college campus across the street.

"Do you agree to follow the Bible above all religious traditions and your personal feelings, as the literal Word of God for your life?" Colton asked me. He looked directly into my eyes.

"Yes," I replied.

"Great. Many churches teach false doctrine. In fact, almost all of them do. If you look in your Bible to Acts 11:26, it tells us that disciples and Christians are the same thing. The word 'disciple' appears in the New Testament over two-hundred and seventy times. The word 'Christian' only appears three times. If you are not doing the work of a disciple, then you are not a Christian. Have you accepted Jesus into your heart or been baptized before, Gene?" Colton asked.

"Yes, I became a Christian when I was younger. I was baptized as well," I responded.

"Turn your Bible over to Matthew 28:18-20. It teaches us that every disciple is required to go and make other disciples. You have to baptize them as well. That means everyone needs to teach the Bible to other people, not just the preacher. We call this the Great Commission. It is a command from God that you must follow. If you haven't done these things, then you aren't really a Christian. If you are not a Christian, then you are really not a disciple. If you are not a disciple, then you are not following God's commands for your life. If you are not following God's commands for your life, then you are going to hell. Do you want to go to hell, Gene?" Colton asked in a serious tone.

"No," I said, shaking my head.

"Do you believe you are a disciple?" he asked.

"I guess not according to what you are saying," I responded.

"Not what I am saying, Gene, according to what God is saying," he added in correction to what I had said.

"Yes, of course," I added to reassure him I was sincere, "What God is saying."

"According to the Bible, the Kingdom of God came around the year thirty-three A.D. It came after the resurrection of Jesus Christ. The Kingdom of God is the church on Earth. Remember, there is only one true church. In Matthew 6:25-33 it teaches us that we need to seek the Kingdom of God before anything else in our lives. That means before our jobs, schools, families, hobbies, and relationships. It also tells us in these Scriptures that if we don't seek the kingdom first and place it above everything else in our lives, then we are disobeying God. God gives us some reassurance in that verse by telling us that all our obligations, worries and lives will be taken care of. We don't have to worry about anything, as long as we are seeking the Kingdom of God first. What is the Kingdom of God, Gene?" he paused to ask me.

"Well, you just taught me that the Kingdom of God is the church," I responded.

"I didn't teach you, Gene, God taught you," he corrected, "and is it just any church that God is referring to?"

"No. You said he is referring to the one true church. You said there can only be one true church that follows the Bible the way that God intended for it to be followed," I answered.

"God said these things, Gene, you have got to remember that," he said, correcting me again, "I am simply just reading the Bible to you. These are God's words, not mine."

"That's right," I said.

I couldn't help but think that he was telling me all of these things, not God, like he kept on insisting. I'll admit that he presented his interpretation of the Bible in a very convincing way, but it was still his interpretation. I concealed these thoughts because they had no use for assuring a stable living situation for myself.

"Open your Bible to James 5:16. In this verse we read that we are to confess our sins to each other and pray for healing. In order to become a true disciple of Christ, you are going to have to confess some of your darkest sins with me. I understand that this can be uncomfortable, but it must be done. There are many sins that we are all guilty of committing such as sexual immorality, adultery, premarital sex, homosexuality, masturbation, sexual fantasies, incest, lust, pornography, abortion, greed, malice, deceit, lewdness, envy, slander and more. Our sin is painful in the eyes of the Lord. Tell me, Gene, have you ever committed any of these sins?"

I sat silently for a moment and thought about his question. I never had to talk about stuff like this in the churches I had attended before. They had always just assumed that everyone was a sinner and moved on with it. The thought of openly telling Colton about what sins I had committed was strange and extremely uncomfortable. I didn't see why it was necessary. I was simply trying to blend in and do what needed to be done in order to give me some more time to find a job and get out of the church. I decided to just go with it.

"Yes, of course I have committed some of these sins. I believe we all have sinned," I said, attempting to sound a little more engaged.

"Can you share some specific times that you sinned?" Colton urged.

I read the look on Colton's face when he said that and realized I wasn't going to be able to fake it through this one. He seemed like he could see right through any of the lies that I would have told him. I wasn't going to be able to lie. I started to confess.

"When I was a little kid," I started, "I stole a little toy car from the neighbors house. The police came and everything."

"Have you ever masturbated, Gene?" he asked abruptly.

The question was very awkward and uncomfortable. I tensed up inside, but I had to tell the truth. He would never believe me if I lied and told him no. I thought of course I have masturbated, who hasn't?

"Yes, I have," I said quietly with my head bowed.

"You are not married, Gene. Have you ever had sex?" he asked firmly.

I thought about the time that I partied up in the mountains with Sean, Lisa and Mel. It was a beautiful night. We had so much fun playing music around the fire and drinking. I thought about Mel and our night together in that tent.

"Yes. I have done that as well," I responded.

"What else, Gene?" he asked with squinted eyes as if he were trying to peer inside my mind.

"I had become very angry with my stepfather when I was young, because he beat me. One day, I saw he had smashed my guitar and the music that I used to listen to. I attacked him and beat him with my fists. I almost smashed his head into the side of a coffee table, but I decided to let him live". I said becoming emotional as I remembered the past.

"Now, Gene, you see the amount of sin that you have in your life? This sin is all part of the darkness. In order for you to become a disciple you have to be forgiven of all these sins and be resurrected with Jesus Christ into the light. Are you ready to continue down this path to becoming a sold out disciple for Christ?" he asked me.

"I am," I responded confidently.

"When Jesus came to the Earth and died on the cross, he did it for you. He did it to pay for your sins. They whipped Him and ripped the flesh off of His body as punishment for the sins you have told me about. Even if you were the only person on Earth, He would have still died for you. The unimaginable pain that Jesus suffered through was all because you stole a little toy car from the neighbor's house. In your head, you might have thought that to be such a little insignificant sin. You might have thought that you were too young. However, that little toy car that you held in your hand was the bleeding flesh of Jesus Christ. You ripped off the flesh from the back of Jesus Christ in the form of a little toy car. Think about that for a moment," he said and then he made a pause for dramatic effect.

The room was filled with a cold uncomfortable silence for a few minutes. Colton stared at me directly in the eyes as if he was scanning my intentions. I became slightly nervous and felt my heart beat speed up. I could hear every movement in the room loudly. I was replaying what had happened in the faded blue house through my head. I no longer saw a little toy car. Instead, I saw the bleeding flesh of Jesus Christ like he had described. I remembered how much damage I had caused from stealing that little toy car. I didn't feel it was insignificant at all.

"Becoming a disciple is a lifelong commitment of your life to Christ," Colton continued after the dramatic pause, "You must be committed to what God commands you to do. He commands you to seek first His Kingdom, which is the church. That means that you must attend every church meeting on Sundays, mid week on Wednesdays, Men's Bible study on

Tuesdays and any other meetings that the church organizes. Your job, school or other obligations take second priority, after the church. The disciples are the body of Christ. We go around the world whenever and wherever we are called to go. God is the head of the church and leads us through the Bible. The Bible is His exact words, there are no private interpretations. Baptism is a requirement for you to become a disciple. You must participate in the death and resurrection of Jesus Christ by physically being submerged into water. That is what the Bible commands. You will devote all of your time, money and energy to the church as God has commanded in His Word. Are you ready for this type of commitment to God?" he asked with bold conviction.

I sat quietly for a moment and thought about that. This church required way more than I thought it would. Colton asked for an unreasonable amount of commitment. I had no idea how I was going to get out of this situation. If I was required to tell a job that I couldn't work almost half the days in the week, then how was I supposed to earn enough money to get out of this place? I felt trapped. I had no time to think of a plan. I had to just flow in the direction that life was taking me, and hope for the best. That is exactly what I did.

"I am ready to become a sold out disciple for Christ," I stated boldly, "I want to devote my whole life to God."

Colton looked up to me with a grin. He reached his hand over and placed it on my shoulder.

"Let me show you one more Bible verse," he said. He held his smile and flipped through the pages of his Bible.

I quickly and enthusiastically flipped through the Bible pages with him.

"Luke 14:28," he stated proudly, "do you want to read that one, Gene?"

I began to read, "Suppose one of you wants to build a tower. Will he not first sit down and estimate the cost to see if he has enough money to complete it?"

"That is what you need to do with your life, Gene," Colton said, "You have to count the cost. It takes a lot to be a disciple. You have to sacrifice many things in your life for God, just like God sacrificed Jesus Christ, His son, for you. You have to make sure that you are ready to stay committed to God and the church forever. You have to seek His Kingdom above anything else in your life like school, jobs, passions, desires and even your own family."

"I am one hundred percent committed and ready to become a sold out disciple for Christ," I stated loudly with fake conviction.

***

"Gene," Colton said very seriously with disappointment in his voice, "I have to talk with you about some things that have been brought to my attention concerning you. It is very important that I speak to you about them now."

Colton's sudden and serious call to my attention frightened me. I had become disquieted from his words. My mind attempted to decipher the reasons why he would need to speak with me so promptly. What had been brought to his attention about me? Did someone catch me doing something I wasn't supposed to be doing? I didn't think I had done anything out of character for being a disciple. Why was he speaking in such a serious and disappointed tone?

It had been about three months since my Bible study with Colton. I dove head first into the church. I more than committed myself. I embodied the life of a sold out disciple for Christ perfectly. I had just finished giving a Bible talk at the university across the street from the apartment. That's when Colton asked to speak with me.

My baptism was performed by Colton in a swimming pool that was near the apartment building. I was baptized a couple of days after I finished studying the Bible with him. I remember everyone was so proud of me and they gifted me a brand new Bible on that day. We sang Kingdom songs loudly and proud for the whole neighborhood to hear.

After my baptism, I spent all day reading every book in the Bible from Genesis to Revelations. Sometimes, I would go without sleep and read overnight. I completed the entire Bible in two months. My knowledge of the Bible had grown so much. You could ask me about anything in the Bible. I knew exactly where to turn. I even had a large amount of the verses memorized. My understanding of the Bible had surpassed most of the members in the church.

Colton assigned me to the university across the street to spread the Bible and schedule studies with campus students. He told me that the goal was to target influential members of society, that way their influence could be used to the advantage of the church. I did that well. I had a consistently large number of students attending my Bible talks, and a lot of them followed up with me afterwards to ask more questions. I was receiving so many requests to personally study the Bible, that I had to ask other members of the church if they could take some of my studies. I was 'a brother on fire', as Colton put it.

I was using my musical knowledge to lead the songs each Sunday at church services and mid-week services. I would direct the congregation to clap to the beat in a catchy rhythm that people enjoyed. I also performed a Kingdom song by myself, with my guitar, while they collected the offering.

I managed to get a job, but just like I had thought, it was difficult to receive enough hours to save money. I usually only worked two days a week due to the restrictive schedule of the church. There wasn't much I could do about that because I had told Colton that I was ready to do whatever it took to follow God. That made it difficult to save money.

Every week, I was required to give ten percent of my paychecks to the church. The church collected the money each week in the offering. On top of the ten percent, there was a second offering called the 'benevolent offering' that was collected in the middle of the week. The benevolent offering wasn't a specific percent, but it was expected that you give 'so much that it hurts'. For those reasons, it made it near impossible to formulate a plan to leave the church.

I embraced the church one hundred and ten percent. I absorbed all the information and did more than what was expected of a disciple. I started to become known as the 'Zealous sold out disciple' in the church. They wrote an article about me that they posted online. All of the churches in the movement from around the world were able to read it. People started using Colton's term, saying that I was a 'brother on fire'. Even the campus students that didn't want to join the church came to the Bible studies simply to hear me speak. I realized that I was a natural when it came to charisma.

I walked over to Colton. I was hesitant on the inside, but I showed confidence on the outside. I was nervous to hear what he had to say.

"What can I do for you, brother?" I asked Colton with direct eye contact. I placed my hand gently on his shoulder.

"It makes me sad to say this," he placed his arm on my shoulder as he spoke, "but the church has decided that it will be for the best."

My heart was beating. I was fighting to keep the outward smile on my face. Naturally, I would have shown concern. I was very concerned.

"You have grown substantially," he continued, "You have shown that you are a true sold out disciple of Christ. You need to work on your pride a bit, amen? But you have really submitted yourself to the Lord. The church has taken notice of this and is in need of a young zealous leader down in San Diego. I know I don't even have to ask you. You have demonstrated that you are willing to accept God's call no matter what it is. You are moving to the San Diego branch of the ministry to help spread the Bible to the universities down there. I wish you the best of luck, Gene. God bless you."

I was relieved. I thought he had discovered that I wasn't a genuine disciple. That I was only doing it to stay off the streets and formulate a plan. That I was waiting patiently for a way out. Thankfully, I was wrong. I then started to feel a bit of shock and surprise. I was moving to San Diego. I had played the part of disciple so well that they wanted to move me to another sector of the church to help out. I thought that maybe this move would present some new opportunities. I was open to anything at the time.

"Wow, what an incredible call from God," I said in a surprised tone with a large smile on my face, "I feel honored to do the work of the Lord, Colton. You are absolutely right, you never have to ask. I will always be ready to do the will of God. I will miss you and the church here in Riverside. When do I leave?"

"Tomorrow," he said with a smile and a chuckle in his voice.

I laughed along with him.

"Tomorrow it is then, brother, amen?" I said with a chuckle.

"Amen," he responded.

***

San Diego was way more beautiful than Los Angeles and Riverside. I would say that San Diego was the epitome of what I envisioned California to look like. The traffic was still bad, but not as bad as it was in the LA area.

I moved into an apartment on a cliffside. It was very close to the ocean so the members of the church would always do their early morning prayer walks on the beach. It was a large three bedroom apartment with a wide open living room area. There were three couches arranged in the shape of a U. There was a large balcony that wrapped around the apartment. I shared a bedroom with two brothers in the church.

I was assigned to the state university in San Diego. I did the same as I had done in Riverside. I created a successful Bible talk. I would have at least twenty students attending each week. I started to grasp a deep understanding of all the other religions like Mormons, Jehovah's Witnesses, and Muslims. I learned about those religions so that I could have educated discussions with them about the Bible or the Quran. It was always in an attempt to convert them to the church.

I picked up a cashier job at a drugstore in San Diego. I was only able to work two shifts per week, like before. The manager at the drugstore would always try and encourage me to pick up a few more shifts, but I was never able to because of the rigorous church schedule.

The leader of the San Diego church had discipled me a couple of times about my Bible talks. He told me that the pride that Colton had been referring to was the fact that I sold myself more than the Bible. He told me that I used my charisma too much, not allowing the Bible to speak for itself. I could care less about his advice because I believed that if I hadn't drawn as many people as I did in Riverside, then the church never would have asked me to move to San Diego. However, I always acted as if I accepted his advice humbly.

I was still waiting for an opportunity to leave the church. It was difficult because the church was forced into every part of my life. It was near impossible to do anything without advice from the church. I still kept an open eye. I had to be patient.

One day, I was asked to attend a Bible study with a guy named Chad. The church warned me about him. They told mc that he could be very manipulative and deceptive with his arguments about the Bible. They didn't allow me to study the Bible with him by myself, instead, I had to go with a more experienced disciple in the church.

We decided to meet with Chad at a park under a tree. The city had placed a concrete picnic table there. That made it perfect to sit down with some Bibles and have a discussion. I went with a brother from the church named Zack. We waited there for Chad to arrive.

Zack was a tall middle aged man. He was balding slightly. He always wore a clean, untucked, button down collared shirt with jeans. He had a careless relaxed sway to his walk and spoke in a calm manner.

Chad arrived at the table and sat down. He walked with excitement and had a little bounce with each step he took. He was taller than Zack but slightly younger than him. His eyes were blue and he had a defined jaw. He had blonde hair with a reddish tint that was styled in a crew cut. He was wearing a large white T-shirt and cargo shorts. He greeted us with a smile.

"What's up, guys? Are you ready to get into some deep Bible discussions?" Chad said eagerly with excitement.

I smiled a little bit at his excitement. I noticed that he seemed genuinely excited to talk about the Bible. He seemed too excited. I was simply there until I could seize my opportunity to leave. He was there because he enjoyed it.

"That's why we're here, Chad. You know it's going to be great, when it is the Word of God," Zack said in an awkward attempt to sound enthusiastic. He was dull compared to Chad's natural excitement.

"Let's start with the Word of God," Zack said as he opened the Bible, "We learn in 2 Peter 1:19-21 that no Scripture came from the prophet's own interpretation. The Bible is exactly as God intended for it to be written."

"Well, that's debatable," Chad chimed in, "technically speaking, all Scripture is simply a translation of the original Hebrew text and the Bible was written by many different men. It was their interpretation of what happened. Like how Matthew, Mark, Luke and John all tell similar stories, but they are their own interpretation of those stories."

"Yes, Chad, but can we agree that the Bible is the true Word of God?," Zack asked, looking at Chad.

"Not completely, but that's fine," Chad said, "How are you so confident that you are right about what you teach and that your church is the one true church? Many religions claim that title."

Zack appeared to be getting a little impatient with Chad's questioning. I saw from the look on Chad's face that he noticed that in Zack as well.

"I'm sorry, Zack," Chad said in a sincere tone, "It's not my intention to ruin your Bible study or anything. I just believe that there is a lot more that we should look into. There are thousands of different religions and cultures, billions of individuals and they all have different experiences. I spent years studying the Bible with the Jehovah's Witnesses and I loved it. I got kicked out for various reasons, but that's fine. I don't think we could ever be one hundred percent sure about anything. If I had to make a bet on it, I would bet that the Jehovah's Witnesses are the closest to the real deal, but I am still learning. You have to question everything. It is essential to learning about life. What do you think, Gene? I haven't heard you speak at all during this study."

Zack was uncomfortable. The Bible study wasn't going the way he thought it would. That was made clear through his facial expressions. He had no control over the direction this study was going and he appeared to be very nervous about that.

I started to like Chad. I really liked the way he cut through the orthodox. He challenged Zack on almost everything he said. His questions carried some good points as well. How could we know? With billions of people and different languages all over the world, is our particular translated version of the Bible really God's Word? What validated the Bible anyways?

"Chad, Gene is just here to learn. He is a younger disciple. He is sold out for Christ and is doing great things. I think it's best if we just stay focused on the Bible study," Zack stated firmly.

"Oh, my bad. I didn't know Gene wasn't allowed to speak for himself," Chad added with a hint of sarcasm.

I couldn't help but chuckle a little at his sarcastic remark. What he said made complete sense and was absolutely true. I couldn't express it outwardly, but I really liked the way that Chad thought. I decided to try and support Zack and get in contact with Chad at the same time.

"Yes, I can speak for myself, Chad," I jumped into the conversation suddenly, "I would love to continue to help you on your journey into the Bible. Why don't I take down your phone number? That way we can exchange Bible verses through text messages. We can discuss anything that you want to."

"Now that's what I'm talking about!" Chad said, raising his voice with excitement.

Chad and I exchanged numbers and I sat silently through the rest of the Bible study. Zack and Chad continued to argue back and forth about religion. I had accomplished my goal. I was content. I wanted to establish a connection with Chad so that I could speak with him someday. Someday, when I was in a less restrictive position to share my true thoughts freely.

The Bible study finished. Zack and I made our way back to the apartment. On the walk back, he didn't talk much. I gave him some encouragement and told him that I thought it had been a great Bible study. I hoped to get him to speak a little more about it. I wasn't lying. I truly thought it had been a great Bible study, but not for the reasons Zack would have considered it to be. He appreciated the encouragement. He told me that some people believe that they are too intelligent for God. He said that they rely on history and science to find explanations for their lives. They are full of pride. He said they will live their lives with emptiness and sorrow in their hearts. Those people lack faith. He said that they are searching for answers. Answers that were discovered by men like themselves. He told me that only God could provide those answers and fill the empty sorrow within their hearts.

***

It was a beautiful day at the university. I was taking a quiet stroll through the campus. I didn't have a Bible talk today, but I still held my Bible in my hand like every other disciple in the church did. There was a light breeze and pigeons hopped around before taking flight into the trees. I was keeping my eye out for anyone that might be willing to learn about the Bible.

I was thinking about Chad and the way that he had expressed his thoughts and opinions. He would flow so freely without a filter on what he said. It had become second nature for me to sensor every thought that left my mind in order to avoid conflicts. I had done it most of my childhood with Jacob. I thought I had escaped it, but instead, I landed into a similar situation with John and the church. In my mind, Chad was the symbol of free thought. I knew that someday I would be able to attain it again.

"Hello, are you?" a man said in broken English, with a strong Chinese accent, from behind me.

It startled me out of my thoughts. I turned around to see who he was. He was a young man, around twenty years of age, with straight black hair that was combed to the side of his face.

"Hi, how are you?" I responded back with a smile.

"What is your name?" he asked me.

"I'm Gene"

"You go school here?"

"No, I am here to study the Bible with people," I said while lifting the Bible in my hand to show him.

He took the Bible from my hand and opened it up to look inside. He then shut it right away, shook his head and handed it back to me.

"No, no," he said with a laugh, "You speak English."

I nodded with a smile, "Yes, I speak English. What is your name?"

"My name, Zhang Wei. English name, Brad" he said proudly.

"Nice to meet you Zhang Wei, or I can call you Brad," I replied.

"Like Chinese food?" Brad asked me cheerfully.

"I haven't tried much Chinese food, honestly," I responded with a slight chuckle.

"Come," he said as he started to walk.

He led me to a brand new white Porsche in the parking structure at the university. It was a five story parking structure and he had parked on the third floor. I had no idea where we were going, though I assumed he was taking me somewhere to try Chinese food.

I thought that Brad was interesting. He obviously had a lot of money and was from China, but he carried himself in a peculiarly genuine way. He was fearless in the way he approached me, despite his language barrier.

We both got into the car and he began to drive out of the parking structure. I had never been in such a nice car. The black leather interior was shining and everything was extremely clean. I realized that it was the same brand of car that my father had told me he crashed with my mother, only newer.

It was a ten minute drive before we arrived at a fancy Chinese restaurant. I became a little nervous because there was no way I could afford a restaurant like that.

We entered the restaurant and Brad ordered in Chinese. We sat down at a nice table near the window. The restaurant was painted with red and gold colors. There were paintings with Chinese writing and Chinese dragons hung from the ceiling. I looked around the restaurant in awe of all the different statues, paintings and handmade fixtures. I had never been to a Chinese restaurant before.

Brad and I ate while he practiced his English for the next couple of hours. I spoke slowly to make it easier to learn. When he responded back, I would correct his pronunciation. I had a lot of fun doing it. We laughed as I taught him curse words in English. He really liked the word 'fuck'.

The bill arrived at the table. He quickly took it.

"My bill," he said with a nod.

I didn't fight him for the bill because I knew I couldn't afford it anyways. I think Brad realized that I didn't have much money and he didn't care.

We drove back to the university. He started to teach me a few words in Chinese and we shared stories in simple English. He told me that he was attending the language institution at the university and that he needed to improve his English before they would allow him to pursue his degree. I told him I could help him whenever he needed me to. We exchanged numbers.

For the next couple of weeks, Brad and I started hanging out all the time. Anytime that I wasn't at a church meeting or work, I was hanging out with Brad and helping him with his English. He would always take me out to eat at various Chinese restaurants all over San Diego. I told the church minister that I was studying the Bible with Brad. I needed to give him an explanation on why I was meeting him so often. He questioned why I hadn't invited Brad to church yet. I told him that his school schedule was conflicting and that it was taking longer because of the language barrier. He warily accepted my explanation.

***

"I'm out!" I shouted at the top of my lungs with excitement.

Brad had his brand new Hummer parked outside the church apartment. He sat in the driver's seat waiting for me. He still had the white

Porsche, but he decided to drive the Hummer that day. I loaded my guitar and my backpack of clothes in the back. The church leader for San Diego was standing outside and watched me load my things with a confused and sad look on his face. I didn't tell anyone in the church that I was leaving that day. They found out as soon as Brad arrived, so everyone was shocked and speechless.

My opportunity to leave the church had come at last. After almost six months of patiently waiting, it had finally come. I seized that opportunity immediately, without hesitation. The church was a cult in my mind. It incarcerated free thought and didn't allow unorthodox behavior. I wanted to be free.

Brad asked me if I would be willing to move into a two bedroom apartment with him. He wanted to live with me so that he could be constantly exposed to English. I agreed immediately and I was more than grateful that he had asked. I told him that within a couple weeks I could find a much better job and pay him for rent. He didn't care whether I paid or not, but I felt better doing it. I wanted to be independent.

"My bro!" he shouted with excitement as I jumped into the passenger's seat.

He had asked me for a word to express friendship, so I taught him 'bro'. He used it all the time from then on out.

"Fuck church," he said with a smile while driving away from the apartment.

I laughed when he said that. It was a laugh of relief. I felt free again.

"Yeah. Fuck church, bro," I agreed.

We drove to his two bedroom apartment. There were four large apartment building sections that formed a square around a large swimming pool and jacuzzi that was positioned in the center. The apartments were painted with a light yellow color. There was a brown trim around all the windows and borders of the buildings. A group of palm trees towered over them in all four corners of the property. There was one that was off centered by the swimming pool.

There was a living room and a large kitchen area. The living room had two large couches aimed at a flat screen TV. A hallway led into the two bedrooms. I didn't have much stuff, so my room remained empty with the exception of a bed that Brad bought for me.

The next week after moving in with Brad, I diligently searched for a better job. I started working at a fancy hotel in downtown San Diego. I worked at least forty hours per week and always took extra shifts any time they needed coverage. I made sure to keep an excellent reputation at the hotel.

I still had my motorbike. It turned out to be extremely useful to travel to and from work during high traffic times. I usually only used my motorbike for work, because most of the time I would go with Brad in his car.

Two months passed by and Brad's English had improved significantly. He passed the language exam at the language institute which allowed him to attend the university in San Diego. He was excited about that.

While I was at work I met a music producer. I started working with him to record new songs that I had written. He wasn't a big time Hollywood producer like I had dreamed about in Colorado, but he was good at what he did. I enjoyed writing and recording music. It had become my passion and I pursued it outside of work. I even picked up some shows in the downtown area.

I started to feel like I was back on top of the world. I had learned a lot about religion and the Bible over the previous six months, but I was glad that that phase of my life was over. The church taught me that I have a natural knack for charisma. That helped me a lot in the hotel industry and life in general.

Brad took me to some crazy parties downtown with all of his Chinese friends. I was the only American kid at most of the parties he took me to. I spent the beginning of one night teaching twenty Chinese kids how to play beer pong. That was hilarious. We played the whole night. Security came and shut down the party. They told us that they were calling the police.

Brad translated that to one of his friends. His friend freaked out. He tied a rope to the balcony, rappelled to the street and sprinted off into the city. Brad and I laughed. We walked out of the front door and passed out on the couches in the hotel lobby for the night.

Life was good, living with Brad.

NINE

The lights blacked out as I was walking down the stairs of the hotel. It was so dark that I couldn't even see my hand in front of my face. Pitch black. I had just signed out at work and was headed to my motorbike in the parking garage. I had the next two days off. I reached in my pocket to use the flashlight on my cell phone. I held it forward, above my head, to light the way.

My shift ended at nine, an hour after sunset. I used my phone light to navigate my way through the parking garage. Usually, it was well lit. The power must have failed. I found my motorbike and started it. I turned on the headlights so that I didn't have to use my phone anymore. I wondered what had happened to the lights.

I drove out of the parking garage into a darkened city street. Downtown San Diego was pitch black. Not one light in the whole city was shining. Even the traffic lights had been shut off. Headlights of a car cut through the darkness. The car turned the corner onto the street I was on. I waited for it to pass and then began to drive into the city.

The street traffic was chaotic. I had only driven ten blocks but I had passed by three car accidents. The accidents were at street lights that no longer worked. I had never seen downtown San Diego without lights. It gave me an eerie feeling. I drove past a few shops that had been looted.

I drove with extreme caution to the apartment. I was worried that someone wasn't going to be able to see me through the darkness. That they might crash into me. Luckily, I made it home safe.

When I arrived, there was no power in the apartment building. I took out my phone to check the news online, but the internet was down. Brad greeted me when I arrived and asked me if I knew what was going on. I had no idea. One of the neighbors walked out onto his balcony and shouted that he heard the power was going to be off for the next forty-eight hours.

I walked over to the refrigerator and freezer and saw that they were not working either. Brad had a lot of meat in the freezer and two large bottles of vodka. I told him that if the power was going to be off for that long then the food was going to spoil. He walked me over to the balcony and showed me a coal barbecue that he had bought earlier. That sparked an idea.

I ran out to the balcony with the two bottles of vodka in my hand and shouted 'pool party' to the rest of the neighbors. We brought Brad's new barbecue downstairs, lit some coals and started cooking. The rest of the neighbors followed.

The party had begun. There were twenty barbecue grills cooking food by the pool. All of the neighbors were jumping in and out of the pool and dancing around with drinks in their hands. There was a beer pong table set up beside the pool. Someone had brought glow sticks that everyone was wearing around their necks. A battery powered stereo was blasted as loud as it would go. A group of Saudi exchange students were smoking hookah by the jacuzzi. There was a large fold out table someone had brought down. We placed the cooked food on it. There was another table that was full of alcohol.

Suddenly, a police helicopter flew over the top of the apartment building. There was a laundry building beside the swimming pool that we all climbed on top of to see where it was going. It hovered over the shopping center across the street and a man started firing gunshots at the helicopter from the rooftop. He was trying to rob the shopping center across the street. We watched as a couple of police officers slid down a rope onto the building top and arrested him.

After the police entertainment, we all jumped into the pool from the rooftop. The party raged on. The pool maintenance guy came to close the pool. It was impossible. He gave up and started to drink with everyone. A random girl told everyone she used to be a stripper in New York and then started doing a strip routine. She stripped completely naked and then dove into the pool. A few other people started to strip after her. The night was wild and the party carried on until the sun started to rise.

I passed out on the apartment floor in the living room at some point. I didn't remember when, but eventually, I ended up there.

It was afternoon the next day when I woke up. My head was pounding and the natural light burned my eyes as I opened them. I stretched out as far as I could reach in either direction and then turned to my side. I jumped inside of my skin a little bit once I had turned. I was startled. There was a girl lying beside me on the living room floor. She was asleep.

She was a short girl with brown messy hair. She was wearing jeans and a white T-shirt. Her makeup smeared from her eyes onto the rest of her face. I was trying to recognize her. I assumed I had met her at the party, but I couldn't remember exactly when. I guess it didn't really matter.

I got up slowly, trying not to wake her. I needed to use the restroom.

"Hey," the girl said suddenly, "Good morning."

That startled me. I turned around and looked at her. She sat up slightly and rested on her forearms.

"What's up?" I said awkwardly.

"You were really drunk last night," she said with a chuckle.

I nodded awkwardly, "I don't mean to be rude, but. . ."

"Melissa," she said interrupting me, "We were hanging out at the party last night."

"Right, Melissa," I said hesitantly.

I realized that I had drunk too much. I couldn't remember hanging out with her at all. I guess that was fine. She didn't seem bothered that I didn't remember anything. She seemed to be understanding.

Brad walked into the room with a sleepy face. He stretched his arms to the ceiling and yawned. He looked over at the two of us sitting on the floor and smiled. He then went to the kitchen and tried to heat water in the electric kettle, but the power was still out.

"Fuck," Brad said frustrated about the power.

He then walked back over to the living room and patted me on the back.

"You are crazy bro," he said with a big smile and a laugh, "Now you have a girlfriend."

He then walked back to his room and shut the door to go back to sleep.

Melissa and I sat there in a pool of awkward silence.

"So you like music," Melissa said breaking the silence, "You played a few songs last night on your guitar. I think you are really good."

"Oh, cool. Thanks," I replied, "So, what do you do?"

"I am attending college and I work at a drugstore downtown," she said proudly.

"Oh, cool. How were you at the party?" I asked.

"I live in these apartments, silly," she said in a mocking tone.

"Oh, right," I responded.

"We should hang out more, Gene. Like maybe just the two of us some time when we are not trashed from drinking all night," she suggested confidently with a laugh at the end.

"Yea, sure. We could do that," I said nonchalantly.

She jumped to her feet and then gave me a big hug and a kiss on the side of the cheek. After, she pranced to the front door and left.

That was the day I met Melissa. I didn't really know what to think about her at the time. She was overly confident and showed an obvious interest in me. I think she wanted to date me. She came across slightly obnoxious, but harmless. I didn't really want to get into a relationship, though. I wasn't attracted to Melissa. She seemed like a nice girl, but my focus was on music and enjoying my life of freedom.

***

"Ok, Gene. Let's do one more take," said Fred through the studio mic, "from the top."

Fred was the studio producer I had met at the hotel. He was a short guy with dark hair he pulled back into a ponytail. He had both of his ears pierced and murals of tattoos on his arms. He wore black jeans and a hoodie with a rock band logo on it.

I had recently played a successful show downtown. I met a record label representative there. He told me to bring him a demo of my music to my next performance. I scheduled some studio time with Fred to help me work on that.

"You are nailing it on the verse part, but once you get to that higher chorus part I'm losing some of the energy in your voice," said Fred to coach my performance, "try it one more time. This time focus on delivering power to that higher note."

Fred and his business partner built the studio with their own hands. It had a large living room with hardwood flooring. There were acoustic sound panels that lined the walls and stage lights that hung from the ceiling. A large window separated the control room from the live room.

The control room had a large soundboard that sat on a desk. Above the soundboard were two computer monitors that displayed the recording program he was using. There were two large studio speakers on either side of the soundboard and a variety of other studio equipment.

Behind the control room was another tiny room the size of a closet. That was the vocal booth. Its walls were covered in acoustic sound foam. It was sound proofed.

I nodded after Fred coached me and placed the recording headphones back on my head. I moved closer to the pop screen that was positioned in front of the microphone and attempted to calm my nervous breathing. I was determined to record the perfect take.

"That's fucking it, Gene! Sing it like that every time," Fred shouted as he jumped up out of his chair and raised his fist in the air.

I smiled with a laugh of relief. It felt great to record a good take. The pressure subsided. I was trying to record the best takes possible, but I realized that I had to chill out in order to achieve that. When I was calm and my voice was loose, I could sing better.

We spent thirty hours over the last week recording three of my best songs for the demo. Fred helped me select them from all the songs I had written. It was a lot of work to record a demo. We didn't stop recording for twelve hours straight on one of the days, but it was worth it. It was an incredible experience.

We finished up for the day. All that was left to do was mixing and mastering. Fred didn't need me at the studio for those tasks, so I left. Now, I had to wait until he was finished. That was difficult because I was impatient.

***

I sped into the parking garage at the hotel and parked in my usual spot. I climbed up the stairs to the employee locker room. That is where I kept my work suit. I threw it on and started up the second set of stairs to the front office.

It was a great day. I had just received my demo back from Fred and it sounded phenomenal. The next show was in a couple of weeks. I was more than prepared for it. I was excited to show these record label representatives what I got.

It had been a couple months since the party at the apartments. Melissa would show up at the apartment almost everyday. I would tell her that I was busy working on music, but she didn't care. She just wanted to watch me. She told me she liked me a lot and hoped that one day we could date. Until then, she was happy to just hang out and watch me write.

Brad thought that I should start dating her. He told me that he thought she was very supportive and always wanted to spend time with me. He said that it didn't matter if I was completely attracted to her or not, because she obviously cared about me. I was skeptical of that theory at first. I became more willing to give it a chance as the time progressed.

"Gene," Rachel said with a smile, "welcome to work."

Rachel was my manager. She was a lady in her late twenties with blonde wavy hair that flowed down her back. Her eyes were bright blue and she had rosy red cheeks. She always wore a clean black business suit with a knee length skirt. She was the kindest manager I had ever had.

"Thanks, Rachel," I responded, returning a smile.

"I have to talk to you about something before you start your shift, if you wouldn't mind spending a few minutes in my office?" she asked in a soft tone.

"Of course, what is it?" I asked curiously.

She smiled and guided me into her office. She closed the door behind us.

The front office had one large room that the supervisors and front office attendants worked in. There was another open room in-between Rachel's office and the large room where they kept the printer. The whole front office was behind a large door that led out to the hotel lobby area. On the other side of that door were three reception pods that faced the entrance of the hotel.

Rachel's office was clean and well organized. I sat in one of the chairs that was facing her. She turned her full attention to me with a large smile and folded her hands on the desk that was in between us.

"We have a new supervisor position opening up in a week," she started to say with excitement, "I have been watching you, Gene. The way you are with our guests at the hotel is incredible. You present yourself in a likable and professional manner. I have had nothing but excellent guest reviews about you. Your co-workers love you. You are always mindful of their needs and help each one of them cheerfully, with a smile on your face. You are a great example of what every employee at this hotel should strive to be like. You take initiative in difficult guest situations that would normally require a manager. You handle those situations perfectly on your own. I can see the natural leader in you. Your charisma, attentiveness and your caring personality will take you far in this world. I see an exceptionally bright future ahead of you. I would like for you to take the new supervisor position."

As she finished her speech I sat there and tried to contain the enormous smile that her words had brought to my face. I was overwhelmed with excitement. I hadn't worked there for that long but she was already offering me a promotion. My day was only getting better. I had received my demo back from Fred and now I was being offered a promotion. I couldn't believe it.

"Rachel," I said in an exaggerated professional tone, "I would be honored to accept the supervisor position."

"I knew you would be," she said with a wink.

After that day, I started training to become a supervisor at the hotel. I received the position as soon as it became available. My pay increased by a decent amount. I was making great money for my age. Life was only getting better.

***

"Gene, that was an excellent performance and your demo sounds great. I believe that we can take your music career to the next level," said the music label representative.

He wasn't lying. My performance was excellent. The whole crowd was clapping along to my music. I was directing them like the conductor of a symphony orchestra. There were other artists that were playing as well, but the crowd cheered the loudest during my set.

They brought me to a back room of the venue. There were two representatives from a well known record label company seated at a table. I was sitting across from them in a portable fold out chair as I listened to their review of the show.

The man that was speaking to me was tall, thin and wore a cardigan sweater. He had stylish reading glasses and his hair was spiked. He wore an expensive wrist watch and designer shoes.

"We would like to offer you a record deal," he continued, "You are a young artist. You write songs and perform your music like many other artists out there. What we are interested in, is your ability to hype up the crowd. You have a way of engaging with people from that stage that could work well in the industry. We have song writers, stylists, and vocal coaches to elevate your act to the next level. We are solely interested in your energy.

We would be willing to offer you five percent of whatever revenue you can generate, after you pay off the studio time, stylists and vocal coaches. It could be a lot of money for you, but that depends on you. You have to want it. You have to be passionate and work extra hard to make it happen."

"Wait, I'm a little confused," I said, squinting my eyes.

"How so?" he asked.

"I would only be making five percent of all the revenue I generate from my music?" I asked with confusion in my face.

"That's correct, Gene. It is a significant amount of money when you consider how much we will have to spend to jumpstart your career. The music industry is expensive, and those expenses have to be paid. The trade off is that you get to do what you love. You get to pursue your passion for music," he replied in a positive convincing tone.

"What happens if I don't make enough money to pay off the studio fees, vocal coaches, stylists and songwriters?" I asked with skepticism.

"Well, nothing comes for free. You would be required to pay it by contract. We can only promise that we will do everything in our power to jump start your career. We are industry professionals and we have all the contacts necessary to do so. It is up to the world, the consumer, whether they will spend money on you or not," he said nonchalantly.

"I see," I said with disappointment, "It's more like a business loan."

"If you choose to look at it that way. I prefer to look at it as an opportunity. A chance to turn your passion into your career," he said with enthusiasm.

"I don't think so," I responded sadly, "I don't want to enter into a contract I can't get out of. I don't want to owe you a bunch of money that I can't pay off. I don't want to become a slave to my passion. Right now, I have freedom. I have freedom to enjoy my life. I have freedom to play whatever songs I choose whether people like them or not. Music to me is more than just a business or a career path. Music to me is therapy. I will not industrialize my soul."

I stood up from the table, grabbed my guitar and walked out of the room.

The music industry was nothing like I had imagined. It was like a scientist and his lab rats. The musicians were just experiments. The goal was to see if they could produce any money. If they didn't, then they would be required to pay back enormous amounts of debt that they couldn't afford. It was the same reason I never wanted to go to college, even though my high school teachers pushed me to do so. This was no different. The teachers thought I was really smart and would do great in college. They never told me that it would leave me with large amounts of debt. This representative thought that my energy on stage was good. That was the only thing he had to justify the expenses needed to start my music career. I would have definitely been in debt to the music industry. Reality hit me. I learned that nothing was quite as simple as it seemed. Nothing was free.

***

"Wow, this place is amazing," Melissa said excitedly, "Look at this amazing view we have from the rooftop."

It had been a couple weeks since speaking with the record label representatives. I was feeling down from that for a couple of days, but I snapped out of it and focused on all the great things that were happening in my life. I had an excellent job. I was bringing in good money as a supervisor at the hotel. I was able to help Brad get into the university and he was doing excellent. I would even help him with his college homework. We still hung out a lot and went on small trips to the mountains, the ocean and Coronado island.

Brad finally convinced me that I should give Melissa a chance. He was confident that she was a good girl and really cared about me. She was there for the show. She tried to cheer me up after I left disappointed from the meeting with the label representatives. That's when I changed my mind and decided that maybe Brad was right. Maybe, she really did care about me. I decided that I should give her a chance. We all went to Coronado island for a bonfire one day and I asked her to be my girlfriend.

The relationship between Melissa and I moved fast. She always came and picked me up in her car to go on dates. We would drive to different places around San Diego. We would often have dinner at nice restaurants. Sometimes, she would surprise me by bringing some food to my work. Within a couple of months, we found a nice apartment downtown. We moved in together.

"It really is, isn't it?" I replied back to her excitement with a smile.

We moved into a downtown apartment at the end of the harbor. You could see everything from there. There was a large aircraft carrier museum, hundreds of private yachts and Coronado island across the water in the background. The scene was like a painting.

We were on the rooftop of the apartment. There was a large pool, jacuzzi, tables and barbecue pits up there. It truly was a nice place.

From the rooftop, we would take an elevator down one floor to our apartment. It wasn't a very large apartment, only a one bedroom, but it was nice. All the appliances were brand new and the layout made it feel more spacious than it was. There was a little balcony that overlooked the city streets. I bought a bunch of furniture and artwork for the walls. There was a little desk with a laptop that I would use to record my music. My guitar hung on the wall like a display.

We decided to sign a one year rental agreement. It wasn't required that we stayed the full year, but if we didn't, we would have to pay a fee to terminate the lease early. I thought that it was a fair agreement.

The new apartment was walking distance from my work. I rarely ever used my motorbike anymore so I decided to sell it. Melissa had got a car from her father as a gift, but she was required to make the payments on it. She struggled paying them because her job didn't pay so much, so I decided to pay the debt for her. I was great with my personal finances so I always helped Melissa with hers.

Life was great. I was able to work on my music all the time. Melissa and I would cook meals at home and then go out to eat a couple times per week. Brad would come over and we would all have beers in the rooftop jacuzzi. I couldn't believe that, not too long ago, I was sleeping on the floor and teaching the Bible to a bunch of college students. Everything was completely different now.

"Gene," Melissa said from the rooftop as we stared over to Coronado island.

"Yes?" I asked, keeping my eyes on the view.

"I think I love you," she said while reaching over and giving me a kiss on the cheek.

I didn't know what to think about that. I thought that it was too soon. I didn't feel the same as her. We hadn't been dating for very long but everything was moving so quickly. I guess it wasn't strange for her to feel that way. I thought about how I should respond. Maybe, I should say nothing and just smile and give her a hug. No, that might make her feel uncomfortable. She had put herself out there in an awkward position. What was love anyways? Jacob and my mother's relationship had also moved quickly. Did it even matter if you meant it or not? After all, it was just words.

"I love you too," I said with an awkward smile and a hug.

I guess it worked. Her face lit up with excitement that she buried in my chest as she hugged me. I remembered what I learned about ignorance while living with Jacob. Ignorance really was bliss, as long as it was true ignorance. If they ever found out that they were ignorant, it would disrupt their bliss.

TEN

My eyes rolled from the back of my head, to the front and then back again. I was disoriented. My stomach fizzed inside with an uncomfortable sting. My eyelids opened and closed slowly without consistency. My brain felt like it was bouncing off the walls of my skull like a racquetball on the walls of the court. I was being dragged backwards by the armpits. I struggled to hold my head up straight.

I stopped moving backwards for a brief moment and collapsed to the floor. I was unable to support my own weight. A door closed in front of me. A familiar, but blurry man lifted me up by my armpits and threw my body onto a large bed. I tried to lift my head but it was too heavy. I was feeling ill. I completely lost control of my basic motor skills. My body felt helpless. I was glued to the blanket. I glanced up at the ceiling. It was rotating above me.

I saw the blurry man at the end of the bed. He was staring directly at me. He walked over to the door and locked it. I heard Melissa through the other side of the door.

"Tim! Is he going to be alright?" she shouted from the other side of the door.

"He'll be fine," the blurry man responded through the closed door. "He just drank a little too much and is embarrassed about that. Poor baby. He doesn't want you to see him like this. I am a pro when it comes to these situations sweetie, don't you worry."

I attempted to open my mouth and speak to Melissa through the door but nothing came out. My vocal cords weren't strong enough to lift my voice. I felt strain and pressure as I continued to try. Eventually, all that came out was a little mumble.

Tim was Melissa's best friend from high school. They used to be on the cheer team together. They would usually hang out while I was at work, or with Brad. He invited us over to his house for a party.

Tim walked to the end of the bed and set his hands on my shins. I was on my back trying to lift my neck to see what he was doing. His hands made their way up to the zipper on my pants. He unzipped them and slowly slid them off. I exhausted myself in an attempt to roll over. I managed to move slightly, but Tim forced me back onto the bed. He removed my underwear and put his mouth around my genitals. I struggled helplessly but my body was too weak.

He moved to the end of the bed and removed his pants. Then, his underwear. I was petrified. Nothing my brain told my body to move was moving. I dry-heaved a few times and my throat became sore.

Tim grabbed me by the legs and flipped me over onto my stomach. My face smashed into the blanket making it hard to breathe. He jumped on the bed and began to force himself into me. My throat strained even more and tears began to drip from my eyes. The blanket that my head was smashed into became wet, and stung, as my face rubbed against it. I closed my eyes tightly in an unrealistic attempt to teleport. Anywhere but here. Please, anywhere but here. Of course, it never worked.

He finished. I laid there like an animal that had just been hit by a car. I twitched a little, but I felt like I was barely alive. I wished that I had been hit by a car instead. I might be closer to death that way. I laid there on my side because my backside was too sore. I stared at the wall in shock.

"Aww… poor baby," Melissa said sympathetically. After putting my clothes back on, he let Melissa into the room. She continued, "Tim told me you threw up quite a bit. You don't have to be embarrassed about that, Gene. We all drink too much sometimes."

She started to run her fingers through my hair and rubbed the side of my arm. She placed her hand on my cheek and noticed it was wet from tears.

“Oh, no! You threw up so much that you started to cry,” she said concerned, but with a chuckle, “I’ve been there before, many times. It is nothing to be embarrassed about. I think it is ridiculous that people think men shouldn’t cry. It is simply a case of fragile masculinity. I think you are adorable when you cry, Gene.”

She wiped the tears from my face and kissed my head. I still couldn’t move. I couldn’t speak. I was devastated. I was numb.

“Tim said that we could stay here tonight,” Melissa said, “He told me we can sleep in his bed. He’ll take the other room. He doesn’t mind.”

If I was able to speak, I wouldn’t be able to. I was speechless. Melissa thought that it was because I had been puking my guts out. Tim knew the truth. She thought so highly of him. He was her best friend. Her cheerleading buddy. The one that was always there for her.

Tim returned to the room with bread and a sports drink that had electrolytes.

“They say that electrolytes help you recover faster, and that bread soaks up the alcohol in your stomach,” Tim said, handing them over to Melissa.

"That's so sweet of you, Tim! You've helped Gene out so much tonight," Melissa said graciously. She grabbed the sports drink and the bread and then hugged him.

I was traumatized. I tried to remember how I got here. I had only taken a couple shots of alcohol and drank one beer. I had drunk way more than that before and never felt this way.

Tim acted as if nothing had happened. He was overly polite. He had a great reputation with Melissa. She had no idea what her best friend was capable of doing and she would never believe it if she knew what he had done. He was so convincing that I began to question if anything had truly happened. I knew it had. I felt it. It stained my mind like dark red blood on a pure white napkin. Everyone at the dinner table would assume that it was wine, but Tim and I knew the truth. The unspoken truth that would haunt me for the rest of my life.

***

Many months had passed since that horrible night at Tim's house. I never said a word about it. I didn't think Melissa would believe me anyways. I was embarrassed it had happened. I was afraid to destroy the one friend Melissa held onto throughout the years. That may have been an excuse to validate my silence, but it felt better that way.

Life dragged on. I received another promotion at work because all the guests loved me, and the staff wanted to see me rise. I wish I felt excited about that, but I didn't. Nothing mattered. I was climbing the corporate ladder without any effort, money came easy. They started rooftop parties for the tenants at the apartment. Melissa loved them. I hated them. It seemed like Melissa loved me a lot. She always wanted me around. It was as if I was the most important thing in her life. On the outside, my life was perfect.

I cared for Melissa, but I felt nothing. I couldn't feel love for her. I couldn't tell her what her best friend had done to me. I told her that I loved her, but I never meant it.

I usually hid the way I truly felt about Melissa. I would bring her flowers, make her food and shower her with compliments. I even helped her with her finances as if we were married. Outwardly, you would believe that we were the happiest couple in the world. Destined to live happily ever after. Maybe, after all of this time, the way that I truly felt was starting to seep out.

"You never touch me anymore, Gene!" Melissa shouted at me angrily, "You spend all of your time on your stupid music projects and then you leave for work. Your music is shit anyways. When you are with me, I feel like I'm talking to a fucking wall. You never want to have sex. You make excuses. You are always too tired. I don't feel like you love me anymore. I thought I was your fucking girlfriend. I can't keep living with you like this, Gene. What the fuck is wrong with you?"

My face was emotionless. I felt exhausted from life. She wasn't wrong. I hated having sex with her. I would avoid it for as long as possible. I understood why she felt like she was talking to a wall; I had nothing to say to her anymore. I almost felt guilty that I lied about my love for her until she said that my music was shit. She told me that she loved my music. She told me that she truly believed I was going to become famous someday. It was all bullshit. We were both lying to each other. My lie may have been worse, but I didn't care.

I started to believe that everyone was full of shit. Everyone was telling a fabricated story to feel better about their lives. I guess I couldn't blame them. Life was miserable. Everything was better than reality. I had constructed the American dream. I had a great job, a girlfriend, a fancy apartment in the city by the harbor, and an area to practice my hobby. I was living my life to the fullest, but it was all bullshit. I wasn't truly happy with any of it. I didn't care about anything anymore. I was only living because I was afraid to die.

I gathered some words for Melissa.

"I think we should break up," I said in a cold tone.

Maybe that wasn't the best way to do it, but I was sick of living a lie. I had lived a lie because of Jacob's rules. I had lived a lie in the church, because I was scared to live on the streets. Now, I was living a lie with Melissa. I didn't even know why I was doing it with her. I was supposed to be free. These should have been the best moments of my life. I guess it was just a habit.

"What did you just say?" Melissa said, trembling. A few tears dripped from her eyes.

"I want to break up," I repeated. My face was stone cold.

She lost it. She threw herself to the floor in a crying fit. She screamed a bunch of nonsense. It wasn't words, just noises. Eventually, she gathered herself and wiped the tears from her eyes. She stood up, straightened her posture and looked at me.

"How could it be so easy, if you truly loved me?" she asked through her sniffles, "You don't even want to think about it?"

Her question made me think for a moment. I guess I would have needed more time if I had truly loved her. That thought had never crossed my mind before because I never truly loved her. She believed that I did, but it was all fake. The decision was so easy in my mind.

"How about this?" I spoke with a little reassurance, "I will go for a walk and when I come back we can discuss it. We can make a final decision then."

"Whatever, do what you want," she snapped back at me.

I didn't respond to that. That answer was good enough for me. I walked out of the apartment and took the elevator down to the street.

I felt a slight relief in my heart knowing that I had finally suggested a break up. It felt good to be honest with myself. I jumped onto the break wall at the harbor and walked along the edge. I looked down at my reflection in the water as I walked. The air was wet from the ocean. There was a refreshing breeze that calmed my nerves. I took a few deep breaths and leaped off the break wall into the grass. I laid with my limbs outstretched as far as they could go. People must have thought I was crazy.

I walked through the tall buildings in downtown over to the highest hotel. There was an elevator that I took to the top. There was an observation deck up there. I enjoyed looking down at the world from above, it reminded me of the mountaintop in Colorado. I stayed there for a while and observed the city below. I noticed a few police cars and an ambulance with flashing lights driving through the city. I could hear the sirens faint wail from above.

I felt calm and at peace with my decision. I really did want to leave Melissa. It would be better for both of us. We had already been together for a year and the lease was about to expire on the apartment. The timing was perfect. I walked back through the city streets to the door of the apartment building. I took the elevator to our floor and walked to the front door. I paused for a few moments outside of the apartment door. I took a few deep breaths before I opened it.

I stepped inside thinking that Melissa was going to be there ready to talk, but she wasn't. I thought maybe she had decided to go for a walk too. I shut the door behind me and went over to the kitchen area. I sat down at the table. I scanned the artwork on the walls and my guitars. I tapped my fingers on the table nervously. I looked over to the front door and noticed that her shoes were still there. I got up from the kitchen table and walked over to the bathroom. Maybe she was in there. I knocked a few times but there was no reply. She might be giving me the silent treatment, I thought. I cautiously opened the bathroom door. When I peered in, it was empty. I noticed an empty bottle of Diazepam pills on the bathroom floor. The lid was on the countertop. I remembered that she would take those every once in a while for her anxiety. Melissa's cell phone was laying on the floor. I picked it up and looked through the last calls she had made. She had called Tim, and then the emergency line. A million chills filled my body like bugs crawling beneath my skin.

Calling Tim was the last thing that I wanted to do, but it seemed to be my only option. I relentlessly dialed his number. When he answered, his voice was like a needle piercing the side of my head. It was hard for me to focus on what he was saying. I managed to pull myself together. He told me that Melissa had overdosed on Diazepam pills. She called him after she had done it. He told her to call the emergency line right away. I didn't respond. I hung up after he told me.

I called the hospital in San Diego and asked for Melissa. It took a while to get through to someone, but once I did, a lady told me that she was on a seventy-two hour hold at the psychiatric hospital. The lady told me that since she had attempted to kill herself, it was necessary that she be monitored closely. She was under twenty-four hour surveillance to ensure she didn't try to harm herself again. I thanked the woman and hung up the phone.

I slowly walked over to the bed and sat on the floor beside it. I couldn't believe this was happening. I thought it would be so much better for Melissa and I to break up. I was only gone from the apartment for an hour. I blamed myself. I couldn't believe what I had done. My cold attitude towards her and the fact that I didn't truly love her. That was why she wanted to commit suicide.

I started to feel terrible. My vision began to blur as my eyes filled with tears. I felt so much pressure pushing against my heart. I cared for Melissa and I wanted the best for her, I just didn't love her. I didn't even know what it meant to love someone. Maybe I did love her, but I wasn't attracted to her. I couldn't understand this concept of love. I sunk deeper into the floor. I stared blankly at the wall.

I had made my decision about the break up, but now I felt horrible about it. I tried to think of what I would tell her when she returned from the hospital. I had no idea, but I had to tell her the truth. I couldn't continue to live in that lie. The truth was such a complicated concept. People wanted to know the truth, but only the truth that they liked. I wanted to leave her. That was a truth that she didn't like. I was wavering in my decision.

The next three days in that apartment were chilling. It carried an eerie feeling of death like an open windy portal to the afterlife. I would look into the bathroom and see visions of Melissa on the floor dying, overdosing. In those visions she would scream at me. She would tell me that it was all my fault. It was hard to fall asleep every night. I wore dark circles around my eyes. I tried to act normal at work, but my manager noticed something was wrong. I broke down crying in her office. She told me it wasn't my fault, that Melissa was selfish for doing such a thing. At the time, I couldn't see it that way.

Melissa returned to the apartment.

"Hey," she said downcast.

"Hey," I replied back.

She walked over to the black futon in the living room and sat down. I stood awkwardly, looking away from her.

"Are you going to come hold me?" she said in a desperate tone.

I didn't answer. I walked over to the kitchen table and sat down. I took a deep breath and then pulled my phone out of my pocket and set it on the table.

"I'm sorry for everything," she said in a contrite tone.

"I still think we should go our separate ways," I said, staring at the kitchen table. I lifted my head and then looked over to her, "I think it would be best if you moved back in with your parents or into your own place."

She didn't answer. She let out a big sigh as she collapsed onto her side.

My phone started to *ring*. I looked over while it vibrated on the table. It was Melissa's father. I answered.

"Hello," I said as I pushed the speaker against my ear.

"Yeah, Gene?" he said.

"Yes?" I replied.

"How is Melissa doing? Is she back at the apartment?" he asked, slightly concerned.

"Yeah, she's here," I confirmed.

"Oh, that's great to hear. Thanks for taking care of her, Gene," he said graciously.

"Um, yeah. . . sure. No problem," I said hesitantly and then continued, "Melissa and I were talking, and I think it would be better if she moved back in with you guys."

"What'd you say, Gene?" he asked as if he hadn't heard the question.

"I said that I think," I started to repeat myself, but he cut me off.

"Gene, Gene. I heard you," he said anxiously and then continued, "but listen, we don't want her back at the house. We can't have her back at the house. She is too much stress on her mother. We can't deal with that right now. The two of you are smart, grown adults. I'm sure you can figure it out. Don't bring her here."

He hung up. He didn't give me a chance to respond. I felt so many things after that phone call. Hopelessness was certainly one of those things.

I felt sorry for her. Her father didn't want her. I was trying to end the relationship. I wanted to move on with my life. That was becoming very difficult for me to do. My emotions were tangled.

"What did my father say?" Melissa asked me as she sat up slightly from the futon.

I was contemplating whether I should tell her the truth or not. I really wanted to be truthful. I didn't want to live with anymore lies. I was torn. How could I tell her that her father didn't want her? How could I say that, when only a couple of days ago she had tried to kill herself? I wanted to melt down, but I couldn't. I forced myself together.

"Well, your father. Um, he said that we should try and work things out like adults." I said, stumbling over my words.

She stood up from the futon and walked over to me. She dropped to her hands and knees and reached her hands out to mine. She looked pathetic and desperate.

"Gene, please forgive me," she started begging with sorrow in her face, "I will never do it again. I was so stupid and immature," her voice began to raise dramatically, "I have grown now. I want to be here for you. I want to be your girlfriend, Gene. I love you. Please! I'm begging you! I promise I will be better. Please? I promise from the bottom of my heart."

I was overwhelmed with her intensely animated apology. It came so abruptly. I was frozen for words. So many things were racing through my head. I couldn't collect my thoughts. I felt responsible for her suicide attempt. After hearing her apology, I was afraid she was going to do it again. I was almost certain that she would. That worried me a lot. I didn't want to be responsible for a dead ex-girlfriend. I thought about her father, and how he said that he didn't want her. Maybe she grew up in a broken home. I could relate to that. I felt pity for her, but stressed at the same time. I didn't know what to do. I wished there was someone that I could ask for advice. I couldn't think of anyone. I was on my own. I wanted to run away, but I couldn't. I had to make a decision.

"Ok," I said in a defeated tone, "I forgive you."

I cringed as I said those words. I didn't know what else to do. I was afraid. I was hopeless. Those words sealed my fate.

***

The three months that followed Melissa's suicide attempt were a lot smoother than I anticipated. We didn't have any arguments. Life carried on and redeveloped into a normal routine. She got a new job, closer to where we lived, as a medical biller. Maybe, she had been serious about her apology. Maybe, she had indeed changed. She started coming to some of my shows again, even though she thought my music was shit. I started to think that I was wrong for wanting to break up. Love might be simpler than I thought. Maybe all it is, is sacrifice. Maybe emotional connection and attraction are irrelevant. After all, the love I had learned about in the Bible was on a cross. Torture. Love, is torture.

In the next couple of months, I quickly learned that I had been wrong about Melissa. She started coming home angry every day. She wanted me to stop playing music. She told me that I was lazy and didn't work hard enough. She said that if I was working more, then I wouldn't have time for music. She smashed one of my guitars while I was at work. It was like Jacob all over again, except that I didn't try to kill her when I got home. I was actually surprised by how calm I was about it. I had lost the power that I felt when I stood up against Jacob. Tim had taken that from me. Love was torture. Life was suffering. I had to accept these grim truths.

Her heightened disgust for my music started at the last show that I played. It was a small coffee shop, nothing extraordinary. She came to watch my performance. I guess that was part of the change that she had promised me. After the show, a woman came to speak with me about my music. She showed adoration, not only for my music, but for me as well. She openly expressed that she was attracted to me and that she wanted to take me on a date. That was when Melissa stepped in. She had heard everything and was furious because of it. I didn't have a chance to respond. She grabbed me tightly, by the arm, and marched me out quicker than that woman could say goodbye. She gave me an ultimatum; music or her. That was the last show that I played. I didn't feel like arguing. I didn't have any more fight left in me. I was dispirited.

After six months, she started to work less. She told me that it was too stressful and that her anxiety would flare up. She wanted to quit. I told her that I thought it would be best if she kept the job while she searched for a new one, that way she could continue to pay the rent. She didn't listen to me. She didn't care. She quit.

After she quit her job, I was responsible for everything. I paid all of the bills, rent and food. I even paid the rest of her college debt. She told me that it was giving her anxiety attacks. Everything gave her anxiety. I was afraid that she would try to kill herself again. For that reason, I always appeased her demands.

She started to tell me that she never received attention from me anymore. She told me that I worked too much and that I was never home to comfort her when she needed me. This situation felt familiar. We had this problem before. I told her that I was sorry, but that I had to work because I was the only one paying the bills. She was unforgiving.

I felt like a slave to her demands. I wanted to break up, but I was afraid to even mention it. I didn't want her to kill herself. I was afraid that I would be held responsible for her death. I didn't want that for my life, but I didn't want her in my life either. How could I reconcile these things? Her best friend had raped me, and her presence was a constant reminder of that. I just wanted to leave. Why was it so difficult? I was depressed, but I carried on.

"Melissa," I said with forced excitement, "You know how you were saying I never give you enough attention because I'm always at work?"

"Yes?" she said curiously.

"Well, how would you like to take a road trip to San Francisco?" I said, trying to sound as enthusiastic as possible, "I have the next four days off from work. We can start driving early in the morning and arrive by the afternoon. We can stay a few nights and then drive back. It's only a nine hour drive."

"Gene, that sounds wonderful," she said with a smile, "I was starting to give up on you. I was starting to believe that you didn't love or care about me anymore."

I wished that she meant those words, but I knew it was all lies. I wish she would leave me. I wished for that everyday. If she left me, then it wouldn't be my fault if she committed suicide. She couldn't blame me for her death, because it would have been her decision.

"Of course not, Melissa," I could hear the insincerity in my voice, "I want to have a special weekend for the two of us."

"You are so sweet, Gene," she said as she stood up and gave me a hug.

We started to pack some suitcases for the trip and I made dinner for the night. I set the alarm to go off at six. I attempted to go to bed early to prepare for the drive, but Melissa didn't let me sleep. She wanted sex. I hated it, every time, but I pushed myself through it to ensure a peaceful night before the trip.

Before bed, I did something that I never do. I prayed. I prayed silently that Melissa would leave me. I remembered what I had thought about as a child, at the first church that I attended with my mother. How I found it interesting that when people reached an all time low in their lives they would almost always, without fail, turn to God or a higher power. People seek a power that is beyond them simply because they feel too weak or powerless to overcome the struggles by themselves. That it is almost always a desperate reach for God and never a voluntary one. That is exactly how I felt at that moment. I finally understood. I was weak. I was desperate. I wished that she would just leave me already.

***

My body began to float into the air, as if gravity had ceased to exist, until the seat belt grabbed me. Glass shards flew from either side of the car. I looked over to Melissa who had previously been asleep. Her seat belt tightened and ripped her from the air before she could float away. I felt the car smack into the ground and then launch back into the air. I looked out of the shattered glass window. We were upside down for a moment. The car rolled over again and launched us back into the air. I started to count each time that we hit the ground and rolled. Six. Seven. Eight. On the ninth time, the car came to an abrupt stop and a cloud of dust filled the inside. I couldn't see anything. Once the dust had settled, I was able to look around. We were hanging upside down, by our waists, from the seat belts.

I unbuckled and dropped to the roof of the car. Melissa was screaming in the passenger's seat. I felt pain in my head and there were cuts all over my arms. I crawled on my hands and knees to Melissa. I unbuckled her from the seat belt. She fell, like me, but didn't move once she hit the roof of the car.

"What the fuck, Gene? What have you done? You've ruined my fucking life," she started yelling at me hysterically.

I didn't answer that. I was disoriented. I needed to find a way out of the car.

San Francisco was a decent trip. She enjoyed the hotel and the city. We went on some city tours and visited Alcatraz Island. We drove down Lombard Street and ate at Ghirardelli Square. For once, I thought that maybe she was satisfied. Maybe I had finally done something right in her eyes.

Melissa didn't want to split the driving on the way back. She told me that she wanted to relax because she was tired from the trip. I agreed to drive us back.

We were passing through a barren stretch of highway. It was empty besides a few semi trucks. There were two lanes; a passing lane to the left and a slow lane to the right. The trucks mostly kept to the right. It was dark because it was late. I attempted to pass one of the semi trucks. I was halfway when it started to turn into my lane. I pressed the brake so that we wouldn't be pushed off the road. I wasn't able to slow down fast enough. The back of the truck tipped the front of the car and we went flying into the air. We flipped nine times on to the side of the road before we landed upside down in the dusty ditch.

"You are such a piece of shit, Gene," she yelled even louder this time. She cried and screamed in pain.

I started digging through the thick patch of dirt that was just outside of the driver's side window. We were trapped. Digging was the only plausible way out. My hands received little cuts from the glass and debris that were mixed into the dirt. I didn't feel the pain as much as I should have because of my adrenaline. I managed to clear a path that was big enough to squeeze my body through.

"You're just going to leave me here!" Melissa shouted dreadfully.

I couldn't speak at the moment. I was unable to produce words. I climbed the ditch to the road and looked in both directions. There wasn't a car in sight. The highway was empty.

After a few minutes, I saw a semi truck driving towards me. I started to jump and wave my arms frantically in an attempt to signal it to stop. It didn't work. The truck flew by me. It didn't even slow down. I reached into my pocket for my phone, but it wasn't there. It must have fallen out in the accident. I ran back to the car and climbed in through the driver's side window.

"You always fuck everything up, Gene!" Melissa greeted me as I re-entered the car.

I started moving my hands through the dirt that had piled up around the shattered windshield. I was trying to feel for my cell phone. I slid my finger over a sharp piece of glass which made me flinch a little in pain. I ignored it and kept searching while it bled into the dirt. My hand moved over the phone.

I lifted the phone from the ground to my face and blew off the dust that had collected on it. The entire screen was cracked. The screen display was flickering in and out. I placed the phone in my pocket and started to crawl out of the window.

"Gene, I think my arm is broken. It hurts a lot," Melissa said in a calm and concerned tone.

"Hang in there," I answered reassuringly. I turned to look at her, "I am going to go outside and see if I can get a signal to call the ambulance."

She nodded and then continued to cry. I proceeded to crawl out of the window.

I found a signal once I was out. The touch screen wasn't working very well, but eventually, I managed to dial the emergency helpline. I told them that I wasn't sure where we were, but I described the route that we were driving from. They instructed me to walk to the nearest mile marker and read it to them. I followed their instructions. They told me it was going to take them about an hour to arrive.

I ran back to tell Melissa. She started crying hysterically once I told her it would take them some time. I did my best to comfort her through the hour, but it didn't help much. It dragged on for what seemed like days.

The ambulance arrived and pulled Melissa out onto a stretcher. They told me that her arm was broken, but other than that she was fine. I was slightly relieved. We took an hour-long ambulance ride to the nearest hospital and stayed there for a couple of nights until the doctor said that she could leave.

Her father came to pick us up from the hospital. I was surprised. He drove us back to San Diego. The doctor told her that it would be best if she wasn't home alone because she would need assistance. I convinced her father to allow her to stay with him. I told him that I had to continue working to pay the medical bills. He finally agreed. She lost her medical insurance when she quit her job. I called my work to try and place her on my insurance plan. Luckily, they were able to do it. If they hadn't, the medical expenses would have been over fifty thousand dollars. Now, I only had to pay a couple thousand.

Every day I would wake up early for work and take public transportation from her parent's house to the hotel. I would come back after work to prepare food for her. She insisted that I help her shower. I would scrub her entire body with soap and rinse it with water. I would shampoo and condition her hair. When the shower was over, I would dry her with the towel. Then, I would dress her and help her to bed.

That routine continued for the next two months.

During that time, I thought about my parents' story. I thought it was strange that my father had been in two horrible car accidents and now, I had done the same. I guess it ran in the family. I injured James and now I had done the same to Melissa. I felt overwhelming guilt for that.

Every time I took care of Melissa she would yell at me and tell me that I was worthless. She would tell me that I couldn't do anything right. She said that I was pathetic. That I was a failure at life. I was starting to believe her. I remembered when Jacob and my manager at Joe's used to say the same thing. I began to think that I was the real problem.

It had been a couple of months after the car accident and two years since I started dating Melissa.

"You're not cleaning my hair correctly, Gene!" Melissa said in frustration.

"Then fucking clean it yourself," I responded harshly.

"Why are you always such a prick? You don't even care about me or my feelings," she said and then began to break down in tears.

I stopped. I had reached my breaking point. I stepped out of the bathtub. I left her there naked, wet, and crying with shampoo suds sliding from her hair. I walked out of the bathroom and left the house. I was about to explode.

I walked a few blocks from her parents apartment to the beach. Her parents had moved out of the apartment complex that they lived in before. I threw myself onto the sandy beach and stretched myself out onto my back. I stared up at the sky. It was night time but the stars were not visible. There was a thick marine layer of fog in the air.

I began to ponder life. I remembered when I used to dream about California. I thought that I would come here and play music on the beach. I imagined playing shows with John and walking up and down Hollywood Boulevard. Now, I hate California. I lost contact with John. He was indoctrinated by the church. I left a decent life in Colorado for this mess. I rarely ever spoke with Blake anymore, but I was sure he was doing better than me. I missed him. I was exhausted. I wanted to give up on everything. I imagined floating off into the foggy ocean and falling asleep. It would be so peaceful in the depths of the sea. I remembered the amount of stress that Melissa's suicide attempt had brought on me. I didn't want that. I was held hostage by her threat to kill herself.

I jumped out of my thoughts for a moment. There was a bird that swooped down from the fog and landed right next to me. It twitched and hopped around on the sand. I watched it for a few minutes as it picked through the sand with its beak. It was sifting through random bits of trash.

Suddenly, it pulled out a live crab. The crab moved its legs in a helpless struggle to break free. The bird jumped into the air with the crab still in its beak and flew off into the fog.

I had a sudden shift in my thoughts. I didn't want to be a victim to Melissa's threats anymore. I didn't care. I wanted to leave her. I couldn't continue my life this way. I helped her with so many things in her life, but it was never enough. I paid for her car. I paid for her college tuition. I provided her with food, water and shelter. I was doing more for her than her parents were. All she did was sit on her lazy ass, talk shit and complain about everything I did. I was over it. I needed to leave her.

I jumped to my feet and started walking back to the apartment. I walked with a passionate stride.

I had made up my mind. I was going back and telling her that it was over. I didn't care if she tried to kill herself. I didn't care if people thought I was a horrible person for leaving her broken. I didn't give a shit about what people thought anymore. I didn't give a shit about what she thought anymore.

I stormed in through the front door of the apartment and walked straight to the back room that she was in. I started to throw my clothes and belongings in a black trash bag.

"You are such an asshole. Do you know that, Gene" she told me as I continued to throw my stuff in the black trash bag, "You just left me there alone, half dirty, in that shower."

"It doesn't matter anymore, Melissa. I am leaving you," I said firmly with conviction.

She lost control of her temper and started to yell.

"You are such a fucking worthless piece of shit, Gene!" she yelled at me as she stood to her feet from the bed.

I ignored her and started to tie the black trash bag. I finished placing all my belongings inside it.

"You can't leave me, you fucking idiot," she began to rant, "You can't take responsibility for anything in your life. You are worthless, Gene. You know, I remember the story that you told me about your parents."

I lifted my head towards her to listen. I wanted to hear where she was going with that statement.

"You are going to be nothing but a fuck up, Gene" she continued her rant, "You are going to be a fuck up, just like your father. Your father crashed that car and ruined your mother's life. You have done the same to me. You will never be anything good in your life. You are a cancer to everyone."

I felt those words as she said them. They pierced deep into my heart, because I felt them to be true. I stopped thinking. I turned off my mind. I discarded my emotions. My heart turned cold.

I lifted the black trash bag from the floor and casually walked out of the room. I felt nothing anymore. I was numb. I felt no pity. I felt no pain. The only thing I did feel was emptiness.

ELEVEN

The water in the harbor was glistening. It reflected the light of the setting sun into the ocean. The view of downtown San Diego from Coronado Island looked as if someone had painted it fresh, right in front of our eyes. The building lights started to become brighter as the sunlight dissipated. Chad and I were sitting in a green patch of grass bordered by little shrubs. It was on the edge, before the land met the water.

"I know it sounds corny," Chad started to say as we stared at the city from across the water, "but I think true love is the ultimate. Nothing beats the feeling of holding a beautiful woman in your hands. It feels like nothing else matters in the moment you two are together. That is what I would consider the pinnacle."

My relationship with Melissa was left in the same black trash bag I carried out of her parents' apartment. I never saw her again after that. I moved out of the apartment we used to share downtown and moved into a more economic one just outside of the city. I bought a new cell phone after the car accident and copied all of my contacts from the old one to the new one. That was when I came across Chad's number. I forgot that I had saved it. I gave him a call and we started hanging out. We met often ever since then.

"Yea, that is pretty corny," I said laughing at him a little, "but I guess I see what you mean. I guess if you could find the right girl, then it could be great. Melissa was definitely not the right girl for me."

"I would even take it a step further," Chad said searching for the new ideas inside of his head, "I would go as far as to say that true love is the main reason people continue to exist in this world."

I turned over to him and raised one of my eyebrows. I was not convinced of what he was saying.

"What about your passions in life? The pursuit of your career and having money? There are people in this world living the dream. They have billions of dollars, drive fancy cars, eat fancy dinners and do whatever they want. They don't even check how much things cost before they buy them."

"Yeah," he said in a high pitched skeptical tone, "All those things are great and all, but those people still need love. Real love. Those types of people have everything except the things that money can't buy. I would even say that money can actually make it more difficult to find real love. People with that type of money have to sift through everyone that is pretending to love them because they are rich."

I thought about what he said for a moment. I turned my gaze back towards the city landscape.

"You know," I started to say while still collecting my thoughts, "I think you're right."

I thought back to when my mother and I were poor and lived in the back of the old station wagon. The times that we would go to the grocery stores to receive free expired food. I remembered how fast my mother and Jacob's relationship had grown. It seemed like they had just met, and within a couple of months, she was already married to him. I remembered the time she showed up to my apartment in Colorado and broke down crying about Jacob and told me her story. The times that she struggled as a poor child in the Dominican Republic. I always wondered if she truly loved Jacob.

"Maybe, it's just my personal bias," Chad said as he tore a few pieces of grass from the ground and threw them in front of him, "I never really pursued love. I was always busy going door to door with the Jehovah's Witnesses. I tried to speak to people about the Bible. Most people didn't want to hear about it. Every once in a while someone showed interest. That was always exciting for me. I truly enjoyed those times, but I think I deprived myself of the experience of love."

"Why don't you try to pursue love now?" I asked reassuringly. I noticed he started to sound regretful and downcast.

He looked at me with a half smile. The type of half smile you give a naive child.

"It's not so simple, brother," he said with a bit of a chuckle, "but I like your optimism. Never stop thinking that way, Gene."

After saying this, he stood up from the grass and started walking towards the street. I got up and followed him. We walked to his car and he dropped me off at my building.

I entered my apartment. I walked into my bedroom and laid on the mattress. It was on the floor in the corner of the room. I stared up at the blank white ceiling. Life was constantly changing. I still thought about my two car accidents and their connection to my father's. I thought about the image Colton placed in my head of that little toy car I stole. The bleeding flesh of Jesus Christ. It was as if my first mistake as a child had predicted my future. That little toy car represented the Volvo station wagon. The poverty my mother and I lived through in the back of it. It represented the truck I crashed into James. It represented the accident with Melissa. It was all bad memories. Almost every tragedy in my life was connected to that little toy car.

I tried to stop thinking about the past. I tried to stop thinking about the horrible memories and the mistakes that I had made. The discussions I had with Chad distracted me from those thoughts. It was impossible to avoid them completely, but it helped. A short while ago I had felt like dying. That life was suffering. Tim had taught me that by raping me. Melissa reminded me of it everyday. I questioned whether I deserved it. Maybe it was God's punishment for my sins. Now I tried to focus on the good. I was free again. I had Chad to talk to, and there was always a focus of change and positivity in our discussions. I had my own apartment. I was a successful manager at a nice hotel. I guess after the discussion with Chad that day, none of those things really mattered. The only thing I was missing in my life was real love.

***

I walked out of the front lobby of the hotel and waved goodbye to the overnight staff. It was a long shift. I started at eight in the morning and didn't leave until ten. It was a fairly quiet night downtown. I noticed as I made my way to the bus stop. I took the same bus everyday. It was a quick ten minute ride to my apartment.

I arrived at the bus stop and waited with the few people that were there. It was the main bus stop. Multiple buses collected people from there.

There was a thin shiny layer of water that glazed the city streets and reflected the street lights. It must have rained earlier. There was steam that rose from the sewage grates and evaporated into the air. The faint sound of horns could be heard in the distance despite the fairly empty street I stood beside. It was most likely coming from the Gaslamp Quarter.

I turned my head when I heard a homeless man grumbling. He wore filthy clothes that you could smell from a distance. He was shaking his fist in the air and yelling at the sky. It was common to see homeless people downtown. Most of them came from the mental hospital nearby. The hospital would release them into the streets with whatever mental conditions that they had. They had to fend for themselves.

I continued to observe the man. He started to walk towards a woman that was waiting at the bus stop. He began to shout at her in slurs that no one could understand. She hugged her purse and moved closer to me. The homeless man followed. I shouted to the man and shooed him away. He relentlessly turned around. He shouted slurs and waved his hands in the air as he left.

"Thank you," said the woman with a strong Brazilian accent.

She looked at me directly in my eyes when she said those words. It gave me goosebumps. She was one of the most beautiful girls I had ever seen. She had wavy dirty blonde hair and wide brown eyes. Her skin was sun kissed to a smooth caramel color.

"Sure," I said. I was trying not to blush, "What is your name?"

"Adriana," she said in a sweet voice, "What is your name?"

"Gene," I said with a smile.

She smiled back. She had one of the most beautiful smiles I had ever seen. Her cheeks raised and her eyes squinted when she smiled.

"Do you live here?" I asked curiously.

"I arrived three days ago," she responded back, "I live in Rio De Janeiro, but I will stay here to study English for three months. I want to receive my certification. It allows me better jobs for my career in Brazil."

"Oh, cool," I said, "Let me know if you need someone to show you around the city or if you need to practice your English."

She blushed a little.

"Okay," she said with a smile.

My bus arrived. She was taking the same bus as me. We sat together and chatted. She told me that she lived with a host family near my apartment. She was going to college to become a chemical engineer in Brazil. She said that many companies had better opportunities if she spoke English. Her English was good. She didn't understand a few words that I said, but she learned them quickly. Her accent was strong, but her speech was clear.

I exited the bus and waved goodbye to Adriana. She didn't get off for a couple more stops. I walked to my apartment with butterflies in my stomach. I was glowing with excitement. I felt a connection between us. I really liked Adriana. I placed my hand on my chest to feel my heart beating. Those moments with her had made my day a million times better. I forgot that I had been working since eight in the morning because I was filled with energy.

I reached into my pocket to grab my phone. I paused. I forgot to ask for her number. I had no way to contact Adriana or see her again. I couldn't believe it. I was too distracted by our conversation. I felt stupid. I wanted to see her again. I had to, somehow.

I thought about the talk I had with Chad. He told me that love was the pinnacle. That day, more than ever, his words made perfect sense. That connection that I felt in those moments with Adriana was incredible. That must have been what Chad was referring to. I was sure of it. I had never felt that way about someone. I no longer thought that love was suffering or torture. That was when I was with Melissa. I still didn't completely understand what it was now, but this feeling seemed close enough.

***

A couple of days had passed since I met Adriana. I couldn't stop thinking about her. I spaced out a few times at work because I was thinking about the day we met. I wished I could see her again.

Chad and I drove to Sunset Cliffs to explore and have our usual deep discussions. It was beautiful there. The cliffs glowed red as the sunlight hit their sides. The waves would crash into the cliffs and throw sparkles of water into the air. We were seated on a large rock enjoying the view.

"I'm just saying that some of the things that they teach us in school should be re-evaluated," Chad said passionately as he continued to develop his thoughts, "For example, what did they teach you about the American Civil War?"

I thought about that for a moment. We were deep into another discussion.

"I remember that it was a war fought by the North and the South of the United States. The Southern states were fighting to keep slavery legal and the Northern states were fighting to make slavery illegal."

"That is exactly what they teach," he said with a bit of excitement before he continued, "but that is misleading. During the war, slavery was still legal in a couple of the Union states, or in the North. Don't you think that the North would have already made slavery illegal if that was the main reason they were fighting the war?"

I had never thought about that before. I assumed that if the North was fighting against slavery, they would have already abolished it themselves.

"Are you sure that it wasn't already illegal in the North?" I asked to confirm.

"It was illegal in most of the North. However, not in Missouri, Kentucky and Maryland," he answered with confidence, "The North was led by Abraham Lincoln. He was a part of what is known as the Union. He wanted the North and the South to be governed by the same power, by one central government. The South wanted to govern themselves."

"So, what were they really fighting for?" I asked.

"That's where it gets interesting," Chad said with building excitement, "Abraham Lincoln owned slaves. A great number of the Union members owned slaves. Those people didn't really care about slavery. The whole war was about control and power. It always has been. There was no diplomatic attempt to end slavery. The first proposed legislation to abolish slavery didn't come until half a million soldiers on either side had already died. The North didn't even have a plan to integrate those slaves back into society after they were freed. You would think that if freedom from slavery was the main reason that they were fighting, then they would have planned for that. They don't teach these things in school. They filter the truth."

I sat quietly and absorbed the information he had given me. He had some interesting points. Why didn't they have a plan for the slaves once they were freed? They never attempted to find a diplomatic solution before they started fighting, which I thought was strange. I thought that war was always a last resort. Why did three of the northern states still have slaves? All of those things seemed a bit strange to me. I thought about what I had learned when I lived with Jacob. How ignorance was bliss, but it had to be ignorance against their will for it to apply. I related that to what Chad said. I related it to what I had been taught in school. Curiosity had disrupted Chad's bliss.

“That is pretty crazy,” I said. I was still thinking about everything.

“Oh, Gene,” he said more enthusiastically, “it doesn’t stop there. Do you remember what happened on September Eleventh?”

“Yeah,” I said. I thought about the classmates that I had to write letters to when I was a child, “There were terrorists from the Middle East that crashed stolen planes into the Twin Towers. They made them collapse to the ground.”

“That is exactly what all the reports said about the incident,” he said, “but they don’t talk about that third building that collapsed.”

“There was a third building?” I asked.

“There was a third building,” he confirmed and continued to speak passionately, “Not only that, how did a couple of airplanes bring those buildings straight to the ground? They looked like they collapsed in a controlled demolition. That is the type of stuff we need to be questioning. Right after the attacks, we knew exactly who was responsible and started a war. It happened too quickly, in my opinion. I don’t have all of the answers to these questions, but I think the answers the government tells us are fabricated. The focus of the American Civil War was placed on slavery, even though that was not the real reason why they were fighting. I believe they are lying about the war on terror as well. I think it’s all about power and control.”

I didn't know what to do with the information Chad shared with me. I thought it was interesting. It made sense. I guess it wouldn't be too crazy to believe that powerful people will abuse their power. I had never really questioned these things. The reason why I liked Chad was because he openly questioned everything Zack told him about the Bible. He didn't simply accept his teachings. He took it a step further in this discussion. He challenged the education system in the United States. He challenged the government system as well. I had only challenged the Bible and direct authority over me, not all the government systems.

"Does that not blow your mind?" Chad said, interjecting my thoughts.

"It is pretty crazy," I said laughing a bit in amazement.

We both jumped off the rock and started to walk along the cliffs. The sun was beginning to set. The light from the sunset made it look like the pictures in travel magazines. The temperature was perfect. Seagulls danced in the air and made the sunlight flicker as they crossed in front of it.

I felt a sudden tap on the back of my shoulder. I turned around to see what it was.

"Gene!" Adriana shouted with excitement.

I couldn't believe it was her. I was astonished at her presence. Her hair sparkled in the sunlight. Her cheeks raised and her eyes squinted the same way that they had when we first met.

"Adriana," I replied back blissfully. I reach out for a hug.

She squeezed my body tightly for a few moments. Then, we silently stared into each other's eyes.

"Did I miss something?" Chad said, looking at us in confusion.

I laughed and introduced him to Adriana. I told him the story of how we met, and how I didn't have a way to contact her. I thought that maybe I might meet her on the same bus again, but it was unlikely. I couldn't believe that we were at Sunset Cliffs on the same day, at the same hour.

"It must be meant to be," Chad said jokingly.

The three of us hung out for the rest of the night. Adriana had a new camera she had bought when she arrived in San Diego. Chad loved photography. He started taking pictures of the two of us while the sun set into the ocean. He told us that sunset was considered the magic hour for photography. He was right, the pictures looked professional.

At the end of the night, Chad gave us a ride home. I saved Adriana's phone number, she made sure of it. I skipped to my apartment with excitement. I knew that I looked ridiculous, but I didn't care. I was on top of the world.

The following three months were the shortest months of my life. Adriana and I spent almost every day together. We took kayaks into a sea cave off the coast of La Jolla. We rented a jet ski and sped through the San Diego harbor and laughed as the water splashed into our faces. I took her to the building tops in downtown to look over the city lights. We took photos and filmed everything.

She stayed the night at my apartment most of the nights. She taught me how to cook Brazilian Brigadeiros and we ate them while cuddled up on the couch while we watched movies. We cooked dinner together and experimented with new recipes. I would sing and play songs on my guitar for her. It rained one day so we ran out onto the street and danced in the rain.

We were devastated when her three months in the United States came to an end. We were worried about how we were going to make our relationship work. We both agreed that there was a strong connection between us. That inspired us to stay together. I saved three weeks of vacation time at work to go visit her in Rio De Janeiro. That vacation time didn't start for the next eight months.

The next eight months passed slowly. We would call each other and video chat everyday. She would study and I would get some work done while we were connected. We would cook together online and show each other what we were cooking. I would play guitar and sing for her through the screen. We constantly expressed how much we missed each other.

The day finally came. I went to see her in Brazil. The flight was long but I was anxious and excited from the very moment it took off until the wheels touched the runway in Rio. I couldn't stop checking the time. Adriana waited for me at the airport with her friends. One of them filmed the moment we were reunited. We held each other for a long time before we left the airport. We went to her house so that I could meet her family.

I booked a nice hotel for the full three weeks. It was the same brand of hotels that I worked for in San Diego. I called them ahead of time to prepare the room as a surprise for Adriana. I sent them the photo that Chad took of us and asked them to place it beside the bed with a welcome note that I wrote to her. They arranged roses in a trail to the bed that formed the shape of a heart. I sent the hotel a cd of all our favorite songs. They had it playing when we entered. I included a surprise song that I wrote for her. I had recorded it in the studio with Fred. I wanted those three weeks to be incredible. I wanted to make up for the last eight months that we had been apart.

We traveled to all the sites around Rio de Janeiro. We drove up to a landscape view of the city where monkeys were swinging above us in the trees. We took a gondola to the top of Sugarloaf Mountain. We walked along the beach at Copacabana and played volleyball. She took me to a nightclub in the city and we partied until the morning. Our lives were like a movie.

On the last day, everything started to change.

We were laying in bed at the hotel. Her attention was consumed by the messages on her cell phone. An hour of silence passed between us. Then, she started giggling at the texts. I leaned over and playfully took her phone from her hand. I was planning to set it down on the nightstand beside the bed, but she quickly took it back and threw it against the wall. I backed away, surprised by her actions.

"Whoa, is everything ok?" I was shocked.

"Why are you trying to take my phone?" she snapped.

"I'm sorry, Adriana," I said in a concerned and slightly confused tone, "I thought I would set your phone down on the nightstand, so that we could spend some more time together before I have to leave."

"Why were you trying to read my messages?" she asked angrily.

"I wasn't trying to read your messages. I simply wanted to spend more time with you," I said reassuringly.

She scanned my expression for verification of what I said.

"Who were you sending messages to?" I asked, now curious from her behavior.

"Just a friend at school," she said quickly.

That was the moment when I started to formulate doubts in our relationship. I thought her behavior was strange. She threw her phone against the wall. She almost broke it, simply because she thought I had read her messages. I studied Portuguese enough for basic communication, but not enough to understand her messages. I could have never understood what she had sent to her friend. I wasn't sure if I wanted to find out. Everything had been so perfect until that moment.

We drove to the airport and gave each other an awkward hug and kiss goodbye. I walked to the plane with a buzz in my heart. Something didn't feel right. The plane ride felt longer on the way back. My mind wandered as I stared out the window. I thought about those messages on her phone. A friend from school? They must have been more than that. I didn't want to believe it, but it seemed too obvious.

My stomach felt sick. I felt like I was going to puke my heart out while it was beating. We had such a great connection. Our relationship was like a movie. Flawless. She even told me that she loved me. I thought for sure that we had the love that Chad always told me about. The pinnacle. I wanted to talk to Adriana about it, but there was no service on the plane. I wanted her to tell me that it was nothing. I wanted to believe her.

***

"I think you are ready for this, Gene. You have developed an extremely effective management style. I want to see you rise," Rachel told me with confidence.

Rachel had been promoted to the general manager of the hotel. One morning, she had asked me to join her for lunch at the hotel restaurant to discuss my career. She was suggesting that I take a front office director position in Maui. It would be a substantial pay raise and beneficial experience to have on my resume.

A month had passed since I had seen Adriana in Brazil. I ignored the incident in the hotel room and we kept dating long distance. We didn't spend as much time on video chat as we used to. Our calls were brief. She always had college projects she had to work on with her friend. I tried not to think about it, but I didn't think that was all they were doing. I could never verify it, so I lived with it.

"I searched for some pictures of the property online," I said with nervous excitement about Rachel's suggestion.

"Gene, you deserve to do well. You do so much for each and every one of your employees. You truly care. That is a trait that is hard to find in the business world," she said reassuringly. She picked up on my nervousness, "I wouldn't be suggesting this to you if I didn't truly believe that you were capable of doing it."

I thought about her words. Maui looked beautiful, that was for certain. It looked like a fantasy world in a movie. The property that she was suggesting I go to was right on the beach. Maui was in the middle of the ocean and there weren't many people that lived there. I thought about Adriana. It would be more expensive to book flights from Maui to Rio. I wish I could confirm if she was cheating on me or not. Without that confirmation, it was difficult for me to let her go.

"Thank you, Rachel," I said appreciatively of her words, "Can I think about it for a few days, before I make a final decision? It's a big step."

"Of course, Gene," she said, "Why don't you think about it and let me know by the end of the week?"

"That sounds great," I said with a smile, "I appreciate that."

Rachel went back to her office and I prepared for the day.

***

"I've been thinking a lot about what I said about love," Chad said. He started into one of our deep discussions, "I think there has to be something beyond just the love itself."

We were at the top of a building we used to climb to look at the city lights. I was sitting down, dangling my feet over the edge. Chad was standing next to me. The sun had already set and there was a blanket of lights flickering throughout the city below. The lights reflected off the small ripples in the harbor as the boats moved gently across the water.

"Like what?" I asked.

"Well," he said as he began to gather his thoughts, "I think that there is a lot of suffering in the world. There are a lot of people that are less fortunate than ourselves. I think that simply being in love is not enough to achieve the pinnacle. That is selfish love. You are only interested in improving your own lives."

"So, what do you think is the pinnacle?" I said curiously.

"The pinnacle," he began to speak dramatically, "is when that love inspires the two of you to want to do more for the world. When the two of you can use the energy of your love for the greater good of humanity. That is the pinnacle."

"Hmm," I said. It was a benevolent concept.

It was an interesting thought. Chad always had interesting thoughts. Every idea that came out of his mouth made me reevaluate my life. I questioned whether I emphasized the right things in my life. It was true, there were a lot of people in the world that suffered. It would be nice to change that.

"What could we do to make the world a better place?" I asked, turning over.

"That Gene, is the question every human being on this planet should be asking themselves," he said. He seemed happy with my question, "I am still searching for the answer myself."

I nodded and looked at the city view. I thought about what would make the world a better place. It was a complicated question.

***

I closed the door behind me as I entered the apartment. It was late, but I was hungry. I went to the kitchen and opened the fridge in search of something to eat. There wasn't anything that looked good. I decided not to eat. I walked over to the couch and sat down. I rested for a few moments from the day. I reached over and picked up my guitar. It was leaning against the couch. I started playing.

I began playing the song that I wrote for Adriana. I stopped halfway through. It didn't feel the same. There was no energy left in the song. My emotions had changed about it. I set the guitar down for a moment and reached into my pocket to grab my phone. I sent a message to Adriana that said 'Oi', the equivalent to 'Hey' in English. I wanted to ask her what she thought about the promotion in Maui.

My phone vibrated right away. I picked it up to read the message. It was Adriana. She responded back in Portuguese. I didn't understand everything she sent, so I copied it into a translator online. Once I read the translated message, I dropped my phone to the floor.

My phone vibrated a few more times from the floor.

The message translated to:

Hey! What took you so long to respond? I sent you a message hours ago. Did I leave my red bra in your room the other night?

It was obvious that the message was not for me. My heart sank.

I knew that she had probably cheated on me the day she threw her phone at the wall, but I refused to believe it. Everything about our relationship was so perfect before that day. There were so many negative things in my life before her, that I wanted to cling to what we had. I saw it as one of the few positives. I felt like I had gone through so much and finally arrived at something true, something real. While I was with Adriana, I focused on the present and the future. She was more than just love to me, she was proof that I could overcome my past.

I never responded to that message. It was the last time I ever spoke to her. There were many times when I felt like calling her, but Chad advised against it. I respected his advice. I looked up to him in a lot of ways.

I went to work the next day and spoke with Rachel. I accepted the promotion. That message from Adriana came at the perfect time. I feared that I would have missed the opportunity if I still had hope for our relationship.

That was the first time I felt heartbreak. Heartbreak was different from pain. It was a different type of pain. I had felt pain many times before, but this was a strange feeling. I felt pain when Jacob hit me as a child. I felt pain when I was raped by Tim. This was heartbreak, not pain.

When I started hanging out with Chad, he gave me a new hope. I used to believe that life was suffering, but he changed that. He inspired me to think differently and search for a reason to live. That reason was Adriana.

She was the symbol of love that Chad told me about, but it wasn't real. I didn't even know what was anymore.

I thought about all the things Chad taught me. How they lied about history in school and that the terrorist attacks in New York didn't make any sense. I thought about all the times that I lied to Jacob so that he wouldn't beat me. I lied to Melissa. I told her I loved her because I thought that would make her happy. Those lies had destroyed everything in the end. Melissa almost killed herself. The accident almost killed the two of us. I almost killed Jacob. Adriana was my punishment for those lies.

I remembered what Chad had told me on top of the city building. The question that we should all be asking ourselves. How can we make this world a better place? That question made the most sense to me, at that moment. I understood suffering. I understood it fairly well, but now I had a taste of bliss. I had a taste of what it feels like to be in love. The feeling that nothing else matters when you are with that person. The original pinnacle.

Chad may have been right. Love is great, but it wasn't the pinnacle. The pinnacle was to use that love to better the world. That is what I wanted to discover. That is what I wanted to find. That is what I wanted to achieve. The pinnacle.

TWELVE

I stepped out onto the balcony of my new hotel. The view was magnificent. The palm trees swayed with the wind as the waves crashed against the shore. There were couples laying together on the beach. Children were running into the water and throwing themselves at the waves. There was a cliff of black lava rock that people were jumping from into the ocean. Birds soared through the sky, just above the palm trees. The ocean was turquoise and it faded into a darker blue the further you looked. It was an island paradise.

I squeezed the railing on the balcony and inhaled a deep breath of fresh island air. I let out a long exhale of relief. I felt so far away from my past. I felt like it couldn't reach me on this tiny island in the middle of the Pacific.

I had been introduced to everyone at the hotel, including most of the staff I would be managing. Everything seemed to function at a slower pace than it did in San Diego. They referred to that as 'island time'. There was no urgency to work. They simply just enjoyed each moment as it came.

When I arrived in Maui, I decided I didn't want to travel by car. I had had enough troubles with cars in my past. I wanted to move on from that and start new. I decided to purchase a little moped instead. That was how I cruised around the island.

"It's beautiful isn't it," a lady that worked at the concierge desk said. She walked over and stood beside me.

"Yes, it truly is," I agreed and smiled.

"It seems so beautiful on the outside," she said in an ostentatious and critical tone, "but that's not the reality. It's a small island, people gossip about everything. They are always watching and judging you. The island will get to you. It will eat you up, if you let it."

I nodded and smiled awkwardly, and then walked away.

I walked to the back office and began to start my work. I was working at the computer when one of the associates came into my office.

"Hi, can I help you with something?" I asked with a welcoming smile.

"So, you're the new manager," he said, judging me with his eyes.

He was an older associate that had been working there for a while.

"That would be me," I confirmed.

"You guys get younger every time they ship you over here," he laughed and continued, "We have burned through a lot of managers at this place. They all come here with a vision to change everything. Most of them quit. It is something that we call 'island fever'. They start missing home, become extremely lonely, and then leave. What are your intentions here?"

I thought about his question. I wasn't really sure. I guess I was just climbing the corporate ladder. I never really thought about what I wanted in the end. I never wondered why I was climbing, I just climbed. I guess it was to make more money, or gain work experience. I didn't really know.

"You know," I said, "to be honest, I'm not even sure myself. I guess I have just continued working, to make more money and survive. I've never had time to think about that."

He crossed his arms together, lifted his eyebrow and grinned a little. He seemed thrown off by my answer.

"You're not sure why you took a management position in Maui?" he asked and chuckled a little, "What are you running away from?"

His question was strange. It was a question that made sense in my head, but I didn't know how he would know to ask it. In a way, I was running from something. I was running from my past. I was searching for the new, the pinnacle, like Chad said. I wasn't sure if, or where I was going to find it, but Maui was where I was starting.

"Don't tell me," he said quickly before I could respond, "Your girlfriend left you."

I laughed a little. Then, I looked up and smiled at him.

"Am I right?" he said, smiling back at me.

"Kind of," I said a little embarrassed, "she cheated on me".

"I knew it!" he said excitedly, "You must be the youngest kid I have ever seen in this position. Tell me, what the hell is a kid your age doing wasting your life away as a manager?"

I never thought about that before. I always just continued to work and make money. I thought that was the normal thing to do, but he made it sound uncommon.

"I don't know," I said, laughing at myself a little.

"I like your honesty kid," he said with a chuckle, "My advice to you is to get out of management. You are in Maui, enjoy yourself. You'll find out soon enough, when you start doing our payroll, that we make just as much as you. Sometimes, we make more money than you do, with a lot less stress."

"Really?" I said surprised.

"Yes, kid," he confirmed, "Maui is different from the rest of the world. On the mainland, everyone slaves away, day after day, to make a living. They say they do it to make their lives better. I say they are wasting time by working too much. It makes no sense. They spend years at jobs that they hate to save up enough money to fly here for a couple of weeks. After that, they go back to the jobs that they hate. You have an opportunity to enjoy the island all the time. That is what you should do. You are young, don't waste your life."

He made the world sound so simple. I felt like what he was saying was true. Why would you spend most of your life working and slaving away just to have a couple weeks of vacation? If you live in paradise, then you can experience it every day. He made it sound like money wasn't so important. Maybe he was right.

***

"You are in direct violation of our contract," a lady in a business suit shouted angrily at me, "We were contracted to that specific room and we are not going to settle for less. Have you forgotten that you are dealing with a group of highly trained lawyers? I will bury this establishment."

It was a nightmare at work. A couple of months had passed since I first arrived in Maui. The management job was stressful. I have worked over eighty hours per week, every week, since I started. I didn't have time to enjoy the island. I hadn't seen anything except the hotel property and the inside of my office.

There was a large group of lawyers that were contracted to stay at the hotel. They were paying a substantial amount of money. They contracted a specific room in the hotel, but it was given away to someone else. The person that was occupying the room was a guest that had visited the hotel, every year, for the last thirty years. Her husband had died while snorkeling in the ocean. She had placed his ashes on the cliff above where he had died. She always stayed in that same room, because she could see that cliff from her room. It was also the room that they stayed in when he was alive.

The sales manager forgot to check the notes about the room before issuing the contract. She promised the lawyer group that they would receive that specific room. She wasn't at the hotel to speak with the group leader, so I had to.

"I sincerely apologize about the situation, ma'am. I will speak with the general manager and we will find a solution promptly," I said apologetically.

"A solution?" she shouted in condescending disbelief, "The solution is clear. You made a mistake, therefore you must evict the people that are staying in that room immediately. I don't understand what is so difficult about that?"

"I understand your frustration, ma'am," I said calmly, in an attempt to validate her anger, "Please allow me ten minutes with the general manager to formulate a plan."

She huffed at me without a response.

I walked over to the general manager's office to discuss the situation. He could care less. He showed no concern for it and simply told me to remove the old lady from the room. He said that the lawyer group was paying more money. He told me that we couldn't afford to lose that contract. I was annoyed and unsatisfied with his response.

I couldn't believe that I had to tell this old lady to move. That room represented so much to her. That was the one time of the year that she was able to mourn the death of her husband. She never asked for anything else. She was a very sweet lady and that was her only request from us.

I returned to the leader of the group.

"Thank you for your patience, ma'am," I began to speak in a soft tone, "May I interest you in a better room? It is significantly larger. It is a suite."

She turned her face and looked me directly in the eyes with disgust. Her face came so close that I could feel her breath. Suddenly, she spat. The spit stuck to my face and started to drip. I slowly lifted my right arm and wiped the spit off with my sleeve. She turned her back towards me and crossed her arms. Her nose pointed to the air above her.

"You will not try to bribe me. I can not be bought," she said with her back still turned, "You will get me what I asked for or I will sue this hotel and you personally. I will win, because I am exceptional at what I do. You will lose everything. I will make sure of it."

I couldn't believe this woman. I couldn't believe that she just spat in my face and then threatened to sue me. I was shocked by the way she treated me. What a horrible human being.

I shouldn't have tried to fix the situation. The general manager already told me to evict the old lady from the room. I really didn't want to do that to her. I thought that maybe there was another way. I was so wrong.

I thought back to what the old associate told me about management. He was right. I didn't know why I was dealing with this. I could just apply for a simple job, like him, and enjoy the island.

I moved the old lady to another room. She was devastated. She said that she understood, but she cried the whole time. It was awkward and the other guests stared at her as she cried. I felt terrible. I never wanted to do that again.

I quit one week after that day.

***

I laid in my hammock staring up at the beautiful night sky. I was on the edge of a seaside cliff. The sky was like glitter spilled onto a black canvas. I saw satellites and comets cut through the sky over twenty times throughout the night. It was silent besides the sound of the waves crashing against the cliff. There were no lights except for the stars above. I rocked gently back and forth in the hammock. Never, in my whole life, had I ever felt so relaxed and at peace.

I received a front office job at a different hotel, just like the old associate had advised. No more management. It was a fancier hotel. He was right about the pay. They offered more than the management position. I had to wait a week before I started the new position, so I was out exploring the island. I decided to spend the night in my hammock on the seaside cliff.

I woke up the next morning refreshed. I was more free than I had ever been. I didn't have a job or girlfriend to attend to. I didn't have to pretend anymore, like at the church and with Jacob. I had no obligations to anyone. No one even knew I was there, on that cliffside. The island was so far from everything, that nothing else mattered. The past was unable to navigate the ocean waters, and therefore it was left on the mainland's shore. There was no judgment. No one knew me for who I was in the past, only for what I was in that moment. The moment was all that mattered.

I rolled up the hammock into a little bag, and hiked back to my moped. I left it on the side of the road. I placed the hammock into the seat compartment and then started to drive along the scenic road.

The hills were covered in a lush green blanket. There were red clay trails that lined the sides of the hills. The road led along the side of the vast blue ocean. Ocean was all you could see in the distance. There were beautiful beaches below that were enclosed by the towering seaside cliffs. Strong waves crashed against volcanic rock formations below. The sun shot a bright yellow ray across the rippling ocean. It was a breathtaking drive.

I started to drive through a small town called Paia. There were many people walking around in their bare feet. They wore hippie style clothing and had braided hair or dreadlocks. Some of them were playing guitar and other musical instruments. There was a small group that practiced yoga at a beach park. A few people walked towards the ocean with surfboards in their hands. I decided to park my moped and take a walk around the area.

"Aloha," a man said from the grass at the beach park.

He was a younger man. He wore baggy hippie styled pants with no shirt. He looked like he hadn't showered in a few days. His hair was in dreadlocks dangling to his shoulders. He sat crisscrossed with his hands resting gently on his knees.

"Aloha," I replied back.

"Why don't you take a seat here on the grass?" he said in a calm voice with a smile, "I can read your energy and predict your future."

He was definitely a strange man, but he seemed harmless. I was curious about what he was going to do. I didn't have anywhere to be. I had all the time in the world. So, I listened to him, and sat in the grass.

He reached out and gently pulled my hands towards him. He turned my hands over so that he could see my palms. He started to study the lines on my hands. He then slowly lifted his head up and stared directly into my eyes. He studied my eyes for a while.

"You are in the process of letting go," he said suddenly, "There are many hardships that you carry within your spirit, but you are open to change. You seek enlightenment. Your spirit is genuine."

I laughed a little and said, "You figured all of that out by looking at me?"

"No," he responded gently, "You told me that with your energy. Your energy is strong."

"Wow," I said slightly interested, "So what does that mean?"

He returned my hands gently to my lap.

"In your energy, I sense that life has been difficult for you in the past," he began to explain, "Life has been difficult enough for you to be open to change. Maui is a vortex of energy. I see a great amount of enlightenment and change in your future."

I couldn't tell if this man was serious, dramatic or slightly crazy. He happened to be right in his assumptions about my past, but I felt like those were general statements. They could have applied to anyone.

He rose from the grass and placed his hands together in prayer form. He bowed towards me and then walked off to the ocean.

I stood there with my head tilted. I was slightly confused about the whole situation. I couldn't understand why he wanted to do that. He didn't ask me for money or anything in return. He just gave me his thoughts and left.

He was right, though. I did have a lot of hardships in my past. I intended to keep them there, in the past. I was looking to change my life in a lot of ways. In some ways, I already did. I quit my management position. Done, just like that. I had worked hard for many years to achieve that position; since I was a young kid in Colorado. I was searching for the pinnacle. I wanted to use the energy of love to make the world a better place. Maybe, that was the enlightenment that he was talking about. Maybe, I was going to find that here.

I went back to my moped and continued to explore the island.

***

The sound of drums thundered throughout the beach. Hundreds of people were dancing and swinging their arms around to the beat of the drums. Many were naked. Some were wearing paint on their bodies. A few wore clothes. The sun was diving into the distant ocean from the sky.

I sat on a tree branch and observed the spectacle. There were small circles of people gathered together. They smoked marijuana and ate food laced with drugs. A few people were out surfing the waves into the shore. The water was reflecting a golden layer from the sun.

The sun submerged itself into the distant ocean. The drums came to a sudden stop. People started to cheer and clap. Some left after the sun had set. Many people stayed.

A large bonfire was lit in the middle of the beach. Everyone gathered around it. There were people with guitars and ukuleles strumming songs. Others would sing along to the songs. A woman stuck the ends of a large stick into the fire, igniting both sides. She began to twirl it around. Another woman was spinning a fiery hula hoop around her waist. A couple was dancing naked together. They slowly orbited the fire.

A man made his way closer to the bonfire. He stood in the middle of the people. The rest gathered around him. He was shirtless and wore only a pair of swimming shorts. Everyone's attention was drawn to him. A few people started to play their drums. Everyone began to clap to the beat of the drums. He swayed gently to the beat and began to sing.

We only have one world

but we fill it with greed

A few will be taking it all

while the rest are in need

We're longing for the peace of the people

but the richest will taint it with evil

It's time that we make the world equal

Unified with love until we succeed

The man finished his song and everyone cheered. They continued to dance around the fire.

The man that sang the song came and sat on the tree next to me.

"Aloha brother," he said with a smile.

"Aloha," I replied looking over to him, "That was a nice song you sang over there."

"Oh, Mahalo. Blessings my brother," he said gratefully.

"What inspired you to sing those words?" I was interested in his thoughts and ideas.

"The world is full of hate," he began to explain dramatically, "Most of that hate comes from money. Money is the root of all evil in this world. There are millions of people and little children starving to death. Why? It is because big corporations and CEOs hoard all the money and resources in this world. They take more than they need. If everyone in this world shared everything they had, then the world would be a better place. There would be plenty of resources for everyone. We have the technology to provide clean water and shelter to everyone in the world. The only reason we don't do this is because of greedy businessmen. They waste resources that could save these people. They allow them to die, with no remorse."

"Wow, that's intense," I responded back.

"And worse," he quickly continued, "They destroy the Earth with their greed. They pollute the oceans, jungles, forests and freshwater rivers. If we don't change now, the world will be completely destroyed. There is so much corruption and power from the wealthy one percent. It makes it hard to change the system. The system they have created is toxic and will destroy us all. They have forgotten what it means to be human. They don't have compassion or love in their hearts for anyone, anymore. We must find a way to heal them. Love can change them."

"How would you change the system?" I asked curiously.

"Well," he began to collect his thoughts, "People are naturally good. People want to help make the world a better place. We don't need money for the world to function. There are enough resources for everyone to have an equal amount of them."

"If there is no money, then why would people want to work?"

"That is a great question," he said with excitement, "Most people believe they work to make money. The true reason they work is for satisfaction. They enjoy the feeling of accomplishment. Everyone in the world would happily volunteer their time. They would only seek satisfaction. The new world system would provide for all of their needs. They wouldn't have to worry about the basics like water, food and shelter. All of those things would be given to everyone on the planet for free."

"Interesting," I said, slightly skeptical of the concept.

"Technology," he continued, "has provided us with robots. They can do all of the jobs that people don't like to do. Robots can build the buildings, farm the food, purify the water and much more. There would only be a small portion of jobs that humans would have to do themselves. That means that if everyone volunteered a small portion of their life to do the work that requires humans, then each person would only need to work for twenty years. The rest of their lives could be focused on doing the things that they love, like their passions. They could spend more time connecting with other people. I believe it is possible to have peace on Earth. We have to come together as one world and one race. The human race. We have to stop dividing ourselves with imaginary borders and unite together."

"Your concepts are very interesting," I said, still pondering what he said, "but how would we be able to unite the world together? You make it sound so simple, but I'm not so sure that it is. There are hundreds of leaders in the world. Who would become the leader of this new one world system that you are talking about?"

"We would elect leaders democratically," he said, still thinking as he spoke, "but the system would be operated by a computer. The computer would be able to track all of the available resources in the world and allocate them equally amongst the people."

"The world has been fighting wars since the dawn of civilization. As a result, it has formed hundreds of nations. Each nation has their own leader. Do you really think that all of those leaders will simply give up their power?" I said skeptically.

"Once we show them how much better the world could be with this new system, they will be excited to be a part of it. Right now, we live in a broken world. We have to heal it. Love and compassion has been lost with-in the current system. Now, we have to change that. We have to inspire people to come together and seek something better for our world. Love will always prevail."

Suddenly, the rhythm of the drums became louder than before. The man and I looked back towards the crowd. He jumped off the tree and began to dance wildly around the bonfire.

I sat on the tree and watched as everyone danced, twirled fire sticks, banged on their drums, shouted and clapped. I started to think about what he had said. I pondered the idea of having a one world system. I thought about what it would be like if everyone shared everything that they had. It was a nice concept. I really liked the idea of a peaceful world. Who wouldn't want to rid the world of suffering? He made it sound so simple.

***

A year had passed since I explored the island and met that man at the bonfire. Life was simple on Maui. I swam with fish and sharks along the reefs. I coasted with the turtles along the current. I went on boats to see the humpback whales leap out of the water and slap their bodies against the surface. I learned how to surf. I went on every hike the island had to offer.

I purchased an ukulele and started a daily routine. I would sit underneath one of the banyan trees and play songs that I wrote. They were inspired by the concepts the man shared with me at the bonfire. I wrote about the one world system and about the spread of peace and love. I thought that maybe through music, I could inspire a change in the world. I did this everyday, even on the days that I worked. If I worked, I would come and play afterwards. People placed money beside me while I played but I tried to give it back. I remembered what the man told me at the bonfire. We don't need money to function in this world.

One day, an older man came over and sat next to me as I played. He was a joyful man with a look of contentment.

"It's great," he said with a big smile, "Your songs are great. We need more of that in this world."

I stopped playing for a minute and smiled back at him.

"Mahalo," I said, "I appreciate that."

Mahalo was the Hawaiian word for thank you. Most people on the island used it instead of thank you.

"You know," the man said. It looked as if an idea sparked into his head, "I work for a man that custom builds ukuleles. He has a little shop here. He told me to look out for new talent. You should stop by the shop next week."

He handed me a business card.

"Prepare a couple of songs for him and then come play them at that address next week," he said patting me on the back, "Aloha to you brother."

The man walked away and left me with the business card. I felt excited. I didn't want to receive money, but that was something different. It was a possible opportunity to spread the message in my songs further. That was what that man at the bonfire told me about. We don't need money in this world, just love.

Once I finished playing my set of songs, I decided to ride my moped over to a little grass area beside the beach. There was a tall tree there. I loved to sit underneath it. I stared out into the vast ocean and pondered my thoughts. It was one of my favorite places on the island.

I leaned my back against the trunk of the tree. I had a little notebook with me and a pencil to write down my ideas. I loved to write songs and stories there. I was trying to think of a new song that I could write for the ukulele shop.

"Aloha," I heard the voice of a woman from behind me.

I turned around to see if she was speaking to me. She was.

"Aloha," I responded back.

She was a short woman in her early thirties. She had brown hair and an athletic body build. She was overly enthusiastic and animated in the way that she communicated.

"May I see what you are writing?" she asked as she sat beside me in the grass.

"Sure," I said, offering her my notebook, "I am writing a new song."

She always stopped what she was doing and looked me directly in the eyes when I spoke. It felt slightly awkward. She took the notebook from my hands and began to flip through it.

"This is great," she said in a chipper tone, "I can see from your writing that you have a true desire to change the world. You are also an excellent writer. I'm sure you will make a lot of money someday."

"Yea," I said slightly embarrassed. I felt a little corny when she said that, "A man told me about these concepts at a bonfire when I first arrived in Maui. He believes that we don't need money in this world, that we simply need to be unified together as one. I had a friend in San Diego that said something similar before I arrived here. He told me that using love to change the world is the pinnacle. That's why I decided to write songs about it. To share the message. I am reluctant to receive money. That's not the reason that I write."

"I can see that," she said giggling, "Do you have somewhere to be tomorrow?"

I thought about my work schedule for a moment.

"No, actually," I replied, "I am free."

"That's excellent," she said enthusiastically, "I know someone that I think you should meet. Are you interested?"

I thought about her invitation for a moment. I had just met her. I didn't know anything about her. She didn't know that much about me. I didn't even know her name. I guess she seemed harmless.

"Sure," I agreed.

"It's pretty far," she said, making sure I was committed.

"That's fine," I reassured, "I have nowhere to be tomorrow."

"Ok, great," she said jumping to her feet, "We can take my car."

I followed her to her car. It was a car that was four wheel drive. We got in and she started driving towards the jungle area on the island.

"You have extremely strong and positive energy," she said suddenly.

"Mahalo," I said and laughed a little.

She glimpsed over at me with a smile and then turned her eyes back to the road.

We drove for two hours before she stopped at the entrance of a driveway. She got out of the car and unlocked a yellow gate that was blocking the entrance. She returned back to the car and we drove in. We followed a long dirt road. It was covered by palm leaves and hundreds of other species of plants that brushed against the sides of the vehicle as we drove.

The end of the driveway revealed a large mansion. It was three stories high and painted to blend in with the jungle. It was the last thing I expected to see in the middle of the jungle. The place was incredible.

It was built in the form of a cylinder. There were large balconies that wrapped around each level of the house. There was a private stream that flowed right beside the house and a little bridge that we crossed to walk to the front door. There was a further extension of the mansion that branched off behind the cylinder part in the shape of a rectangle. The place was enormous.

We entered through the front door which revealed the inside of the cylinder part of the mansion. The whole area was open, with a long chimney directly in the center. It was filled with large windows. There was a staircase that spiraled up the edge of the house, with an entrance to each floor. There was a shiny black grand piano at the end of the staircase. From the top floor you could see all the way to the ocean through miles of jungle. It was positioned on the top of a hill.

I was amazed at where she had brought me. I couldn't imagine how much a place like this would have cost. It had to be worth millions.

An older man casually walked down the spiral staircase. He had pure white hair that was to his shoulder in length. It was brushed to the back, out of his face.

"Hi, sweetie," the man said.

"Hi, daddy" the woman said happily, "I brought someone for you to meet."

He looked over towards me and smiled as he continued to walk down the stairs.

"My father is the person that I wanted you to meet," she said excitedly, "I know you said you don't like money, but the things that he has done with money are incredible."

The man laughed as he heard his daughter speak about him and approached me with a handshake.

"She is referring to the global project that I am working on," the man said proudly, "I am a quantum physicist and an inventor. I have been inventing new technology since I was a child. The technology that I have developed will provide free energy to anyone in impoverished countries throughout the world."

"Wow," I said, fascinated, "that's incredible."

"Thank you," he said humbly, "The idea was inspired by a Tesla coil. I believe the whole universe is like a Tesla coil. I fund this project through my other inventions. I have patents on touch screen technologies and a variety of radar systems. I sell these technologies to governments throughout the world. Many of those technologies are currently being used. I heard my daughter mention that you don't like money. Money is not what you have to worry about. Money is simply the system we use to exchange resources, time, ideas and more. When people want to support your ideas they can give you money. That allows you to buy more resources. Evil is what you should be aware of. Why don't you stay for dinner and we can chat more about these concepts?."

"That sounds great," I said with excitement, "I would be honored."

The three of us continued to discuss the concepts of a system with money and a system without. He showed me pictures of the free energy villages he built in various countries throughout Africa. He showed me the water catchment systems that he created. They absorb the water in the air and convert it to fresh water. He explained quantum physics and shared some of his theories.

We decided to cook together. We made pasta while we chatted. He began to discuss religion and God. He attempted to prove God's existence through science, which I thought was an interesting combination. He believed that every human serves a certain purpose in life. He related it to how every living thing has some sort of contribution to the ecosystem. We then discussed the concept of multiple universes and time travel as we finished cooking dinner.

We sat down at a long dinner table positioned in the giant cylinder room. As we ate the pasta he continued to share his knowledge and his ideas with me. He drew out diagrams and little sketches explaining his theories. I was impressed with how intelligent he was. He explained everything so clearly.

After dinner we moved the discussion to the top floor. We looked out at the view while we talked. He told me stories about his life. He revealed that he was a billionaire. He told me about meetings that he had with leaders from all around the world. He met with presidents, kings, queens and prime ministers to sell his technologies. He told me that some of those leaders were corrupt but many of them meant well. His influence was widespread.

I learned so much from him. It was interesting to talk with someone that was rich. Someone that was part of the 'one percent' that the man on the beach told me about. He didn't appear to be evil at all. This man was truly trying to make a difference in the world. In fact, I thought he was doing more than most people I talked to. He was doing more than all of the people that told me we needed to change the world. It was a paradox.

"Why don't you stay the night?" the man offered.

"If you don't mind?" I asked graciously.

"Not at all," he said with a smile, "It's getting late. That will be all of the discussions for today. What you do in your life matters. When you think in abundance, not scarcity, you are in a position to change in the world."

I nodded and then walked up the spiral staircase to my room for the night. It had a beautiful view. You could see all of the stars over the ocean. The jungle was a silhouette.

I stayed awake and stared at the view. I thought about everything that happened. Life was crazy. I started under the banyan tree, playing music. I took a trip with a woman that I didn't even know. I still don't know her name. I met her father, who is a billionaire. We had profound discussions throughout the night. I didn't know his name either. I thought about his views on money. I was so reluctant to accept it from anyone. They may have supported the concepts that I sang about, but they still supported it with money. I attempted to reconcile these thoughts before I drifted to sleep.

***

I followed the instructions on the business card. I had my ukulele with me. It led me to a little shopping center in Lahaina. There was a little ukulele shop that I entered. I didn't see the man that had given me the business card, but I was sure that this was the place.

"You must be Gene," a middle aged man said smiling.

The man wore a Hawaiian shirt with sunglasses. He was in white shorts and flip flops.

"Yes, that's me," I said surprised, "How did you know my name?"

I never told the man that gave me the business card. I didn't even know his name. I couldn't figure out how he knew my name.

"It's a small island," he said with a chuckle, "Everyone knows you, Gene. You are the banyan tree ukulele guy. I'm the store owner here."

"Oh wow," I replied, "I didn't know people paid much attention to me under that tree."

He laughed at what I said, "People are always watching."

I thought back to what the concierge lady said at the hotel. Maybe she wasn't so crazy after all. She was right, the whole island sees everything.

"I like the way you play," he began to say, "I want to custom build you an ukulele. I think it would be great if you recorded some music with it. We will figure out the best wood to use, the type of strings you like and the body design. That will help promote my ukulele brand."

"Mahalo," I said humbly.

"I've typed up a contract for you," he said and handed me a three page document, "You can read it over yourself. It basically says that you agree to record some music using the ukulele I will build for you."

"That sounds great," I said excitedly, "I'll read it over now."

"While you do that, I'm going to walk around the shopping center and grab a few things. I'll be back," he said as he left the store.

I stood at the counter of the store reading over the contract. The store had a display of ukuleles lining the walls. The counter I was at had a glass display case with hand made wooden watches. Outside of the store they had sets of tables and chairs for people to sit at.

"Gene!" I heard the store owner call from outside the shop.

I left the contract on the counter and walked out to the tables. He was standing there with a girl. She was an incredibly beautiful girl. Her dark brown hair had a reddish glow from the sunlight. It was arranged beautifully in a long French braid that flowed down the center of her back. Her skin was smooth like silk. Her eyes were wide with a mesmerizing glow. She wore a short strapless sundress that revealed her delicate shoulders. She had a little brown ukulele in her hands. She held it above her heart.

"This girl asked me if I knew someone she could play ukulele with," he said pointing his thumb towards her, "I told her she should come to my shop and play with you."

My heart warmed and started to beat a bit faster. My gaze never left her. She stood there and looked towards me. She quickly looked back down at her ukulele, and then back up towards me again. Her cheeks produced two rosy red circles on either side.

"Well," the store owner said bursting into the moment, "I'll leave you two to it."

He walked back into the store.

"I'm Gene," I said in a soft, shy tone.

"I'm Caro," she responded back with the same tone.

I could tell by her faint accent that she wasn't from the United States or Maui.

"Where are you from?" I asked.

"Argentina," she said with a grin.

"How long are you visiting for?" I asked curiously.

"I'm not sure," she replied giggling, "I've been here for a couple of months. I love it. I want to stay as long as possible."

"You don't have a job or anything you have to go back to?"

"Nope," she said cheerfully, "I'm just traveling the world."

"That's incredible," I said in amazement, "I'm jealous."

She laughed when I said that.

"How can you be jealous?" she asked, taken aback, "You live in paradise!"

"Yea true," I said laughing a little, "So, do you want to play some ukulele?"

She nodded and we sat down at the table. We played popular songs and she taught me some songs in Spanish as well. We laughed when I couldn't pronounce the Spanish words correctly. We sang together and played for the next couple of hours. The hours that passed felt like a couple of minutes.

"Hey," I stopped playing for a moment, "If you're not doing anything tomorrow. Would you like me to show you some of my favorite places on the island?"

She looked up with a smile.

"I would love that," she responded.

"You don't mind riding on the back of a moped, do you?" I asked.

"No," she said with a chuckle, "I've ridden on the back of a motorbike before."

I smiled and she smiled back.

***

The wind blew in our hair as we cruised through the Maui roads on my moped. She hugged me tightly from behind as I drove.

We stopped at the beach and snorkeled for a while. We swam together through schools of bright colored fish and waved to the turtles. I had seen all of these things before, but being together with Caro made them feel brand new again.

We climbed up my favorite hike on the island and looked out to the view. You could see a large section of the island from the top. We played ukulele and sang a few songs there before we returned back.

We picked mangos and bananas from the trees and ate them on the ocean cliffs. We dangled our feet off the edge and told stories of our pasts. She told me of her upbringing in Buenos Aires. She told me the reason that she came to Maui. She had been dating a guy from Europe for a couple of years. The relationship seemed perfect, but he left her without warning. They planned to start a life together in Europe. She even purchased flight tickets to go. She was devastated and decided to fly to Maui instead.

I thought about her story. It seemed like we both came to Maui to start new lives. I don't think either of us had any idea what we were looking for. We were simply searching for something new, something different.

I decided to call in sick at work so that we could spend more time together. We drove to a beautiful beach that was secluded. We climbed down some black volcanic rocks to arrive at the beach. No one was there, just the two of us.

The sun was beginning to set into the ocean. We brought a blanket to sit on. We held each other on the blanket as the sun started to sink into the ocean. We played ukulele together and sang out to the ocean waves as they crashed against the shore.

I gathered sticks while she continued to sing and play. Her voice was angelic. It sent chills through my body with every note that she sang. She sang with passion and a brightened smile on her face. She glowed in the sunset.

I started a fire and we cooked some potatoes. After we ate, we laid together on the blanket and stared up at the sky. We were waiting for the stars to appear.

"What do you think the purpose of life is?" I asked her while we continued to stare at the sky.

"Why does life have to have a purpose?" she replied.

"I guess it doesn't" I respond back, pondering her answer.

I wasn't expecting the answer. She made an interesting point. Why did life have to have a purpose?

"You don't constantly have to be chasing after something in your life," she said while she continued to look up at the sky, "Life is full of little insignificant moments that carry no meaning or purpose at all. They are often beautiful moments. You can miss out on them when you're constantly chasing after something else."

A few stars started to appear.

I felt like what she said was true, but hard to accept. I lived my whole life believing that I had to chase after something. I was chasing the pinnacle Chad told me about. I was trying to make a change in the world, like the man at the bonfire had told me. She spoke beauty to the simplest things in life. The things that we miss during that chase.

"There doesn't have to be a higher purpose or meaning to our lives," she continued, "Look up at the billions of stars and planets in the universe. Humans are a small insignificant part of that. There is so much more beyond ourselves."

The sky was beginning to fill with a lot more stars than before. The fire crackled quietly in the background.

"Humans are the only species that try to search for a higher purpose or meaning for their lives," she continued, "You watch the animals and they simply enjoy the nature around them. I think you should enjoy every moment of your life and spend time with the people that you love. Life is beautiful and simple. People complicate it."

I laid quietly and pondered her words. Even the billionaire scientist believed that everyone has a purpose in life. She made life sound so simple and beautiful. She was right about the animals. They don't chase after complicated goals or attempt to find deeper meaning for their lives. They simply exist and enjoy their existence. Her mindset was so contrary to everything I learned throughout my life.

"So, what do you want to do with your life?" I asked her.

"I want to travel the world," she said. She turned and looked at me with a smile, "I want to enjoy my life."

The sky was full of stars and the Milky Way was visible.

"Can I come with you?" I asked. I turned to her with a smile.

"I would love that," she replied.

We cuddled closer together. It was still just the two of us at the beach. The waves continued to crash against the shore as the fire crackled in the background. It was dark. The only light came from the stars and the fire. We began to kiss each other's lips and remove our clothes. We made love into the night and fell asleep together under the stars.

THIRTEEN

I stood on the edge of the highway wearing a backpack and my ukulele. My thumb was up in the air, visible to the passing cars. Caro was beside me with a backpack and her ukulele. The sun beat mercilessly down on us. It was extremely hot. We had been standing on the side of the road for hours.

Caro and I had been dating for a couple of months now. After the night on the beach in Maui, I decided to quit my job and go travel the world with her. I placed some clothes into a backpack and took my ukulele. I had some money saved from my job, but not too much.

I recorded the music for the ukulele shop before I left. They liked it so much that they decided to make Caro an ukulele as well. I left them a stack of CDs to pass out. They wished us well. They dropped us off at the airport and we boarded a one way flight to Australia.

We were hitchhiking our way down to Melbourne to board a flight to Tasmania. We sent emails to jobs throughout Australia and received a reply from a small restaurant in Tasmania. The restaurant was on an island next to Tasmania called Bruny Island. The population of Bruny Island was about five hundred people. Significantly smaller than Maui.

An old truck pulled off to the side of the highway. A man rolled down the window and shouted out to us.

"Where you's all headed?" the man shouted in a heavy Australian accent.

"We are trying to get down to the airport in Melbourne," I said as I walked up to his window.

"Righty-o! You could just jump in the back," he said pointing his thumb to the cargo bed of the truck.

We both climbed into the truck and leaned against the back windows. We held onto our backpack's and ukuleles as he pulled back onto the highway. He began to drive South towards Melbourne.

We spent eight hours in the back of the truck. He stopped a few times to fill up the fuel tank and use the restroom. We drove through larger cities and smaller towns. There were many stretches of nothing but vast hills in the distance. The landscape gradually changed from dry desert to lush green the closer we got to Melbourne.

Melbourne was filled with green trees and towering skyscrapers. The man dropped us off fairly close to the airport, so we walked the rest of the way.

Once we arrived at the airport, we booked our flights to Tasmania. We spoke with the manager of the restaurant through email. His name was Ash. He told us that once we arrived at the airport in Tasmania, he could drive us the rest of the way.

We arrived in Tasmania and Ash picked us up in his car, just like he said he would. We drove for another hour before we arrived at a ferry boat. He drove the car onto the boat and we took a thirty minute ride to Bruny Island.

Ash was a tall awkward looking man with black hair and a baby face. Some of his teeth seem to be slightly rotten. He had a beer belly and wore an old fuzzy sweater.

We drove off of the ferry boat and began the drive towards the restaurant. The island was beautiful. There were little kangaroos that hopped across the island landscape. It wasn't a tropical island like Maui. They said it snows in the winter. There was rough terrain and tall cliffs towering against the seaside. We drove across The Neck of Bruny island. The Neck was a thin strip of land that separated the North and South seas.

We arrived at the restaurant. There were only two buildings. One was the restaurant and the other was a tiny convenience store. A little further from the restaurant was a little house near the ocean. It was a three bedroom house that was shared by some of the staff.

Ash told us that there was a little water tank for the house which was filled once a month. We had to limit the amount of water we used to shower, cook, clean and drink. The food on the island was extremely expensive and limited. We would assign one person to drive to Tasmania every two weeks with an order of groceries for everyone.

Ash dropped us off at the house and showed us our bedroom. The room had a hardwood floor and a double size bed. There was a little window that looked out to the backyard where the water tank was. He told us the weekly rent for the bedroom would be taken out of our paychecks. He then told us that he would send us our work schedules via email and left.

"Hello, I'm Harriet," a woman said with a British accent. She poked her head into our room.

Caro and I introduced ourselves to her. She was in her early thirties. She had blinding pale white skin and her hair was a blonde tangled mess. She wore a sleeping robe with pajama pants and looked exhausted.

"So, listen," she started to speak in an irritated tone. "You two are a couple, and your room is right next to mine. I don't want to hear the two of you having sex with each other late into the night. Usually, I live in a large castle back in England. The walls aren't so thin there. Here, the walls are very thin. I came here because I am writing a book and need this secluded island to help me write. Don't make any noise when you are in the house, otherwise, I can not focus on my writing. As long as you respect my simple requests, then we shall get along fine."

Caro and I stared at Harriet with disbelief in our eyes. She was a very intense person with an overwhelming personality.

"That's very interesting," I said with an awkward smile of encouragement, "What are you writing about?"

"Well," she said flattered with herself, "I am writing an incredible book. I am related to royalty in England. That means that success is in my blood. You will have to wait until I am finished. It is a magnificent tale of love, honor, courage and determination. I'm sure you would love it."

Caro and I looked at each other. We tried to hold back our judgmental laughter.

"Can't wait to read it," I said with an awkward excitement.

Harriet left the room.

Caro and I began to unpack some of our clothes and hang them in the closet. We set up the room to our liking and then started to get ready for bed. It was a long day of traveling and it was getting late.

There was a little hallway outside of our bedroom that led to the other rooms and the shared bathroom. Caro and I went to the bathroom to brush our teeth before bed.

"I'm sorry," Harriet said while abruptly poking her head into the bathroom. She made us flinch a little, "It's just that I'm writing an important part of my book. I need quiet. I can hear you two brushing your teeth from my room. Could you please keep it quieter? Maybe, you could shut the door all the way."

Caro and I looked at Harriet holding our toothbrushes in our hands. We were puzzled by her request.

"Sure," I mumbled with my mouth full of toothpaste.

She slammed the bathroom door and went back to her room.

Caro and I looked at each other with shared confusion. We finished brushing our teeth and made our way back to the bedroom.

We started to snuggle underneath the covers and drift to sleep. There was a sudden *knock* on the wall behind us. It startled us. We sat up in bed and listened.

"No love making tonight!" Harriet shouted from the other room, "I need complete silence to focus."

Caro and I looked at each other and quietly giggled a bit. We laid back down and fell asleep.

***

I set the stack of dirty dishes that I had picked up back down on the table. I looked outside of the restaurant towards the parking lot.

The restaurant had glass walls so that you could have a clear view of the ocean. The dirt parking lot was visible from inside as well. I watched as Harriet drifted her car into the dirt parking lot. A huge cloud of dust floated into the air from her aggressive entrance. She quickly exited her car, leaving the door open, as she stormed into the restaurant.

Caro and I had been working at the restaurant for a couple of months. We bussed tables. We received a paycheck each week and used that to purchase our bi-weekly rations of food. We saved some for future travels.

The island was beautiful. Caro and I had explored most of it. We chased the little kangaroos around to take photos. We even found a pure white kangaroo with red eyes. There was a lighthouse on the edge of the ocean that we visited. We took night photography there. The views were incredible. One of the nights, there was a geomagnetic storm and we saw the Aurora Australis reflecting off the ocean.

Unsurprisingly, no one liked Harriet at the restaurant. She was extremely demanding and was difficult to work with. Ash gradually started to cut her hours each week. This week she didn't have any.

"Ash!" she screamed at the top of her lungs.

Ash was standing at the bar and looked over to her.

"I haven't received my hours for this week. Tell me, why is that?" she said in an aggravated tone.

"I thought you needed to write your book?" Ash said in a condescending tone.

"Get fucked," Harriet snapped angrily, "You know that I need to keep a couple of shifts."

"You're done here," Ash said nonchalantly, "No one wants to put up with your shit anymore. You're fired. Finished. G'day."

Harriet gasped in disbelief. She swung herself around and furiously marched out of the restaurant. She jumped into her car and slammed the door. She started to drive off until she crashed into a car that was parked beside her. Her right headlight shattered on the ground. She jumped out of the car and started to walk back to the house.

I continued to work. I brought the dishes to the dishwasher and then returned to the restaurant tables to wipe them down. I watched as the last customers walked to their car. It wasn't the car Harriet crashed into. I wondered who's car she had hit.

I was looking out of the window when a group of motorcycles pulled up to the restaurant. Their motorcycles roared and left a cloud of dust behind them as they approached. They were rough looking men. They had shaggy beards and all leather motorcycle gear on. The backs of their leather jackets had large confederate flags. They swung open the restaurant door with force and walked up to the bar.

Ash was still standing at the bar when they approached. They started to have an intense conversation. I tried to listen to what they were saying while I continued to work. It was hard to understand them because they spoke with rough Australian accents. The conversation had come to an end. Ash handed them a black leather bag. They carried it out of the restaurant with them and jumped back on their motorcycles. A cloud of dust filled the restaurant window as they drove away.

That was extremely shady, I thought. I wondered what was in the bag and why he handed it to them. I also couldn't believe that Harriet crashed into that car and just walked away. It had been a wild afternoon at the restaurant.

Caro and I finished our work shifts and started walking back to the house. It was a short two minute walk. We saw our other house mate, Christian, as we approached the house. He was running out of the house naked and full of soap suds.

Christian occupied the third room. He came a month after we met Harriet. He traveled all over Tasmania in a van and decided to stop in Bruny Island to work. He was twenty three years old. He used to attend college in the United States but decided to drop out. He flew to Australia and started traveling instead.

"Fucking Harriet!" he shouted as he ran towards the ocean.

Caro and I laughed and continued to walk towards the house. We opened the front door and walked in. We walked over to the living room and sat on the couch. Harriet stepped into the room with a sinister smile on her face.

"Ash can fire me, for all I care," she said in a snobby tone, "Now, no one will have water."

Caro and I looked at each other confused.

"What happened?" I said curiously.

Christian burst back in through the front door and ran to the living room. He had a towel wrapped around his waist that was dripping water on the floor.

"Fucking bitch!" he shouted. He seemed irritated but he was humorous about the situation.

"I'm not a bitch, Ash is," Harriet said in a pretentious tone while tilting her head upwards.

"What the fuck are you talking about, Harriet?" Christian asked in an angry laugh, "You drained all of the fucking water for the whole month. You didn't bother to tell me that you were doing that before I got into the shower. I had to finish bathing in the ocean. What the fuck is wrong with you?"

Harriet didn't respond. She stormed off to her room and slammed the door.

"What's up guys?" Christian said to us in a chuckle of disbelief.

"We just got off from work," I said and then laughed at the situation.

"Well," Christian said, "We're all kind of fucked now. Harriet threw a temper tantrum. We have no water left for the next three weeks."

"I can see that," Caro said laughing, "So what do we do?"

"I say we leave," Christian said with a smile, "Fuck this shit."

"Yea," I agreed, "I think this place is a little shady. Today at work, I saw Ash give a black leather bag to some rough looking biker guys."

"No shit?" Christian said surprised, "Did they have leather jackets with confederate flags on them?"

"Yea, they did," I said, shocked that he knew.

"A lady I was serving at the restaurant told me that those guys are involved with one of the most dangerous biker gangs in Australia," Christian said, "Apparently, Ash works with them to move drugs, launder money and other shady shit."

"What?" Caro burst in with a worried look on her face.

"Yea," Christian said, nodding.

"Yea," Caro said uncomfortably, "Let's leave."

"Can we ride with you in your van?" I asked Christian.

"Of course," he said, "Let's get the fuck out of here."

The three of us quickly packed all of our belongings. Caro and I placed everything back into our backpacks and loaded them into the van with our ukuleles.

"Should we tell Harriet or Ash?" Caro said as we were getting ready to leave.

Christian and I looked at each other. We both shook our heads.

"Nah," Christian said as he started the van.

We left the house. We drove to the Bruny Island ferry to leave the island.

***

Caro and I were swimming as fast as we could, just under the surface of the ocean. Beside us, there was a giant whale shark. The whale shark was beautiful. It had rows of white dots along the sides of its body. It moved gracefully through the water and waved its back fin side to side. The mouth of the whale shark was open wide as it swam. It was collecting plankton.

A few months passed since Caro, Christian and I left Bruny Island that day. Christian dropped us off at the airport and he continued traveling in his van. Caro and I took a flight to Perth and started hitchhiking up the west coast of Australia.

The journey was incredible. We passed by a lake that was bright pink in color. The smell of the lake was awful, but the color was vibrant. We camped out at beautiful white sand beaches. The sunsets lit up the sky in a fiery red color with darkened gray clouds. The kangaroos were much taller than they were in Tasmania. They were quicker too.

We stopped in Broome. We met a lady along the way that told us to come visit her there. She wanted us to watch her house while she traveled to the Outback for work. She was showing us the whale sharks before she left.

Caro and I climbed into the boat. We couldn't keep up with the whale shark, it was too fast. The boat turned around and started to head back to shore. Caro and I held onto the railings of the boat as the sea water splashed into our faces. We gazed out into the ocean. There were vast patches of red jellyfish floating on the water's surface. They looked like little red bubbles. Australia was beautiful.

We returned to the ladies car and she drove us back to her house in Broome. She handed us the keys to the house and told us she would be back in a couple of days.

She had a friendly Australian Shepherd that we pet and played fetch with. Tilly was her name. Tilly cuddled with us while we watched movies on the couch. When we made food, she always came to the kitchen to see what we were cooking. We always tossed her some food because if we didn't, she would steal it from the counter anyways. We didn't mind.

We used the days to explore Broome. We went to Cable Beach and watched the sunset. It was picturesque. There was a thin layer of water that settled on the beach sand from the tide. It reflected the sky above like a mirror on the beach. There was a group of camels that crossed through the mirror. The camel's images reflected the sunset as a beautiful silhouette.

The last day we went to Gantheaume Point. We saw footprints of dinosaurs that had been preserved on the cliffside. We stayed for sunset and ate some food.

We returned to the ladies house. We started to think about what we were going to do next. We didn't really have a plan.

Christian called us to see how our travels were going. We told him everything. He told us about his travels as well. He took a boat with his van from Tasmania to Melbourne and drove up the East Coast of Australia. He told us that he found a sweet potato farm that we should work at. He said it was a family owned farm and that we could make good money. Caro and I thought it might be a good idea. We were starting to run out of money. We considered it.

We packed our backpacks. We were prepared to leave once the lady returned the next day. We locked up the house and went to sleep.

We woke up early the next morning so that we would be ready to greet the lady when she returned. I sat up from the bed and swung my feet off the side and rested them on the floor. I rubbed my eyes and sat for a moment. I looked over to where our backpacks had been before. They were gone.

I jumped up from the bed and shook Caro awake. She woke confused and groggy.

"Our backpacks are missing," I told her with a worried face. My stomach was twisting.

"What?" she said, jumping out of her grogginess.

We got up and walked through the whole house. We were greeted by Tilly. She jumped up on us and licked us. We gave Tilly some pets and hugs and continued to look through the house.

The back door of the house was open. Someone had broken the lock and walked in while we were sleeping. I became nervous. The reason we were there was to watch the house. I couldn't believe it.

"Our passports were in those backpacks," Caro said in distress.

"Shit, you're right," I replied, still searching through the house.

I opened the front door and walked out onto the driveway. Our backpacks were lying there. They were opened and some of our clothes were pulled out of them.

"I found our backpacks," I shouted to Caro from outside.

She ran out and we both started to check our backpacks. To our relief, our passports were still there. All our cash was missing and they took Caro's necklace but they left the ukuleles behind. For some reason they took my deodorant as well. We thought that was strange. After we checked our backpacks the lady pulled into the driveway.

"Everything alright?" she said, shouting from the car.

I walked over to the driver's side window.

"Someone broke into the house," I said nervously, "We locked everything, but they broke the lock on the back door."

"Bloody bastards," the lady said as she got out of the car, "I'll check all my secret spots and see what they snatched from me."

She seemed fairly calm about the situation and didn't blame us for it. We walked with her around her house to check for her belongings. They took all of her cash and a few pieces of jewelry. She was satisfied that they didn't steal more than that.

"Drug addicts," she said suddenly after she finished checking the house, "They only took cash and things they could trade for drugs. I work with a lot of these types of people in the social work that I do. It's sad, truly."

"Really?" I said curiously, "What do you do at work?"

"Yea," she responded back, "I work with a lot of Aboriginal families in need. It's only been a handful of years since Aboriginals were counted as part of the population here in Australia. I believe it was in 1967. Before that, they were barely considered humans. It was terrible. They are not accustomed to the Western culture. Some of them still live out in the Kimberley in indigenous tribes and practice Aboriginal law."

"Wow," I said with interest, "What is Aboriginal law?"

"Well," she replied, "It's the ancient law practiced by the Aboriginal tribes. It is a complicated and sensitive topic. My friend is in the Australian police force. He has been to the tribal land to monitor their practices. One time, a member of the tribe stole something. They punished him by having his calf muscle removed with a hook. My friend said that he couldn't watch. It was too gruesome. He had to turn away."

"Ouch," I said as if I was feeling the pain, "That's an intense punishment for stealing."

I thought about the little toy car I stole when I was a child. I couldn't imagine having my calf muscle removed because of that.

"Yea," she said in agreement. She scrunched her face, "You would think that they wouldn't want to steal if that was their punishment. The problem is that the western culture of Australia is mixed with their culture. The punishment for stealing in our culture is minimum. You might spend some time in jail, but most likely, you'll only have to pay a fine. That is a huge contrast to having your calf muscle removed with a hook. When they integrate into the western culture, a fine or jail time isn't a deterrent from the crime."

"That's sad," I said with sympathy.

"Yea, it truly is," she said looking down to the ground, "They also don't drink alcohol in the tribes. They don't have it. Aussies love to drink, and we drink a lot. When the Aboriginals integrate into our culture they often become addicted to alcohol and drugs. Many of them overdose. It's horrible. Those are the cases that I work with. The children and families of those people."

"Wow," I said, absorbing what I had learned, "That is great that you are there to help them out."

"It's tough work," she said while she pet Tilly, "It can be emotionally difficult, but someone has got to do it."

I nodded and reached over to pet Tilly as well.

The three of us prepared lunch and continued to chat about Australia. Once we finished, the lady drove Caro and I to the airport. Caro and I decided to fly to the farm Christian had told us about. We needed to make some more money for our travels.

***

"You bloody cunt!" Ron yelled from the forklift inside the sweet potato washing shed.

Ron was the owner of the sweet potato farm we started working at. He was a tall Australian man who wore a fishing hat and vest. He spoke with a strong Australian accent. Sometimes, we couldn't understand anything that he said.

We had been working on the farm for a few months. We spent as little money as possible to save for our travels. The farm was secluded. It was an hour drive to the nearest town.

There were living arrangements on the farm that looked like the abandoned aftermath of a nuclear disaster. You would never know that people actually habited the area. We slept in a room that had been cut out of an old rusty shipping container. One container had six rooms. There wasn't very much space. Caro and I were fine with that.

There were makeshift showers that were installed in a smaller rusty shipping container. There were only two showers to share with everyone that lived on the farm. We were covered, from head to toe, with a thick layer of red dirt after working with the sweet potatoes. For this reason, it would be difficult to go without a shower. There were long lines for the showers everyday.

There was an outdoor kitchen area that had a propane tank hooked up to some camp stove burners. Those camp stoves sat on top of an old wobbly fold out table that was nearing its end. There was a large piece of scrap wood laid on top of a few stacks of cinder blocks to form a surface to eat on. Surrounding the surface, was a bunch of buckets and old beaten up chairs that we would sit on to eat. That was our kitchen table. You could say that the place had character.

The farm was huge. There were large square fields of sweet potato vines planted in neat rows. There was a large reservoir that was used to water the sweet potatoes. You could see it from the kitchen. Some of the fields were a couple kilometers away. The farm had a bunch of old beaten up cars and trucks. They would be illegal to drive on the streets. We only used them to drive around the farm.

Some of the cars were missing doors and side view mirrors. There were windows smashed out of a few of them. There was a truck that thundered loudly when you started it because it was missing part of its muffler. That's the truck Caro and I used. None of the seat belts worked.

Christian was right, it was a family farm. Ron had lifted his sister's car off the ground with a forklift. She drove over to talk to him about something, and whatever it was, really pissed him off.

"Put down me fucking car!" Ron's sister shouted in a thick Australian accent. She waved her hand in the air and jumped up and down in front of the forklift.

Ron started to drive his sister's car out to the side of the dirt road. He would have run her over if she didn't eventually move when he got too close.

"You want me to put down your bloody car?" he yelled at her with a smile and a chuckle.

Suddenly he jerked the forks on the forklift shaking her car from it. The car came crashing to the ground. It landed upside down in the red dirt. A cloud of dust floated into the air from the impact.

"You fuck wit!" his sister yelled furiously.

I watched for the next couple of minutes while they yelled insults back and forth at each other. She even threw a few punches at him. Eventually, the two of them left to continue their quarrel elsewhere. The rest of us continued to do our daily work. Believe it or not, that was pretty normal for the farm. There was a deep rooted family feud amongst Ron's family. All of us experienced the drama of it on a daily basis.

There were a couple of different types of jobs on the farm. First, we would all stand on a rusty hand made digging machine. That machine was attached to the back of a tractor. We would grab the sweet potatoes and place them into large bins as they came up from the ground onto a conveyor belt. Those bins were then carried over to the sweet potato wash shed. At the wash shed, those bins would be dumped into a large machine that would spray off all the dirt. We had to trash the rotten sweet potatoes and package the good ones. A few times during the week, we would go out to the empty fields and hand plant the sweet potato vines in neat rows. They would take a couple of months to grow. That was a normal day's work at the farm.

There were always a handful of dramas. There were two groups of people that worked on the farm; local Australians and backpackers. The backpackers were people from all around the world that came to explore Australia and work. The local Australians were exactly that, local Australians. Some of the Australians had been working there for their whole lives. They didn't like the backpackers very much. They were always griping about how we were going to steal their jobs or how we were a lazy bunch of workers.

A few of the Australian workers were addicted to methamphetamine and would have random fits while they were working. They would start screaming loudly in a mumbled Australian accent. We could never understand it. Then, they would storm off and reappear randomly throughout the work day. Sometimes they didn't reappear until a couple days later. The others usually showed up a little tipsy from the night before or from the alcohol they drank that morning. They were a pretty miserable group of people that would grumble and complain about everything. However, every once in a while they would lighten up.

One of the Australian ladies lives in a motorhome on the farm. She calls it her 'donger', but pronounces it 'donga'. I drove the loud truck with the missing muffler past her donger one day. It was on the way to the field I had to work in. Apparently, I drove past too fast. She came chasing after me in her car. She screamed obscenities and waved her fist out the window while she drove. When I finally arrived at the field, she came running towards me with a large boot knife. I thought she was going to stab me. She didn't stab me, but she slashed every tire on that truck. The tires were flattened to the rims. She told me to never drive near her Donger again because dust gets into it. I apologized and promised I never would. Ever since that day, she considered me her favorite backpacker. She was always kind to me. To this day, I still have no idea why.

There was a unique character that was a mix of the two groups. He was an American that was traveling from the United States, but he was also an Australian. He had dual citizenship for both countries. His name was Aaron.

Almost every girl, whether backpacker or local Australian, thought Aaron was attractive. Aaron not only had the looks, but he had the charm as well. He was constantly complimenting people and making them smile. He came from a wealthy family. His dad had large corporations in both the United States and Australia.

Aaron and I hung out quite a bit outside of work. We became good friends during our time at the farm. We would have deep conversations that were similar to the conversations that I had with Chad in San Diego. Aaron reminded me of Chad in a lot of ways. He would go with Caro and I to get ice cream and insist on paying for us. He always offered us food or drinks whenever we were in the kitchen. He was an extremely nice guy.

He told me the story of his past and how he struggled with a heroin addiction. He told me that he overcame the addiction on his own. He believed strongly that anyone that wanted to get off drugs could do so, as long as they made the decision within their hearts. In his mind, there were no excuses. He was always positive about life.

"I'm sorry, Gene. I'm here for you if you need anything," Aaron said in a sincere tone. He sat next to me and rubbed my back.

I had just received an internet call from James. He told me that he was diagnosed with stage four cancer and didn't have long to live. I had only met James once in my life, when I crashed into him. I became sad and worried when I heard the news. I remembered when I had almost killed him in that car accident. That was such a tragic day. I decided that I had to fly back to go see him. I wanted to help him in whatever way I could. Although, he always refused help.

"Thanks, man," I replied mournfully.

"I hate seeing you like this, Gene. Why don't we take the day off and go get some ice cream?" Aaron said with a smile to try and cheer me up.

I agreed. Caro came along with us and we discussed our plans. She agreed to fly back with me. I asked James when we should go and he suggested in two weeks. Caro and I booked our flights and decided to continue working on the farm until we left.

I was grateful for Caro and Aaron's company. The ice cream trip cheered me up. I was still sad about James, but he always spoke as if nothing was wrong. He said he was a fighter, and that it was going to take more than cancer to kill him. The last time I heard him say those words was in the emergency room. However, this time he didn't sound as confident as before.

***

A French couple arrived halfway through our time on the farm. At first, they kept to themselves and rarely talked with anyone. People would try to make conversation with them but they ignored them or brushed them off. Many of us thought that they were rude because of that. Eventually, they became more social.

I noticed that the French couple would fight a lot. I never understood what they were saying, because they would argue in French, but I could tell they were angry with each other. They seemed to move past these fights, because I always saw them hugging and kissing a few days later.

Theo and Lily were their names. Theo was more shy than Lily, but he always tried his best to make Lily happy. It was sad to see how helpless his efforts were most of the time. Lily was more outgoing and confident. She had a very stubborn personality and always pushed for things to go her way. She seemed to have set high expectations for Theo as a boyfriend. I believed that to be part of the reason they fought so much.

The whole farm had a day off from work. Almost everyone went down to swim in the reservoir. I stayed back to relax and play my ukulele in the kitchen. I could see everyone jumping into the reservoir in the distance while I played. I noticed that Aaron stayed back as well. He came over and sat next to me while I played.

“You only have to put up with this place for a couple more weeks,” Aaron said with an encouraging smile.

“I don’t think it’s so bad. I kind of like it here,” I said, still strumming the ukulele, “I am only going back because I have to see my uncle.”

“Yeah, that’s true,” Aaron said nodding, “So you’re not really bothered by the rumors and the bad things that people say about you on the farm, then?”

I stopped playing and looked over to Aaron with curiosity.

"I didn't know that people spread rumors or said bad things about me," I said surprised, "I don't even know what bad things they would have to say about me?"

"Yea," Aaron said looking down to the ground and then back up to me to continue speaking, "I always stick up for you. I tell them that you're the coolest guy I know. I tell them that they shouldn't be saying those things."

"Thanks, bro," I said appreciatively, "but what do they say about me?"

"It doesn't even matter bro," Aaron said, patting me on the back, "I think you are an incredible person. Do you really care about what they say about you? I mean, you're leaving soon anyways. They are silly rumors. Does it really matter?"

I thought about what he said for a moment. I was surprised to hear that people talked bad about me. I couldn't remember doing anything to make anyone angry. The only time that I did was when I drove the truck past that ladies donger, but she said she liked me now. She told me that I was her favorite backpacker. I guess Aaron was right. I was leaving in a few weeks so it didn't really matter. They are just silly rumors. It still slightly bothered me, but I just ignored the feeling.

"I guess you're right," I replied to Aaron, "I really don't care about the rumors. Like you said, I'm leaving soon anyways."

"Exactly bro," He said with a smile.

I got up and walked to my room. I wanted some time alone. I sat in the entryway and began to write in my notebook. Caro was swimming at the reservoir. I was thinking of something to write about. I started to jot down a few song lyrics that came to me. While I was writing, I heard someone walk near the room. I turned to see who it was. Lily was stepping into her room. I smiled over to her and waved.

"How are you doing, Lily?" I asked looking up from my writing.

She flinched when I spoke. She was startled that I acknowledged her presence.

"Good," she said in an awkward tone.

"You didn't want to swim either?" I asked to make a little conversation.

"Not really. I'm not feeling very well. I just want to rest," she said nervously.

"Yeah, same," I agreed.

She nodded awkwardly and then entered her room.

I noticed that Theo wasn't with her. He must have been at the reservoir. I returned to my writing. I continued to search my brain for ideas and wrote them down as they came to me.

Suddenly, Aaron tiptoed his way over to Lily's room. He looked as if he was trying to avoid attention. He noticed that I was watching him. He looked over to me and smiled with an awkward wave. I smiled and waved back. He entered Lily's room. I thought it was strange but I continued to write. I had too many ideas on the tip of my mind.

Caro and I had one week left on the farm before our flight to the United States. It was early in the morning and everyone was getting ready for work. We had already finished our breakfast so we were waiting for everyone else. We were seated on the buckets in the kitchen staring out towards the reservoir. There was a slight morning chill in the air and a layer of fog that hovered above the reservoir. It was a beautiful morning.

Lily marched up to me with outrage in her eyes.

"Why the fuck are you spreading rumors about me, Gene?" she shouted in accusation.

"What are you talking about?" I asked with complete confusion on my face.

"Don't fucking play stupid with me, Gene," she said irritated, "You are telling everyone on the farm that I am a slut. That I slept with Aaron. That I cheated on Theo!"

"I never said any of those things to anyone," I said confidently. I was still confused by her accusations.

"You are a fucking liar, Gene!" she shouted, "You were sitting there writing in your stupid little notebook when Aaron came into my room. You were the only one there. He only came to my room to give me some medicine. I told you that I wasn't feeling very well. Why would you make up these bullshit lies about us?"

"I'm telling the truth, Lily" I replied, "I never said anything about you or Aaron. Aaron is my friend."

She stormed off in anger.

That really bothered me. I started shaking a little from the intensity of her outcry. I was extremely agitated. I told her the truth. I was pretty sure that she had slept with Aaron. He wasn't just bringing medicine to her because I heard everything. However, I never told anyone about it, with the exception of Caro. I kept my mouth shut. I didn't care. I remembered that Aaron told me not to worry about the rumors. I told him that I didn't care about them. This was difficult for me to ignore. I hated rumors. I wondered who was spreading them.

Everyone started the beat up vehicles and we drove to work. We started in the wash shed because we hadn't finished washing the sweet potatoes from the day before. I was working with Aaron to pack the potatoes. There was a girl working near Aaron and I that packed the potatoes as well. She was a local Australian that usually kept to herself and never really talked much.

"Everything alright, bro?" Aaron asked. He noticed that I was agitated.

"Not really, man," I said, attempting to conceal the frustration that was building inside of me.

"What's going on, Gene? You can tell me," he said in a comforting tone.

"I don't know why, and I don't know who, but someone is telling everyone that I am spreading rumors about you and Lily. That you are sleeping together. I would never do that. It is none of my business, and you are my friend," I said venting my frustration to him.

"Bro, don't even worry about it. Don't let it get to you. Remember? You told me that you really don't care about the rumors," he said, attempting to calm me down.

"I know. You're right," I said shamefully, "but it really does bother me. I don't know why?"

"You're probably just stressed out about your uncle," he said reassuringly. He was attempting to validate my frustration, "That is some pretty devastating news to hear all of the sudden. You are holding yourself together extremely well."

"Yea, maybe you're right," I said remembering the sadness I felt when I received that call from James.

"I've got you, bro," he said with a smile while rubbing my back, "but hey… I've been keeping my eye out for you. You see that quiet Aussie girl over there? The one working at our table?"

He pointed his finger at her. She was looking down at a sweet potato that she held in her hand. Even though she was close to us, she couldn't hear us talking. The wash shed was extremely loud.

"Yea?" I said curiously and looked over to her.

"Well," he continued in a quieter voice, "I am positive that she was the one that started that rumor. She pretends to keep to herself but she hears everything. She seems all innocent on the outside, but she talks behind your back when you're not looking. She is trying to turn the farm against you. She has nothing better to do with her life. That is why she gossips. It's like a hobby for her. She enjoys it."

The blood began to pump through my veins. I was filled with anger. I couldn't believe that she would do that. I never did anything to her. I never even talked to her in the wash shed except to say ‘hi’. I know Aaron told me that I shouldn’t let the rumors bother me. I know that he said I was leaving soon, but I couldn’t help it. I had to confront her about it. I had too much emotion built up inside of me. I was on edge. I was furious. I stormed over to her.

“Why would you tell people that I said that about Lily and Aaron?” I asked her loudly in frustration.

“Don’t fucking talk to me like that you little shit!” she yelled back throwing the potato onto the floor, “I don’t even know what the fuck you are talking about!”

The whole wash shed stopped working. Everyone was focused on the two of us screaming at each other. Lily ran over to us and Theo followed. There was a circle of people and tension was building. Aaron tried to calm me down but it was too late.

“Then why did Lily start yelling at me this morning? Why was she accusing me of things I never said?” I shouted to the crowd of people around me, “Who is spreading these lies?”

Lily stepped up to me in anger.

“You are the only fucking person that was there!” she shouted angrily at me, “You are fucking jealous, so you spread lies”.

I started to steam. I was furious.

"I didn't give a shit about you and Aaron fucking when Theo was at the reservoir!" I shouted at her.

She slapped the right side of my face and pushed me back with both of her arms. She spat on me and cursed at me in French. I didn't care. I stood my ground firm.

"I never said a word about it," I yelled, "But now that everyone believes that it was me, maybe I should start telling everyone that you did cheat on Theo. It was none of my business. Now, someone has made it my business."

Lily launched herself towards me. She swung her fists aggressively in the air. Theo grabbed her arms and held her back from attacking me. He was holding back the tears from his eyes as well. He seemed really bothered by what I said about Lily and Aaron. I'm sure that was hard for him to hear.

"Well, Aaron told me that you said that," Lily shouted angrily. She was becoming tired from resisting Theo's grip.

"Aaron?" I said, shocked with confusion.

We both paused to catch our breaths. We were quiet for a brief second. I looked around for Aaron but he had already left. No one knew where he had gone.

"Yea," she said beginning to calm down, "Your fucking friend, Aaron."

I couldn't believe it. I flashed back to all the conversations I had with Aaron. I remembered when James called me about his cancer. Aaron was so kind and comforting to me about that. He was one of the nicest people I knew. I considered him a good friend. I started to think about what he had said about not becoming angry with people who spread rumors about me. I don't think those rumors ever existed. Not until after he told me that. I realized that he had set me up. He set me up in hopes that I wouldn't care if people talked about me. That way, he could tell people that I was spreading a rumor about him and Lily. He wanted it to be a rumor from someone that was leaving so that no one could verify it to be true. I was the only person who had witnessed what they had done. I was the only person that could verify it. He used me. The problem was that I actually did care about the rumors. I told him that I didn't, but inside I truly did.

"Let's go, Theo," Lily said abruptly. She was irritated with the situation, "We need to leave this fucking farm right now. Fuck these people. It'll just be the two of us."

Lily and Theo left the farm that day and never returned. I never found out what happened between the two of them. I didn't care anymore. I knew the truth. Lily knew the truth. Aaron knew the truth. I think Theo considered the truth in his heart, but he loved Lily too much to believe it.

Everyone except Lily and Theo went back to work that day as usual. After work, Caro and I made some dinner and ate it in the kitchen area. Aaron walked into the kitchen cautiously with a smile. I ignored his presence but he sat down next to me anyways.

"That sucks that these people are saying these things about you, Gene," he said sympathetically, "You know that I would never spread rumors or lies about you right?"

I cringed inside as he spoke. On the outside, Aaron was the most attractive, friendly, caring, compassionate, charismatic person I ever met. Now, I knew him for what he really was. Everyone that I had asked confirmed that the rumor came from Aaron. It was indisputable. I decided to play along with his game of lies.

"I know bro," I said, patting him on the back, "I appreciate everything you do for me."

He smiled at me.

"I thought you told me you didn't really care what people say about you," he questioned, showing a bit of concern.

I couldn't believe that he was saying that. It was as if he knew that I knew what he had done. He lied indirectly through his responses. I really hated lying. It was as if I was back with Jacob or in the church. I lied about what I liked just to make him happy and to avoid some beatings. I lied to Colton just so that I wouldn't be kicked out onto the street. I guess life was full of lies. Life was full of bullshit. We were all guilty of it, including myself.

"I think you were right," I said sorrowfully, "I was just stressed about my uncle's cancer and I exploded."

"I'm sorry, bro," he said rubbing my back, "It must be extremely difficult for you."

I learned so much from Aaron and the type of person that he was. I used to think of him as a great friend. I told him everything about my life. I believed he was the most genuine person I ever met. He was so kind. It was all a lie. A facade. He completely deceived me.

I didn't care for religion. I especially disliked my experience with it, but one Bible verse reminded me of Aaron.

. . .They come to you in sheep's clothing, but inwardly they are ferocious wolves. -Matthew 7:15

Aaron was a ferocious wolf disguised as an innocent little sheep. I believed that he was more dangerous than Jacob. I knew that Jacob wanted to harm me. I knew that I would come home and he would beat me until I was shaking on the bathroom floor. I expected him to hurt me. His intentions were clear. I knew who he was. I had no idea who Aaron truly was. I had no idea that Aaron was going to betray me. I thought of him as a close friend. He always told me that he was there for me. He acted so genuine. He was the last person that I would have ever suspected to do this to me. Aaron didn't spit on me like Lily did. Aaron didn't slap me in the face like Lily did. Aaron didn't shove me like Lily did… but because of his lies those things happened.

I wondered if Aaron knew that I would have reacted the way that I did. Maybe, he didn't expect it at all. Maybe he thought that he inspired me to not care about the rumors through our talks. I even told him that I didn't care, so it was hard not to blame myself for everything. His intentions might have been good. He thought that I didn't care. My response was all the confirmation that he needed to feel justified in spreading those rumors. His actions were self-centered, but maybe he didn't mean any harm. I questioned whether it was my lie that caused everything, or his. It was difficult for me to reconcile these thoughts.

"Yea," I said nonchalantly.

Aaron stood up and looked over to Caro.

"He'll be fine," Aaron said. He patted my back and then exited the kitchen.

Those words stung my ears and sent shivers down my spine. I flashed back to when Tim had said the exact same words to Melissa, after he raped me. I remembered how he acted like nothing had happened, just like Aaron did. Tim taught me that life was suffering. Aaron confirmed that life was a lie. I was beginning to believe that we're all full of shit.

FOURTEEN

Caro and I stood outside of James' little pink house. I had never been there before. I had only seen the house from a distance when I went to visit my father. I only went as far as the accident.

The house was beautifully landscaped. There was a nice grass yard sectioned off with rock borders. There were trees that he planted to cover the perimeter of the house. The paint on the house was professionally done. There was beautiful white trim around the windows and doors. A little wooden swing was attached to a tree that stood in the middle of the yard. I would have never expected his house to look that nice. It was a huge contrast to my father's house.

I felt nervous coming to see James again. The old guilt that I had from the car accident started to resurface. My nerves buzzed underneath my skin like bees. I walked up to the door and knocked. Caro and I waited for an answer.

Tiffany opened the door. For a moment, I didn't recognize her. Her face was sunken a bit around her cheeks and she lost some weight. She didn't look like she was doing very well.

"How have you been?" I asked her.

"Oh, hum. How have I been, you ask? You don't know anything about what the doctor has taken. You think it's always something, but nope. I'll tell you what, though, the bastards are eating candy as we speak."

I looked at Tiffany with complete confusion. I had no idea what she was talking about. She twitched when she spoke and she seemed to be agitated about something. I wondered what had happened to her. Suddenly, James came slowly walking to the door.

"Tiffany," he said in a low raspy voice, "Why don't you get up out of here? Go to your room for a minute, ok?"

"I can go to my little fucking room," Tiffany said irritated and spazzing, "I will defeat the mother fuckers and burn the witches to the ground."

She marched to her room slamming the door behind her.

“I’m not sure what the fuck is wrong with her,” James said in a low raspy voice, “Shit, the doctors don’t even fucking know.”

James was pretty thin. Small patches of his hair were starting to fall out. There was a feeding tube connected to his stomach that hung below his shirt. Despite all of that, he still produced a little smile when he saw us.

“When did she start acting like that?” I was concerned.

“I don’t remember when the fuck it happened,” James said while guiding us to the kitchen table to sit down, “but I have a suspicion that it was when she was with her druggie friends. I think they took too much of that shit. She hasn’t been right in the head ever since. It’s like she died. That’s not her. That’s a completely different person. Her brain is fried. Fucked.”

“That’s terrible,” I said in a downcast tone.

“Yea,” James said. He stared at the ground for a moment and then looked up to me with a depressed laugh, “but what the fuck can you do, right?”

“Yea,” I agreed with a depressed half smile.

“Well,” he said. He wanted to change the subject, “Who is this fine young lady?”

“I’m Caro,” she said softly, in a shy tone.

"Nice to meet you, Caro," James said with a chuckle.

"You as well," Caro said with a smile.

"Well, Gene," James said, and then coughed a few times, "I might as well tell you a little bit about myself. I might not be able to fight death this time. I don't need to tell you my whole fucking life story and shit, because who gives a fuck? I'll just share some stories with you so that you know a bit about your uncle. Hopefully, it will be good for something. This cancer shit fucks you up pretty badly."

"Yea, I can imagine," I said looking down at the floor.

"They zapped my fucking body with radiation to try and kill the cancer. I don't think that it worked. Now, I can't eat from my mouth. I have to pour food in this little fucking tube, it's disgusting."

James lifted the tube hanging from his stomach and showed it to us. He began to share some stories.

"I have always tried to make the best of life as it comes," James began, "People will try and tell you shit like, 'God only gives you as much as you can handle' but it's all a crock of shit. God doesn't give a fuck what you can handle. He just gives it to you, like he gave it to me.

I like to tell things straight. Exactly the way they are. Too many people in this world bend the truth so that it rings better in their ears. Fuck that. I tell it how it is.

I started out selling drugs when I was young. I quickly realized that I was going to get shot if I continued down that road. I thought that I was such a fucking badass until I was staring down the barrel of a gun. After that, I tried to find other shit to do. I considered myself somewhat of an entrepreneur. I had a lot of ideas. Whether those ideas were good or not, is for you to decide, but I made a lot of fucking money.

I started a bunch of strip clubs. Many people saw that as immoral or degrading to woman, but they don't know what the fuck they are talking about. I provided opportunities to those women. I constructed some bullet proof glass booths that I would rent out. All the money the girls made was for them to keep as long as they paid the rent. I had girls coming from decent paying jobs because they made more in my booths. Some girls would bring home six figures in those booths. A lot of them pulled themselves out of tough situations and started new lives for themselves with that money. I even helped out your mother. I gave her a booth for a while. I didn't fuck around either, I had top notch security for the girls safety.

The problem was that there were gangs that ran some strip clubs as well. They didn't treat those girls with respect. They would abuse them and take their profits. Dirty mother fuckers. Many of the girls at those clubs started to leave and rent booths at my clubs. It was better for them because they worked for themselves. The gangs didn't like that at all. They fucking hated me for it.

I was chased down by gangs in New York. Eventually, I had to move the business to a different state. The gangs followed me. They pushed me further and further, state to state, until I reached San Diego. There, they told me that they would kill me if I didn't shut down my clubs. They had a gun to my head when they told me. I had to get out of the business. I wasn't going to lose my life over that shit.

Apparently, shutting down the clubs was not enough because one of the gangs put a bounty on me. I had to lay low for a while so I moved out here. I bought this land with all the money I made from the businesses. Your father was in prison and he wasn't going to be out for a while. I figured that when he got out, I could have a nice place for him to live.

Life hit me hard out here. I had a son with down syndrome, Tiffany lost her damn mind, my wife wanted to leave me and I got diagnosed with stage four cancer. Now, I'm in debt up to my ass. I just laugh as the shit piles up because what the fuck can I do about it anyways?

I started a painting business out here. I would drive into the nearest town and paint all the houses and small businesses in the area. I had to stop taking so many jobs when the cancer hit me. That is one of the reasons for my debt. I don't give a fuck about the debt anymore. The doctor says I don't have long to live anyways. It's just a lot of shit to deal with, you know?"

James paused his story for a moment and started to pour a protein shake into the feeding tube connected to his stomach. He then continued, "The important thing to take away from all this shit is that life is precious. Don't ever fucking waste your life. I had been chasing the wrong things. I was chasing the goddamn American dream, but it's all bullshit.

I spent my whole life chasing money. I thought that I would have a nice house, job, car, white picket fence with a little dog running in the backyard. Instead, I got fucking cancer. I wished I would have just enjoyed the simple things more. I wished I would have spent more time exploring the world or spending time with the people that I love. In the end, none of the shit I was chasing even mattered. None of this shit is coming with me when I die.

The past is the fucking past though. I don't want to waste more time regretting the shit that I never did. I'm an old fucker now and I really don't care anymore. I think you're doing it right, kid. Australia must be nice. Keep doing shit like that. You'll be happier for it in the end. Trust me.

I want to show you something."

James finished pouring the protein shake down his feeding tube and slowly stood up. Caro and I got up and followed him. He walked out the front door and led us to the side of the house.

There was a newer Volvo station wagon parked on the side of the house.

"You see that shit?" James said smiling and laughing, "isn't she a beauty?"

"Is that your car?" I asked.

"Fuck no," James said laughing as he started the engine, "It's yours."

"James," I said with concern, "This is your car. Selling this could help you pay off all your debt."

"Fuck my debt," James said laughing. He then went into a coughing fit for a moment. He gathered himself and continued, "I won't live long enough for the debt to matter. You and your girlfriend should take it. Go see the fucking world. Don't ever let the past keep you from living. Enjoy every moment that life gives you. You don't want to end up like me or your father do you?"

I looked over to James and smiled. He patted me on the back and smiled back.

I thought about his story for a moment. It seemed pretty irrelevant, but I guess there was a bit to learn from it. He really didn't care what people thought of him. He didn't just say it like I did either, he actually meant it. He really didn't care.

He was a bit unorthodox and rough around the edges, but he actually seemed to care about the people he loved. He bought a house for my father, he helped my mother earn money for herself, he continued to work as much as he could through cancer to support his family. Now, he was giving me this brand new car.

I wondered if he knew that this car was a newer model of the old Volvo station wagon my mother and I had lived in. I had a moment of nostalgia. The little toy car I had stolen was nothing like the old beaten up

Volvo station wagon but it had carried the same feeling of regret. James was right, I shouldn't spend time regretting the past. This new car was similar to that little toy car. I remembered thinking how it was brand new and no one else had played with it before. It wasn't broken or used like the other toys. This new car was just like that little toy car. It represented a brand new start. I should let go of my past.

"Get the fuck out of here!" James yelled at me while pulling himself up from the driver's seat, "Don't waste your life. Go out and enjoy every moment of it."

I gave James a hug and shed a few tears. He pushed me away after a moment and started walking to his house. I noticed a few tears from his eyes as well.

Caro and I got into the car and drove. I wasn't sure where we were going. I just drove.

Hours passed since we drove away from James' house. The scenery was beginning to look familiar. We drove down a long interstate highway that consisted of a couple lanes going in our direction and a couple going opposite to us. The highway led us to a long winding road that ascended up a tall mountain. I looked over at Caro. She was resting her chin on the inside window ledge, watching as everything below started to become smaller. I could smell the Ponderosa pine trees and a tiny hint of vanilla emitting from their bark. Large rock boulders and pine trees blurred as we drove past.

I started to slow down and pull off to the side of the road. Caro and I were pretty high up and everything below looked like a miniature model of what it really was. I stopped the car and pulled the hand brake. We flung our doors open and stepped onto the gravel road beneath us. I felt the nostalgia in the air. It was the same place I had been when I was with my mother in the old Volvo station wagon.

Caro and I jumped up onto the hood of the car and dangled our feet off the edge. The view was magnificent. There was a slight breeze in the air that blew a fresh scent of vanilla from the trees. Caro's hair blew with the breeze. I placed my arm around her as we gazed out to the world below us.

I realized we had been through a lot together. It had almost been a couple of years since we met. Every moment was precious and beautiful. The day at the ukulele shop. The night on the beach in Maui. I thought about all the crazy experiences we had traveling through Australia. She even came with me to visit James. Love was always complicated in the past. I never understood it. I remembered what Caro told me in Maui. Life is simple, people complicate it. Maybe love was like life. Simple.

"Caro," I said looking over to her.

She turned and looked me in the eyes.

"Yes?" she said softly.

"I love you," I said with a smile.

"I love you too," she said smiling back at me.

We kissed, held each other and then continued to look down at the world below us. I finally felt at peace. Everything that happened in my past didn't matter anymore. I was no longer chasing a meaning for life. I was simply enjoying every moment of it. I was alive and with someone that I loved. That's all that mattered.

"Why don't we go to Argentina? We could visit your family," I said suddenly, still gathering my thoughts.

"You mean in this car?" she said, surprised by my suggestion.

I thought about that for a minute. I didn't really think about driving there in the car. I just meant that we should go. I hadn't really thought anything through. It was just an idea.

I remembered the times that I lived in the back of the old Volvo station wagon with my mother. I remembered that brief moment on the mountaintop that I felt it didn't matter that we lived in the back of the car. I thought about how my mother and I had nothing except for each other. I loved that feeling. I remembered how that feeling disappeared once we had moved in with Jacob.

"Yea," I said with a slight smile, "In this car."

"Okay," Caro said with a chuckle.

"We can buy some blankets and sleep in the back," I started to say with excitement and vision, "We can go and see all the beautiful places in this world. We can drive through Central America and South America, all the way down to Argentina."

"That sounds great!" Caro said, smiling with excitement.

We watched the sun begin to set on the world below us.

I pondered life with Caro in my arms. I felt like I came full circle from where I had started. I used to think that life in the back of that old Volvo station wagon was my punishment for stealing the little toy car. I didn't think that anymore.

FIFTEEN

Caro and I lay cuddled up in the back of the new station wagon. We had been traveling down the Pan American Highway for the last year. The sun was starting to rise from the Andes mountains. The sunlight reflected off the snow caps causing the peaks to sparkle.

We had driven to the top, and stayed the night at the Pastoruri Glacier in Peru. It was freezing but we had piles of blankets and each other to keep us warm. The glacier was beautiful and had a large lake that chunks of ice broke off into. Our journey wasn't finished yet but we had already experienced so much.

We started the journey from the top of that mountain in Colorado right after I mentioned the idea to Caro. We never looked back. We drove up North and visited the vast lakes of Michigan. We continued up the coast of Maine and ate blueberries at the top of Cadillac Mountain. Down the East Coast, we stopped in New York to watch a Broadway musical. After the musical we stayed the night in Buffalo at a gas station parking lot.

A woman's car broke down at the gas station. Her children were waiting in the back of the car worried. We helped them get their car started and she insisted that we follow them to their lake house. The lake house was beautiful. Lake Erie was in their backyard. There was a beach full of colorful glass stones and shells. They took us out on their boat, we had dinner and then stayed the night. The next day we continued driving down the East Coast.

When we arrived in Florida, we stopped at a place called Crystal River. We swam with giant manatees in the transparent water. We used paddle boards to explore the beautiful river.

We ran barefoot through the pure white sand dunes in New Mexico and camped under the stars in Arches National Park. We hiked through the Grand Canyon and climbed to the top of Mount Rainier. We traveled down the Pacific Coast Highway in California and drove through the giant redwood trees.

We crossed into Mexico through the Southern border of the United States. Mexico was beautiful. We saw the ancient ruins of Chichén Itzá and swam in hundreds of cenotes. We swam in the clearest fresh water I had ever seen at Lake Bacalar.

Life was incredible living in the back of the station wagon with Caro, but we still had our challenges throughout the trip. We were driving through Chiapas when we were stopped by a large group of men with machetes. They blocked the road with long boards that had nails pointing out of them. Luckily, we managed to offer them a little bit of money and they allowed us to pass.

We continued through all the borders in Central America, until we made it to Panama. We drove to the end of the road and realized that we could not cross into South America by car. The Darién Gap stood in our way. It was a dangerous stretch of undeveloped swampland and forest. The locals told us the only way across was to ship our car on a boat.

We waited in Panama while our car was shipped to Colombia. It took two weeks. We took a flight to Colombia to collect our car there. Colombia had the kindest people I had ever met in my life. We made friends in Guatapé. They made us local food and took us on hikes around the area. We celebrated independence day with them and got sprayed in the face with foam. They threw fireworks onto the street and everyone danced to avoid the explosions. Colombia was incredible.

We entered Ecuador and we were greeted with vast beautiful green hills. It rained the day before we arrived and we didn't know what that meant for our travels. We got stuck on a dirt road in the middle of nowhere. There was no one around to help us. We had to use sticks and rocks to try and get the car out. We laid them in the deep mud in an attempt to create a platform for the tires. It took us hours before we were able to succeed. Once we got the car out of the mud, it wouldn't start. We were filled with mud all over our faces and clothes. We were exhausted. Eventually, we finally got the car to start and continued our journey.

We drove to the top of Cotopaxi, an active stratovolcano in Ecuador. There was a beautiful view that was slowly covered with a cloudy mist. We decided to camp overnight and continue the next day.

The next day we started to drive down the volcano. The engine made a loud sound like a gunshot. Everything shut off and we rolled down the volcano. The engine died. We were towed to a local mechanic and spent ten days camped there while he tore apart the engine. He was able to fix it. He was kind to us and didn't charge us much for the repairs. He was inspired by our story.

When we first entered Peru, there were tall mounds of trash along the coastline. The cities were dirty and filled with piles of junk spread throughout the ground. Everything changed as we drove toward the Andes Mountains. Peru was one of the most beautiful countries we drove through. That led us to the Pastoruri Glacier.

"Buenos días," Caro said, turning over to me with a tired smile.

"Buenos días," I replied smiling back.

We crawled from the back of the station wagon to the front. I crawled to the driver's seat and Caro climbed to the passenger's seat. We heated some water with an electric kettle. It plugged into the cigarette lighter in the car. I poured us each a cup of hot co-co. We sat there and sipped it as we stared out the window at the view.

I set my hot co-co down for a moment. I reached into the back to grab one of the ukuleles. I began to strum some chords while Caro continued to sip her hot co-co. I thought about the dreams I once had of playing in front of a huge crowd. The biggest crowd in my dreams was no comparison to the life that I had now. This life was much better.

I thought back to all the things that I had to overcome throughout my life. All the struggles. I remembered that I used to believe that life was suffering. I believed that life was a lie. That it was all bullshit. I didn't think about those things anymore. That was all in the past. Life was simple. Life was beautiful. Everything was so tranquil at the top of that glacier.

Made in United States
North Haven, CT
02 December 2022